# OBSESSED

## BOOKS BY JAMES PATTERSON FEATURING MICHAEL BENNETT

*Shattered* (with James O. Born)
*The Russian* (with James O. Born)
*Blindside* (with James O. Born)
*Ambush* (with James O. Born)
*Haunted* (with James O. Born)
*Bullseye* (with Michael Ledwidge)
*Alert* (with Michael Ledwidge)
*Burn* (with Michael Ledwidge)
*Gone* (with Michael Ledwidge)
*I, Michael Bennett* (with Michael Ledwidge)
*Tick Tock* (with Michael Ledwidge)
*Worst Case* (with Michael Ledwidge)
*Run for Your Life* (with Michael Ledwidge)
*Step on a Crack* (with Michael Ledwidge)

For a preview of upcoming books and information about the author, visit JamesPatterson.com or find him on Facebook, Twitter, or Instagram.

# OBSESSED

A Michael Bennett
Psychological Thriller

# JAMES PATTERSON
## AND JAMES O. BORN

Little, Brown and Company

New York Boston London

Copyright © 2023 by James Patterson
Excerpt from *Lion & Lamb* copyright © 2023 by James Patterson

Hachette Book Group supports the right to free expression and the value of copyright. The purpose of copyright is to encourage writers and artists to produce the creative works that enrich our culture.

The scanning, uploading, and distribution of this book without permission is a theft of the author's intellectual property. If you would like permission to use material from the book (other than for review purposes), please contact permissions@hbgusa.com. Thank you for your support of the author's rights.

Little, Brown and Company
Hachette Book Group
1290 Avenue of the Americas, New York, NY 10104
littlebrown.com

First Edition: July 2023

Little, Brown and Company is a division of Hachette Book Group, Inc. The Little, Brown name and logo are trademarks of Hachette Book Group, Inc.

MICHAEL BENNETT is a trademark of JBP Business, LLC.

The publisher is not responsible for websites (or their content) that are not owned by the publisher.

The Hachette Speakers Bureau provides a wide range of authors for speaking events. To find out more, go to hachettespeakersbureau.com or email hachettespeakers@hbgusa.com.

Little, Brown and Company books may be purchased in bulk for business, educational, or promotional use. For information, please contact your local bookseller or the Hachette Book Group Special Markets Department at special.markets@hbgusa.com.

ISBN 9780316499576 (hc) / 9780316565981 (large print)
LCCN 2022944748

Printing 1, 2023

LSC-C

Printed in the United States of America

*For Jack,*
*making his way in this brave new world of ours*
*—J.P.*


*For my remarkable children,*
*John and Emily*
*—J.O.B.*

# OBSESSED

# CHAPTER 1

**THE NYPD BOAT** lurched and I almost slipped on the deck.

The waves made a monotonous slapping sound against the boat's hull, like an uneven drumbeat, as we cut through the choppy water. I sucked in a deep breath and could practically taste the Hudson River. The toxic odors of rotting fish and garbage didn't do anything to help the nausea I felt. I prayed it would pass.

One of the officers assigned to the boat tapped me on the shoulder. He grinned and offered me a piece of beef jerky.

"Very funny, asshole," Detective Terri Hernandez said as she snatched the jerky from the smirking cop and gave him a shove. "We're here to work. There's a woman's body out there." She turned to me. "You okay, Mike?"

"Never better. Fresh air, the sea. Who could ask for more?"

She smiled and said, "That's called karma for all the pranks you've played."

Terri was trying to distract me. That's why I like working with her. I was on edge, terrified that I'd recognize the body we were on our way to recover.

Suzanne Morton, a friend of my oldest daughter, Juliana, had gone missing three weeks ago. The last place anyone saw her was at a prestigious acting class in SoHo. Suzanne and my daughter had been in a few classes together in the past. The NYU sophomore kept a busy schedule but never missed an acting class. She had been a good influence around my house, encouraging my younger daughters to pursue their passions.

I'd spent hours with Suzanne's parents. I had first met them six months ago when we attended a short play both the girls were in. Since Suzanne's disappearance, they'd asked me over and over again what the NYPD was doing to find their daughter. I understood. If your child is missing, you want the whole world to stop and go look for them.

As a parent of ten kids, I always seem to have something to worry about. At least none of them was missing.

I didn't need to use my imagination to worry about what might have happened to Suzanne. I'd seen enough as a homicide detective. It felt like a knife in my abdomen every time I pictured the young woman, her light-brown hair framing a beautiful face that had deep dimples when she smiled.

I felt a change in the engine just as the pilot looked over her shoulder. She yelled in my direction, "Wind chop is really bad today! I'll get as close as I can."

I looked out over the whitecaps and spotted a figure floating in the water. A second boat, a Zodiac inflatable-hull outboard, discharged a diver. Recovery takes a lot of resources.

We idled alongside the body. Now that we were closer, I could see more clearly that the body was a woman, floating facedown in the water, with waves of long hair fanning out around her head. She was wearing a sparkly black cocktail dress that had attracted sea life. A fish nibbled at something in her hair.

Terri stepped behind me. "Is it her?"

Salt spray stung my face as I watched the grim procedure to recover the body. I shrugged. "Can't tell yet." I appreciated Terry's reassuring hand on my shoulder.

The female crime-scene tech on our boat pulled the winch line so the diver could attach it to the recovery basket. The wire basket was over six feet long, with sides tall enough to keep a person firmly inside. I was relieved to see the care they used. They didn't know about my possible connection to the victim. They were just professionals.

Against all sound judgment, I stepped closer for a better look.

The other crime-scene tech, a doughy guy in his mid-thirties, leaned over the edge of the boat. He'd been the first victim of the beef jerky prank. All it had taken was a quick whiff of the smelly, dried meat, and the tech had vomited over the side of the boat. But now he showed great concentration and focus, leaning so far out of the boat his face almost touched the water.

I heard a helicopter in the distance. When I looked up, I noticed it was a news helicopter. I hoped to God they didn't try to get too close and film the body coming onto the boat. I couldn't imagine a family ever seeing that on TV, but reporters continue to amaze me.

I heard one of the crime-scene techs say they were bringing the body on board. I took a deep breath and steadied myself.

# CHAPTER 2

**I WATCHED THE** crime-scene technicians and police diver struggle in the choppy water. My stomach lurched as I stepped over to help. Forensic scientists and crime-scene investigators can be territorial. The crime-scene tech waved me off.

Then the male crime-scene tech slipped during a particularly rough wave. He grabbed the basket holding the body. It tipped. I tensed, expecting disaster.

The other tech sprang from the deck and managed to straighten the basket. At least temporarily. When the winch holding the basket swayed, the basket came forward onto the boat deck.

That's when it happened.

The body tumbled onto the deck of the patrol boat with a sickening thud. I kept my mouth shut. It was an accident, and conditions were dicey. It could've happened to anyone.

One of the basket's black straps fluttered in the wind as both crime-scene techs carefully picked up the body, turning her so that she faced up. We all stared at the victim for a moment as the female crime-scene tech kneeled and meticulously brushed wet strands of hair away from the woman's face.

It was not Juliana's friend. But whoever she was, this young woman had been stunning. Not just pretty or cute but an honest-to-God beauty. Long, gorgeous dark hair, a straight, petite nose, and high cheekbones. She hadn't been in the water long. She was fully clothed, and even still had her high heels strapped on. She looked like a peaceful angel lying on the deck of the boat.

Terri Hernandez leaned in close to me. She said in a low voice, "This is really similar to a body we found in the Bronx about two months ago. Both pretty, both in formal wear, and both discarded like an old fast-food container." She stepped past me and pointed at the body on the deck. "Looks like a puncture wound in the chest. It's small but noticeable." Terri turned and added, "See the red soles on those heels? This girl has really expensive taste. Those are Christian Louboutin stilettos, and the dress looks like a Gucci."

I just nodded. I always need a few minutes after recovering a body. I tried to picture the circumstances that led to the victim's death. There was something about being dumped in the water that felt extra evil. It's one of my nightmares. I said a quick, silent prayer for this poor woman.

At the moment, the only thing I could think of was catching whoever killed her.

The crime-scene techs took photo after photo from every angle.

The male crime-scene tech looked up from the body and said, "No ID of any kind. I'd put her age between nineteen and twenty-two. We'll try to get her fingerprints back at the lab. We'll see if she ever applied for a government job or has ever been arrested, but we might have a hard time figuring out who she is."

I shook my head. "Somebody's missing her. She'll match a missing person's report. We'll know in a day or two who she is." The thought of this girl dying alone caused a wave of sadness to pass over me.

I'd promised myself that if these kinds of feelings *didn't* come to me whenever I saw a body, I'd know it was time to retire.

# CHAPTER 3

**BY NOON, I** was headed back to my office. Every time I walk through the doors of the Manhattan North Homicide unit, in an unmarked building on Broadway near 133rd Street, I am thrilled not to work anywhere near One Police Plaza.

I was hoping there would be more information waiting for me at my desk. I also intended to track down our criminal intelligence analyst to help me sift through the data from my newest death investigation.

I headed to the seventh floor, where my squad took the center of the space, with half a dozen small offices and interview rooms ringing it.

I slid behind my desk and took a moment to make a few entries in my notebook and just think about what to do next. Even though we've moved on from physical case files to an electronic system called ECMS, Enterprise Case Management System, I still trust my own handwritten notes.

Then I hustled to my boss's office. Harry Grissom's tall and lean frame fit well behind a desk, and I knew that sitting eased the discomfort he always felt. Harry favored his left side when he walked, the result of a knife wound that had severed his femoral artery when he was a young patrolman. He never complained, but it was clear from his gait that it was painful for him to walk too long.

I realized Harry was starting to show his age lately. The creases around his eyes were now cracks. The mustache that drooped below his mouth, contrary to NYPD grooming policies, was now almost completely gray. Recently, I'd heard whispers that the big shots at One Police Plaza wanted Harry to retire. I hoped it wasn't true. Work was all Harry knew. I worried that without the NYPD, Harry, with three ex-wives and no kids, might become one of the many suicides in the police ranks. It's an issue no one inside or outside police agencies wants to talk about. The pressure of the job can be intense. But the pressure of *losing* the job can be overwhelming.

Harry gave me a little wave and his version of a smile. "What do you got?"

I filled him in on the recovery from this morning, and told him about Terri Hernandez's mention of a similar victim. "I'd like to work with Terri on this and look at both homicides together. Just in case we're dealing with another serial killer, I don't want anything to put us behind the eight ball. For a change, I wouldn't mind being a step ahead of an asshole like this."

Harry gave me a nod. That meant to move full speed ahead. Other lieutenants might ask for memos or extra admin, but Harry's nod carried a lot of information. It told me to catch this killer any way I could. I almost ran from his office before things could be slowed down.

I looked toward the criminal intelligence analysts' room as I left Harry's office and felt my first relief of the day. Sitting by himself in the corner of his office was Walter Jackson, arguably the best analyst in the NYPD.

Without a doubt, Walter was the *biggest* analyst with the NYPD.

He stood six foot six and was every bit of three hundred pounds—the word *imposing* didn't completely capture the thirty-five-year-old African American. The big man's smile tended to lift everyone's spirits. Walter had always been interested in helping his community, but he didn't like some of the risks associated with being a police officer. He found he had a knack for piecing together information and solving puzzles when he studied English literature at Virginia, so when he saw a job announcement for criminal intelligence analyst, he thought he'd give it a try. Now he was a legend in the department.

I popped my head in the room. "Hey, Walter, I just caught a homicide and I've got a lot of information to put together. Any chance you're free?"

"I got plenty to do, but it's tough to turn down a new homicide. What do you need?" he asked.

I stared at him. He didn't say anything.

He returned my stare as he slowly smiled. "What is it?"

"That's one of the first times you've ever answered a question without a pun."

The big man laughed, his belly jiggling. "I bet my daughter, Janine, I could go a week without making a pun. I have to give her a dollar every time I slip up. Whether she hears it or not."

"What made her want to bet?"

"I asked her, when does a joke become a *dad* joke?" He paused, then added, "When the punch line becomes apparent."

I guess most dads share a little bit of the same sense of humor, but I couldn't help but groan at that one. I didn't tell him I'd use that pun almost as soon as I got home.

I gave Walter the recovery information I had and what I had learned from Terri Hernandez about her homicide in the Bronx. Walter didn't have to be told what needed to be done. He'd call the medical examiner's office to get the latest information, track down all the outside sources, like news stories, on the other homicide. Then he'd give it to me in a concise manner.

In short, it's people like Walter Jackson who make homicide detectives look efficient.

# CHAPTER 4

**I'D BEEN IN** the office less than an hour, searching the ranks of missing persons, hoping to find a match for the girl we had pulled out of the Hudson, when a shadow fell across my desk like an eclipse. I turned to see the towering figure of Walter Jackson.

He eased down onto the hard, wooden chair across from my desk. Walter never sat down with force. He'd learned better, after a similar city-purchased chair had once crumpled under his weight. Now he instinctively tested each chair.

He gently placed a photo on my desk. It was clearly a recent picture of the beautiful victim from this morning. It hurt my heart a little to see her smiling in the photo. I said, "That was fast."

"Me and Fotomat promise to develop photos in less than an hour."

"Jesus, Walter, Fotomat? You're not that old. How do you even remember them?"

"You're not much older than me and you remember them." He looked at the photo. "I got lucky. The ME's office picked up immediately. They have a fingerprint scanner connected directly to the FBI. Turns out the girl had once applied to work at a preschool in SoHo. We were able to match her fingerprints to that application.

"Her name is Estella Abreu. Nursing student at Pace. Lived in East Harlem with her family on 116th Street." He bent his head for a silent prayer. Walter did that any time he talked about a recent homicide victim. A common practice around people who deal with tragedy every day.

"Good work, Walter."

"Autopsy is scheduled for tonight. Aurora Jones is the assistant medical examiner on duty."

I was glad to hear it. Aurora was a hell of a coroner. I nodded and looked at Walter. "That's outstanding. Can you see if there're any connections between this victim and the one from the Bronx? When you have more information, we'll compare them."

Walter didn't waste a second. "The girl in the Bronx, Emma Schrade, was a student at Juilliard. There is one connection right there. Both were students. Emma was a soprano." He tossed an envelope onto my desk.

I opened it to see a bright-eyed blonde with a spectacular smile. "Where did these come from?"

"I just pulled them off the internet. I printed them so you could take them on interviews. I saved the original photo in ECMS."

"Walter, just when I think you're out of surprises, you pull one more out of the hat. This is impressive for just a few minutes."

"I've got two daughters. You think I'm not motivated when I see a photo of a girl who's been murdered? I don't understand how you guys ever sleep at night. I'd be consumed with all the leads that come into a case like this. How do you handle it with your ten kids?"

"It's definitely a balancing act. Between sports, homework, and just trying to spend some time with them, this is a tough job."

Walter shook his head. "I don't know how you do it, Mike. With your crazy-ass cases and all those kids, how do you find time in the day?"

"It's all about being efficient and keeping moving like a shark. I'm afraid if I ever stand still, it'll kill me. Believe it or not, I also start coaching my daughter Fiona's basketball team this week."

"All school officials see when they look at me is a potential football coach," Walter said. "No one can believe it when I tell them I've never even seen a football game all the way from beginning to end." He sighed. "I don't know that I'd give up my steady daytime hours and comfortable desk for your job. I'd already be burned out and barely able to talk to my family."

"Walter, I know your family. It doesn't matter if you talk to them or not, they'd be talking to you." We both laughed because we both understood what it meant to be true family men.

"I know what you mean. Questions at work, questions at

home. Sometimes you want someone to answer *your* damn questions."

I nodded. "Elementary school math and science can baffle me."

Walter paused. "You mean like what weighs more, a gallon of water or a gallon of liquefied butane?"

"They weigh the same, right?"

Walter grinned. "No, butane is lighter fluid."

I groaned and said, "You owe your daughter another dollar."

"Totally worth it."

# CHAPTER 5

**I STUDIED THE** information Walter Jackson had come up with on both victims. It was during times like this, slouched at my desk, that I appreciated the padded chair I'd bought for myself. The city didn't care if hours at my desk hurt my back.

As usual, Walter Jackson's packet on my homicide victim was outstanding. The right criminal intelligence analyst makes any case easier. Walter always sticks in little bits of information other analysts might ignore, putting in data on siblings and old addresses, giving investigators more options to pursue when starting out on a case.

Sometimes, as a homicide detective, you've got to recreate the victim's world in your head. You've got to be able to live their life and see the world through their eyes, at least briefly.

I was deep into Emma's and Estella's worlds and was startled when my phone rang. The kids had installed a new ringtone, the start of the piano solo from Eric Clapton's original "Layla." As soon as I heard it, I remembered that my wife, Mary Catherine, was going to call me after her doctor's appointment.

The first words out of my mouth were "How'd it go?"

Instead of a concise answer, I heard a series of shrieks and laughing in the background.

Using my razor-sharp detective skills, I made an assessment and said, "You have the kids with you?"

"Only sixty percent of them. We're on our way to buy some school clothes."

"I thought you were going to call as soon as you were done at the doctor's office."

"Things got crazy and I was running late."

I heard my youngest child, Chrissy, whine that she wanted to talk to me. That started her sisters Fiona and Shawna doing the same thing. I could barely hear Mary Catherine as she tried to explain things in code.

"Michael, I know I said I wanted to go to this first appointment on my own, but there was a lot to absorb. It was almost like the…" She searched for another word. "The cashier was trying to talk me out of any purchase."

I was careful with my reply. I said, "To be clear, the *doctor* tried to talk you out of *fertility treatment.*"

"I have no idea why crime is rising with brilliant detectives like you running around."

I snorted a laugh. I didn't want her to think I was trying to influence her one way or the other about her efforts to get pregnant. Finally, I came up with "How do *you* feel about it?"

"I really don't know. I think I'd like you...to come next time."

I knew her pause was a last-second change from *I'd like you at the next doctor's appointment.*

All I said was "Anything you want."

"I think about how great our life is now in a home filled with children." Mary Catherine paused to yell at the kids. "Everyone quiet for two minutes!"

I heard Trent sneak in an "Or what?"

The silence over the phone was terrifying. I knew those kids were facing the toughest of Irish glares. I felt sorry for them.

She came back on the line and her voice betrayed no hint of anger. Mary Catherine said, "I look at it two different ways. I think how happy another"—there was a pause—"*visitor* would be in our house. I also think we have the perfect balance now."

"No matter what, we can't lose. We have a great life, and a baby would make it better."

Mary Catherine said, "I thought irrepressible optimism was supposed to be my thing."

We both laughed as she broke the tension. We chatted for a few moments about the rest of our day. Then I built up the nerve to tell her, "Listen, I caught a homicide earlier today. I'll probably be home late." A homicide detective's spouse hears this phrase dozens of times a year. But it felt harder to say, knowing she was having a rough day.

There was silence for a few moments on the other end of the line. Then Mary Catherine haltingly asked, "I know you've been looking for Juliana's missing friend, Suzanne..."

"No, it wasn't Suzanne. Suzanne's father left another message for me this morning. I've been over to Missing Persons at One Police Plaza several times, hoping to find out something. So far there's nothing on her. But Suzanne wasn't the girl we fished out of the Hudson."

"Oh, my Lord. Someone dumped a body in the river? That's horrible."

I try not to bring home the terrible things I see on my job. I guess I have achieved my goal because Mary Catherine was still reeling from the few details I had told her. I never want my family to become numb to the horrors that happen. Just like I don't want to lose sight of what each homicide means, especially when the victim is young. Somewhere a family had lost a child. Every homicide victim means potential that won't be reached. I know in my heart someone feels the loss every time a person is murdered.

Mary Catherine said, "Don't worry about a thing, Michael. I have a plan for the afternoon that includes helping the twins with a project, then showing Ricky how I make my Irish stew."

Her kind understanding—especially when she said things with that light Irish accent—made me want to rush home that much faster.

# CHAPTER 6

**TERRI HERNANDEZ MET** me in East Harlem near where Estella Abreu, the young woman we'd pulled out of the Hudson, had lived. I caught Terri up on everything I'd learned about our victim.

"The only address listed for her is this one, with her parents, on 116th Street. A patrol sergeant made notification almost as soon as we knew who she was."

We were about to do one of the most challenging things all homicide detectives do: interview the family of a homicide victim. You never know what you're going to find. A family in denial. A family grieving so deeply they can't focus. A family so shattered by the loss of the child they don't know how to cope. There's a wide array of responses to losing a family member to homicide, and none of them are positive.

"You know I did some work not too far from here. Did a

year in Narcotics that, for a time, had me coordinating with officers at the Two-Three," Terri said.

"Is the neighborhood better or worse than back then?"

"Same. Still tough. Right over there is where a convenience-store robber shot at me."

"What happened to the shooter?"

"He ran and ended up shooting a cabdriver. Then he took the cab and went on a high-speed chase. The New Rochelle cops finally got him with Stop Sticks. He was booked, but since he didn't hit me and the cabdriver survived, he got time served and two years' probation."

I said, "If the shooter had hit you, the judge would've given him another month or two for sure."

"I don't think people realize how close most cops are to just stepping away."

"I hear ya. All we can do in the meantime is our best. Maybe if we did a better job, this neighborhood wouldn't be so rough."

Terri pointed down the street. "Over where those guys are selling dope was the site of my biggest fistfight. Place looks about the same. For a girl to get out of here and go to nursing school is really something. Her parents have to be special." She shook her head and added, "And this is their reward? Makes you wonder why we all try so hard. Shit happens no matter what."

All I could do was nod. I'd been thinking about this most of the afternoon. This beautiful young woman, studying to be a nurse at Pace University, and suddenly everything was taken from her. It made me sad, but it also made me angry.

# CHAPTER 7

**WE PAUSED OUTSIDE** the building, a five-story apartment complex a few blocks from the East River. It was quiet on the street this time in the early evening. A few people were coming home from work. There were no kids playing outside. That said all that needed to be said about the neighborhood.

A man standing by the steps saw us pull up and immediately called someone to let them know the cops were here.

Terri said, "Relax, we're not here for you or any of your petty crimes."

The man looked insulted and relieved at the same time.

We climbed up two flights of stairs to the Abreu family's three-bedroom apartment.

As we walked, Terri asked, "Any indication why Estella was so dressed up, or where she was going? Some kind of university function?"

"No. Nothing like that. Still checking."

I took a deep breath to prepare myself for what we were about to do. The apartment door was open, and we could hear people talking inside. I knocked lightly, hoping someone would notice me at the open door. I'd seen scenes like this play out too many times. Still, there was something positive in seeing people here, comforting grieving parents.

I spotted a couple I assumed to be the Abreus together on a small love seat: a short, pudgy man wearing a work shirt with the name RAUL stenciled across his left breast, sitting with his arm around a small woman dabbing her eyes with a handkerchief. She had the same long dark hair as Estella, and I could see a strong resemblance.

One wall looked like a shrine to Estella, with photos from her First Communion and soccer trophies all set up on a library table in the corner of the room. An elderly woman who I thought might be Estella's grandmother silently arranged more photos on the table.

A young man came to the open door and said, "May I help you?"

I leaned in close and told him who we were and why we were here. He appreciated the quiet introduction. He motioned us inside, then said to the couple on the love seat, "Tio, I think you need to talk to these people."

A few minutes later, we were in a bedroom with Mr. and Mrs. Abreu, sitting on a bed covered by a thick, vibrantly colored comforter printed with birds nesting in trees. We'd waited for Mrs. Abreu to compose herself in the bathroom. It looked like she could've used a couple more minutes.

We started slowly. Grieving parents don't usually come up

with the details that can really help in an investigation right away. We chatted about their daughter's life. That is always the best route to information.

Mrs. Abreu spoke with a thick Spanish accent. "My Estella was not just pretty, she was *beautiful*. Since the day she came into this world. Smart as a whip too. She was also nearsighted, and she started wearing glasses at six. She always chose stylish frames, but she tried to not wear them for pictures. Without them she was almost blind. She could wear contacts for a short while."

Mr. Abreu kept nodding. "Estella is sweet too." He froze. Then eked out, "I mean she *was*." Then he started to cry.

We went back to short questions about friends, interests, and relationships.

After a few minutes of simple questions, Terri Hernandez asked Mrs. Abreu, "Do you have any idea where Estella was going last night? She was dressed up like she was going out on the town."

The grieving woman shook her head. After blowing her nose into the handkerchief, she looked up and said, "When Estella went out yesterday evening, she was dressed in casual clothes. I don't know anything about being dressed up."

Terri politely asked if she could see Estella's bedroom and closet. I followed along as Mrs. Abreu led us to the third bedroom. All eyes followed us as we walked through the crowded living room. There was no question who we were or why we were here. These people expected results.

I watched silently as Mrs. Abreu showed Terri Hernandez her daughter's room and closet.

After rooting around for a minute, Terri pulled a shopping

bag out of the closet. She looked to Mrs. Abreu for approval. The middle-aged woman nodded, and Terri opened the bag. Inside was another bag, which held a long, flowing designer gown. She stood up and held the dress almost to her chin so it just barely cleared the floor. It was a dark green and looked like what someone would wear on a red carpet at the Oscars. It would make anyone look elegant. Especially someone like Estella.

Terri said, "When did Estella wear this?"

Mrs. Abreu took a tentative step forward. She reached out and felt the material between her thumb and forefinger. She focused on the dress for several seconds, then turned to Terri. "I have never seen this."

Terri took some photos of the dress, then carefully folded it and put it back in the bag. She left it in the corner of the closet.

Estella's mother had a vacant stare. It was like we weren't even in the room with her. Without hesitation, Terri wrapped her arms around Mrs. Abreu. The woman started to sob.

We stood in silence for minutes while Mrs. Abreu let out the emotion of the worst day she was ever going to have. Terri continued to hug her. When Mrs. Abreu recovered, we headed back into the main room, where her family had gathered. Everyone looked at us to make an announcement. Instead, I awkwardly eased toward the front door. Mr. Abreu acted as my escort as people parted to let us exit.

I left my card and told them we might have more questions and let them know it was okay to call me anytime.

Mr. Abreu stepped out, grabbed my arm. He said in a low, shaky voice, "Tell me, Detective. Who could do something like this to a beautiful girl like Estella?"

"I don't know, sir. But you can bet I'll do my best to find out."

# CHAPTER 8

**IT HAD BEEN** a long day, and I was still going. I threw down two Butterfinger Minis just to give me some energy. The quart of coffee I'd downed since midafternoon sloshed around in my belly as I pulled my city-issued Chevy into an official parking spot in front of the NYC Health Department building on the corner of First Avenue and 30th Street, a block from the East River. This was one of three forensic pathology centers run by the New York City medical examiner. The other two were in Queens and Brooklyn.

No one is ever happy to go to the medical examiner's office. But we'd caught a break. The assistant medical examiner on duty, Aurora Jones, could turn around a long, shitty day. With her charming Jamaican accent and sparkling smile, Aurora always lifted spirits, especially if people were looking tired or depressed. Maybe it was her job. Maybe she was around those kinds of people too often. Whatever the reason, I was looking forward to seeing her.

I met Aurora at her office on the third floor. I always smiled at her sense of humor, like how she decorated the cluttered cave with posters of *Night of the Living Dead* and *The Walking Dead* opposite one for *Shaun of the Dead*.

At just over five feet tall, she sprang from her chair and hugged me. It felt like I was hugging one of my kids.

Aurora stepped back. "You look like shit, Bennett."

"Wish I didn't feel like it too."

She poured a cup of the harsh Dominican coffee she liked. It felt a little like drinking Drano with some coffee flavor. But it revived me. At least for a moment.

As we walked down the hall at Aurora's blistering pace, I said, "Terri Hernandez said she'd wait for us at the examination room."

Aurora let out a quick laugh. "She's probably looking for Jeff Alter. He's a tech. If I was fifteen years younger, I'd hang out near there too."

I never thought about Terri's dating life. Maybe because we got along like old buddies. As Aurora and I continued our fast trot downstairs, we caught up with each other about our families. Especially her son, who was in his second year at UMass. He was a backup player on their basketball team but still earned a full scholarship.

I said, "I'm going to need more than a few scholarships to get all my kids through college."

"Maybe you'll get lucky and only a few of them will get into college." She cackled.

"I can't keep up with their homework now. The twins' math

is almost incomprehensible to me. I remember when I was in school, I once asked my teacher, Sister Sheilah, when I would ever need to really use algebra."

"What was her answer?"

"She said, 'You won't, but some of the smarter kids will.' That one little insult pushed me to study and get an A in algebra. I think Sister Sheilah is still proud of that little quip. I see it in her smile every time she greets me."

"If I didn't know you better, I'd say that sounds like a massive inferiority complex."

We got to the hallway with the examination rooms. I saw Terri playing with her hair as she gazed up at a tall young man, but as soon as she saw us she straightened up and led us into the room where the autopsy would be performed.

I'd been dreading this moment. As a professional homicide detective, I've seen my share of autopsies. These rooms and their equipment are not made for comfort. As Aurora once said, "When a patient complains about the uncomfortable tables, I'll change them."

I try to not think of the victims while a medical examiner slices open different parts of their bodies and pulls out their organs. I view it mainly as an exercise in gathering evidence. This case felt a little different. I'd met Estella Abreu's family. I'd seen photos of the beautiful girl who reminded me of my own daughters.

Aurora set up her recorder, and Jeff, the tall forensic tech, started taking photos. I could hear Aurora speaking into her recorder and the occasional grunt or mumble as she looked at every aspect of the body. Instead of walking right up to the table, I hung back and averted my gaze. I knew there was an unclothed body stretched out on the steel table. It almost felt like an invasion of privacy looking at a naked woman without her permission. It didn't matter if she was dead or alive. That's just how I felt at the moment.

Instead, I went through paperwork to make sure that Estella's dress and shoes had been saved as evidence. The chances of finding anything on the dress were remote. The salt water in this part of the Hudson River does a good job of washing away DNA. But you never know.

A little over an hour after she started, Aurora, Terri, and I huddled at a desk on the far side of the examination room. Aurora's scrubs had a few stains on them from her recent work. It didn't seem to bother her. She said, "I understand you're wondering if the victim from the Bronx homicide might be related to this."

"We're interested in any similarities."

"I reviewed the case notes on that one after you called. As far as a physical examination and mode of death, there's no similarity. Emma Schrade, the victim from the Bronx, died from strangulation. This girl died from a puncture wound directly beside the sternum and between her fourth and fifth ribs. It left only a small hole in the dress."

"How big was the knife?"

"I don't think it was a knife. It was cylindrical. Relatively long. Almost like"—she paused as she searched for the right word—"a round metal rod. Maybe a kitchen tool. The victim in the Bronx wasn't stabbed."

Aurora continued: "Whoever stabbed this girl was powerful. They struck her with such force that it damaged the cartilage in her chest. The weapon was long enough to skewer her heart. The blow probably stunned her so badly that she bled out before she even knew what happened.

"Emma Schrade was strangled by a similarly powerful assailant. Parts of her windpipe were crushed. That indicates a killer who has strong hands—and who apparently doesn't stop once they start."

That last statement sent a chill down my back. It was exactly what I was afraid of.

# CHAPTER 9

**I WAS HAPPY** to be headed home after a day like this. It wasn't even that late. The kids would still be awake. That's what I needed about now. Kids.

I parked my city-issued Chevy Impala in the garage across the street from my apartment building on the Upper West Side. I had to take a moment to breathe and center myself. I know that sounds a little like a hippie in the Rockies, but I didn't want to bring home the tragedy of a day like this to my family. The fact that I was so exhausted would make it worse. I gulped some air and took a swig from a 20-ounce Coke I'd bought after leaving the medical examiner's office.

I cherish any time with my family. I have to. It's the same story with almost every cop. Few of us can count the number of holidays and family gatherings we've missed.

Being with my kids would ease the heartbreaking experience of seeing a beautiful young woman on a medical
examiner's slab. As soon as I opened the door and heard feet
running toward me, my mood soared.

Somehow I caught Shawna in midair as she leapt up to give
me a hug. I'm pretty sure the younger girls will give up their
practice of jumping at me like a missile before I get too old
and frail to deal with it. I'm not about to tell anyone to stop
it. How many people have someone who loves them so much
they jump into the air to greet them?

After I made it into the living room, delivering hugs and
kisses along the way, Fiona bounded up to me wearing basketball shorts and a Holy Name jersey. "I'm ready to play as soon
as we start practice."

I grinned. She was so excited, she was talking as fast as an
auctioneer. Enthusiasm could be contagious. I liked seeing it
in my middle schooler.

Fiona continued in that rapid-fire style. "I've been prac-
ticing in gym class every day. Sister Elizabeth says I have a
good jumper and sense of the court. She says since I'm tall, I
would be a good center. But I did some research, and if I want
to go to college on a scholarship, I have a better chance as a
point guard."

I held up a hand. "Hold on there, Steph Curry. Let's play
our best and see where it takes us."

She nodded like she was electrified. "Good plan. Are you
as excited as I am?"

I don't like to lie to my kids, so I just smiled and said, "I
will do my best to be a good coach."

The twins, Fiona and Bridget, looked alike in the face.

Maybe in their mannerisms. That's where the similarities stopped. Bridget was reserved and preferred quiet activities. Fiona gravitated to anything she was good at, sports or academics. If she had a talent, Fiona used it. She had played basketball with the boys over the summer and never complained about them being rough. She really was tall. Maybe she had some talent that could be developed. I just hoped I was qualified for the task.

# CHAPTER 10

**I SPENT A** few minutes with Mary Catherine in the kitchen, away from the kids, wolfing down a few bites of left-over Irish stew from their dinner earlier that evening but also checking to make sure she was doing okay.

She said, "I'm fine, really. I worry about you while you're working. I'm a little tired. You know, the usual."

I kissed her and listened to an abbreviated account of the day. I was constantly amazed by this beautiful woman. She managed to guide all ten kids through most days with barely a hitch.

Mary Catherine said, "Ricky and Eddie did have a problem. You should go talk to them."

I held my questions.

As Mary Catherine told some of the younger girls to get ready for bed, I stepped into the living room and got a good look at the boys. I froze. Ricky had a black eye and Eddie had a cut lip. I knew brothers tended to roughhouse, but these two had never been the least bit aggressive. The injuries were from someone else.

Like any father, I could already feel my blood pressure starting to rise. Who would lay a hand on my kids? "What happened?" I almost shouted.

Eddie said, "Some boys punched Ricky so I jumped into the fight."

This sounded improbable. I turned a flat stare at Ricky.

He blurted out, "It wasn't really a fight, Dad. They just came up and punched us both out of nowhere. They both looked a little older than us. We didn't recognize them."

"Where, exactly, were you?"

Eddie said, "Sometimes we like to shoot hoops across from the school and down the block a little bit. Not as many rules there. Feels like we're doing something dangerous."

Ricky interrupted him. "But it's not dangerous. It just *feels* dangerous." He looked directly at Mary Catherine and said, "We're both very careful all the time."

I said, "Yes, we know you're the most conscientious young men in the city. I don't care that you were playing basketball off campus. You should be allowed to walk around the Upper West Side without being accosted."

I got a few more details. The bullies hadn't demanded anything or stolen anything.

Mary Catherine looked at the boys seriously and said, "I don't want you getting in fights."

Ricky said, "I don't want to get in fights either."

I tried to hide my smile as Mary Catherine and I said they

should at least try to reason with boys like that. It was nice to be on exactly the same wavelength.

But it didn't last long.

Mary Catherine said, "And if reasoning doesn't work, run away. Find your great-grandfather or one of the nuns."

Before I knew what I was saying, I held up my hands. "Sometimes you need to get a good lick in yourself. Bullies don't like it when people fight back. You may not win the fight, but you might discourage them."

Mary Catherine said, "Are you sure that's the right thing to do?"

"No. This is one of those situations when you use your experience. I don't want to see these boys become doormats or afraid to engage with anyone." I could tell by the look on Mary Catherine's face how strongly she disagreed with me. I was sure we'd have a discussion about it later. My American mentality versus her Irish mentality. Or perhaps it was much more of a mother's mentality versus a father's mentality. I didn't want to see anyone bother my boys. But I did want them to stand up for themselves.

I decided to talk to my grandfather about it as soon as I could.

# CHAPTER 11

**THE NEXT DAY,** I picked up Terri Hernandez in front of the Four-Six on Ryer Avenue in the Bronx, where she'd been catching up with one of her friends at the precinct. We scooted north on the Bronx River Parkway until we were on the edge of Scarsdale, New York.

Terri said, "I hate leaving the city for the snobby people in Scarsdale."

"C'mon, how many people from Scarsdale have you ever even met?"

"A few. And I feel bad for this grieving family. I don't count them as snobs. I just don't like the vibe. Too many white people clustered together makes a girl like me nervous."

Westchester County sat just a little north of the city, but the atmosphere and attitude were entirely different. I gawked at the impressive houses as we cut through Scarsdale to the home of Lisa and Robert Schrade, parents of Emma Schrade, the young woman found strangled in the Bronx two months ago. Terri had been working the homicide.

The house where the Schrades lived sat at the end of a cul-de-sac on a hill. The second story was nestled in a cluster of elm trees. The yard was perfectly manicured. The circular driveway had a Cadillac SRX and a Chevy Volt with the spare donut tire on the front driver's side.

I said, "You know the difference between a dead-end street and a cul-de-sac?"

Terri gave me a look. She knew me, so she tentatively prompted, "No, what's the difference between a dead-end street and a cul-de-sac?"

"About a hundred thousand bucks."

Terri let out a laugh. She said, "That's clever. Did you just now come up with that?"

"I wish. I read it in a *MAD Magazine* ages ago and I've been waiting to use it ever since."

Terri let out a whistle as we stepped out of the car. She said, "I've been here three times. Each time it feels like this place is bigger."

"It's a relative shack compared to the neighbors."

"You telling me you couldn't raise your ten kids here?"

"I could raise my kids anywhere. But you're right—they'd have fun up here. If you know anyone who wants to give me a house, I'll consider it."

Terri knew our apartment had been inherited by my first wife. She even knew about the trust in place to pay the taxes on our Upper West Side apartment. The chances of getting a deal like that twice in a lifetime seemed pretty slim.

We stood on the front porch for a moment as I checked a few notes. Someone inside the house was playing the piano. They were good. Just as Terri was about to push the doorbell, the door swung wide. A woman wearing a light-blue blouse and dress slacks with running shoes said hello to Terri, who in turn introduced Dr. Lisa Schrade to me.

She said to Terri, "I'm on shift in about an hour."

"This shouldn't take too long. Is your husband home as well?" Terri asked.

"Let me see. Middle of the week, middle of the morning, of course Robert's here," Dr. Schrade said over her shoulder as she led us down a long, tiled entryway. Each tile had a hand-drawn image of nature. There were birds, deer, and some of the tiles were just trees.

"Who's playing the piano?" I asked. "It's lovely."

Dr. Schrade said, "That's our younger daughter, Lauren. She hopes to get into Juilliard just like her sister." She added, "Emma was the first student from her school to get into Juilliard in more than ten years. She had an excellent GPA and had very high SATs." Clearly, Dr. Schrade was proud of her daughter's accomplishments.

I realized this was how I must sound talking about my kids. With ten, I had a lot of choices of what to brag about. But Juilliard was a huge accomplishment. My stomach fluttered at the thought of one of the younger kids wanting to attend Juilliard. I wasn't certain, but I guessed my entire annual salary might barely cover tuition.

At the end of the entryway was a small music room to one side. A girl of about sixteen, with long, light hair, didn't look up from her practice. We followed Dr. Schrade to a pleasant patio at the rear of the house. Ferns spilling over narrow planters gave the patio a wilderness vibe. Robert Schrade sat at a small, round table, sipping a glass of iced tea. Dr. Schrade's husband was almost the complete opposite of her. Long hair drooped over the collar of his stained polo shirt. Streaks of gray shot through his shaggy beard. I remembered reading that he was some sort of part-time acting coach in the city. I guess it was Dr. Schrade's salary that paid for this nice house and the tuition at Juilliard.

We all sat around the glass-topped patio table with a pitcher of iced tea. Terri got right to our questions as soon as both of the Schrades were sitting comfortably.

The family may have been coping with the death of their older daughter, but there were obvious strains in the marriage. I didn't know what Mr. Schrade had been like before his daughter was murdered, but he seemed lost now, while Dr. Schrade clearly forced herself not to roll her eyes every time her husband spoke.

After all these years talking to the families of homicide victims, I understood their pain. The homicide may have occurred two months ago, but it was still an open wound for these poor parents.

My quick assessment of the emotional state of the Schrades was that Dr. Schrade seemed like she was using work to occupy herself. Her husband was a different story. He shambled along and didn't add much to our interview. He would be the one to worry about. Mr. Schrade looked like he'd been knocked for a real loop.

We went over some of the earlier questions Terri had been asking. The parents had paid Emma's bills, and she had earned a little extra money singing at weddings and other events.

Throughout the interview, I listened to the haunting piano music from inside the house. I glanced over at a table with some photos of the sisters. I picked up the first one.

Mr. Schrade said, "I was just going through a few old photos. That was Emma when she was about fourteen."

Dr. Schrade said, "You can see she had pretty bad acne back then. We finally got it under control, but she had a few scars. I would tell her she wore too much makeup as she got older, but I realize she was just trying to cover her old scars. That acne really bothered her. Funny what affects each of us the most." Her words trailed off as she thought about her daughter.

Mr. Schrade added, "You've seen the more recent pictures of her. She really blossomed once she got to Juilliard. She was a striking girl and no one ever noticed a few blemishes."

Terri tactfully said, "I know we've talked about this, but now that you've had time to think about it, did Emma ever mention a boyfriend or relationships?"

Both of her parents shook their heads in unison.

Dr. Schrade said, "I know she was dating and going out on occasion, but we never talked about any specific boys. Emma liked her independence and privacy. She was very careful never to post anything personal on social media."

As we walked back into the house, and they stopped for a moment so Terri could take down a new phone number, I glanced into the music room just as Emma's sister took a break.

I decided to take a chance.

# CHAPTER 12

**I STEPPED INTO** the piano room, which had dark, mahogany paneling and a high ceiling. I wondered if it had been designed for acoustics. I could hear Terri still talking with the Schrades in the foyer.

I approached the girl at the piano and smiled. I said, "I wish I could say I knew what you were playing, but it was beautiful."

Lauren returned my smile. She looked like her sister. I noticed a few wisps of acne on her cheeks.

"I only know classical music from watching Bugs Bunny or hearing commercials for classical music on TV," I told her. "Beethoven's 'Moonlight Sonata' is one of the few classical songs I can identify."

Without saying a word or missing a beat, the teenager played the first few bars of the "Moonlight Sonata." It was like she was a different person as she focused for a few moments.

"Ha, just like the commercial, only the sound really carries in here."

The girl spoke for the first time. "My parents spent a fortune to build this room just right for my sister's singing. They didn't want it to go to waste, so now I'm supposed to practice in here hours a day."

I said, "Your name's Lauren, right?"

The pretty girl nodded.

"Do you want to go to Juilliard like your sister?"

Lauren shrugged. "My parents definitely want me to. Just like they forced Emma to go."

"Wasn't it your sister's dream to go to Juilliard?"

Lauren took a moment. She appeared to be a serious young woman. "Emma wanted to be a star. She'd have preferred going on *American Idol* or *The Voice*. She only went to Juilliard because our parents insisted. Like they're doing with me."

"What would *you* like to do?"

"I dunno. I'm not sure what I want to do yet."

I let out another smile. She sounded just like some of my kids. "That's the right answer. Worry about what you're going to do with your life when you get a little older."

Lauren turned in her seat to look at me directly. "You're trying to find who killed Emma, aren't you?"

This wasn't a random question.

I paused, nodded, and said, "Detective Hernandez and I are working on it."

Lauren said, "This whole thing sucks. Emma could be bossy and even a little mean, but she was a pretty good sister. I miss her."

"Were you guys close?"

"There were four years between us. But we bonded together against my parents. It was kind of fun."

"Did Emma ever talk to you about boyfriends or dating?"

"No. Emma didn't confide in people. She liked doing her own thing, not answering questions about it. She had a few fights with our parents about being careful in the city and checking in at least once a day. She didn't like that at all."

"Do you think she had a wild personal life?"

"I doubt it," Lauren scoffed. "Emma was pretty focused. My parents paid for her apartment and food but didn't give her much for fun. That annoyed her and she complained that the city was so expensive.

"She also told Dad he couldn't crash at her place after his acting classes on Tuesday and Thursday nights. She just wanted her independence, but I think it hurt his feelings."

Emma's sister had given me some insights, but that wasn't why I'd wandered into the music room. I said, "How are you doing through this whole thing?"

She shrugged again. It made me wonder if all teenagers were trained to shrug in exactly the same way. She said, "I guess I'm doing okay. My parents aren't quite right. Especially my dad. He never missed one of Emma's school concerts."

I wanted to leave this girl on a positive note. I said, "Can you play me something I wouldn't expect?"

"Like what?"

"I don't know—I wouldn't expect it."

A smile slipped across her face. She turned back to the piano and started playing a haunting melody that wasn't quite classical music. The deep chords resonated inside the room. I could feel the performance suck me in. It was phenomenal.

She wrapped up the song after about two minutes. She looked at me and said, "That was 'Solace' by Scott Joplin, but I played a version that was arranged by Marvin Hamlisch."

I almost couldn't speak. I felt like this young woman had opened a new musical door for me.

I heard Terri finishing up with Dr. Schrade. I waved to Lauren and she gave me a genuine smile.

# CHAPTER 13

**AFTER I DROVE** Terri back to her car, I decided to pay a visit to an informant who'd helped me break some of the biggest cases of my career. He was a little high maintenance to use too often—not so bad that I had to pull all the green M&M's out of a bowl, more like having to deal with an unending stream of minor bullshit, such as his asking to get out of parking tickets or hoping I'd arrest one of his rivals.

I had to balance the value of his information against the cost.

About six years ago he'd legally changed his name from Ronald Higdon to Ronald Higdon, Esquire. He spelled out the Esquire. It wasn't illegal, unless he was caught claiming to be an attorney, or acting as someone's attorney. Anyone who knew him recognized it was just another scam.

About the time he changed his name, he also helped me make an arrest in a nasty drug homicide on the Upper

West Side. Two bodies in an alley with no ID. The homicide investigation was stalled. After a day of stumbling around with no progress, I called Ronald. He came up with the victims' names in less than two hours. The next day, he had the shooter's name for me. In return, he asked to have his criminal record erased. That didn't happen. That *couldn't* happen. So he'd settled for getting off probation early. Believe me, it was a good trade.

Ronald ran his uncle's pawnshop on West 127th Street, a couple of blocks from the famous Apollo Theater. Higdon's Pawn and Jewelry had been in the same spot nearly sixteen years. I was certain that Ronald fenced stolen property through the pawnshop, but it was more of a gut feeling than real information. And frankly, for the kind of help he'd given me in the past, I was prepared to overlook the assumption.

I knocked on the shop's front door and waited for Ronald to buzz me in. The place was roomy for a New York pawnshop. Clean, but not fancy. The concrete floor was painted with thick gray paint. The shelves, holding assorted electronics and collectibles, didn't match. The shop didn't have nearly as much inventory as other pawnshops I'd seen, which reinforced my belief that Ronald was using the place for things other than short-term loans on people's personal belongings.

The lean man behind the counter gave me a smile. A gold tooth twinkled in the light. He was about my age and had seen some tough times. I have never asked him about the scars on his face or the bullet wound on his wrist. That is sort of the way a relationship with an informant works: you don't get to know them too well and don't ask too many questions.

Ronald came from behind the counter and shook my hand.

He wasn't quite as tall as my six feet three inches. Maybe six foot one. But he was sturdy. And he had a strong grip.

"What brings the city's best homicide detective to my humble shop today?"

I smiled. He used a good narrator's voice with precise enunciation. There weren't many informants with a delivery like that and a college education to back it up. Ronald had bragged about how he worked hard at having no discernible accent. I knew it had more to do with tricking people on the phone than any sort of interest in self-improvement.

I gave him a rough overview of the two homicide victims. I was careful not to give him any details he might use for other reasons. You never want an informant to create a suspect from the facts provided. He even made a few notes as he nodded.

"I'll start making calls right away. I got more and more people around the city. What are you interested in me asking about?"

"Anything unusual. Anyone who might hang with a younger crowd. Or, if we're lucky, someone's talking. Maybe a street person saw something. You know the drill—anything that might help."

"This isn't my usual kind of thing. I don't mix with a crowd that talks much about college girls. But I'll see what I can do."

"And what will your help cost the city, or me?"

The way the smile slid over his face, I knew he had an answer ready.

Ronald said, "I'm in a little bit of a bind. There's a lady down in SoHo who claims I told her I was an attorney. She said she listened to my advice on a minor civil matter. Now she's being sued for two million dollars and is blaming me. A Detective Matthews in the First Precinct says what I did is criminal and he's not done with me. Could you have a talk with the good detective?"

"Let's see if you make any progress first." I was about to tell him I'd make a phone call to the detective to see where he was on the case. Instead, I was startled by someone rattling the door violently.

I heard Ronald mumble, "Goddamn, not now." He hit the buzzer to avoid his door being shattered.

Three young, buff men rushed into the pawnshop. One of them said, "You owe us two grand for those little metal people."

The Brooklyn accent, the dark hair, and the tattoos on his arm all told me this was probably an Italian kid raised in Bensonhurst. In all likelihood, so were his buddies.

The young man who spoke glared at me and said, "We got business here. You need to get your ass moving."

I chuckled and said, "I don't think so."

# CHAPTER 14

**I MADE AN** effort not to move or show my intentions in any way. The young men from Brooklyn stared me down. Maybe no one had ever told them no. That was the problem with about half the people in the criminal justice system. Their parents told them they could do no wrong and they took it to mean they could do anything without consequences.

Clearly, Ronald didn't want to talk to these guys in front of me. He was trying to calm them down and get them to come back later.

The guy who'd been doing all the talking, the one in a tight T-shirt with a tattoo of the devil on his left forearm, looked at me and said, "I told you, get out."

"And I said, I would prefer to stay here." I tried to keep a pleasant expression on my face. But no matter how you looked at it, we were in a standoff.

Now the second young man stepped forward. He was about twenty-two. Tall and ripped. The gold crucifix around his neck dangled outside his Snoop Dogg T-shirt. His sharp brown eyes stared right at me. "Listen, mister, we got business with Ronald. It don't concern you."

Another Brooklyn kid trying to act tough. I kept my face neutral and said, "Thanks, but I'll refer you to my earlier answer: I think I'll stay."

The young man inched closer to me. He wore checkerboard Vans like a surfer, and the rubber soles squeaked a little on the painted concrete floor. He growled at me, "Do you know who my father is?"

I said, "No, does your mother?" The insult took longer to sink in than I thought it would.

When the young man realized what I'd said, his eyes bulged, and he took another step toward me. That's when I calmly moved a barstool with my foot. It was part of a four-piece set with some kind of bird etched into the contoured seat. Ronald had bought the whole set on sale for $199. I'd been expecting one of the Brooklyn boys to advance. That's why I'd hooked my foot through the leg of the stool before I ever opened my mouth.

The young man stumbled on the stool for a moment, then had a change of heart. He eased back toward his friends. They looked like football defenders in formation. They were ready for a fight.

Some of this was my fault for having a little fun. I decided to take a different tack. I said, "I can't leave. I'm Ronald's attorney."

The young man with the devil tattoo said, "I thought he *was* an attorney. He's got an *Esquire* at the end of his name."

I looked at Ronald Higdon, Esquire. It appeared he did tell *everyone* he was a lawyer. I turned toward the three Brooklyn-ites. "Why does he work at a pawnshop if he's a lawyer?"

"He said he was tired of the bullshit in the criminal justice system."

"We all are. But that doesn't give you the right to barge in here and threaten him."

"He gave us three hundred dollars for some little metal people."

Ronald mumbled, "Figurines."

"Whatever they're called. We found out the four of 'em were worth about twenty-five hundred bucks, not a measly three hundred. We want the rest of the money." He dropped his voice and added, "Now."

He pulled an old-school straight razor from his pocket. He flicked it open to let us all get a good look at it. The whole idea of an edged weapon like that is to instill fear. It was working.

# CHAPTER 15

**INSTEAD OF GOADING** the young men any further, I did the lame, adult thing: I pulled out my ID. I let them see the badge and said, "NYPD. Do you boys want to spend a few days at Rikers?"

All three of the young men laughed.

I had to ask. "What the hell is so funny?"

"A cop telling us what to do. The mayor of New York City says cops can't do shit no more. We didn't do nothing that you could arrest us for. This is a private matter."

"It would've been, except you had to go and pull the razor. I'm not going to let anyone get cut while I'm standing right here."

One of the punks said, "Then you should probably leave."

Another added, "That would be the smartest move for you."

"I doubt any of you know the smartest move for yourselves,

let alone someone else. Do you really want to make this a police matter?"

The young punk kept the razor open in his hand. "There ain't even bail no more. You can arrest me, but I'll be hitting the clubs in a couple hours. You guys ain't the big cheese no more. We are."

I canted my body slightly and kept my right hand loose at my side, in case I needed to draw my pistol. I didn't want to do it. It would escalate the situation. But I wanted to be cut by a straight razor even less.

I was so concentrated on the man with the razor that I didn't notice Ronald leaning back to press the button to open the door. I jerked my head up at the loud buzzing sound, and saw the door burst open. Two men and a woman rushed into the shop.

The new arrivals were all Black. Both the men were older than the Brooklyn punks. Maybe in their mid-thirties. The woman was a little younger than her companions. She was tall with broad shoulders, and had wild hair with pink highlights shot through it like lightning.

I saw the smile on Ronald's face and knew these were friends of his. The looks on the punks' faces were phenomenal.

The tallest of the new arrivals, who had to have at least fifty pounds on any of the Brooklyn boys, looked at my informant and said, "Everything all right, Ronald?"

"That depends on how you look at it. These three just busted in here, threatened me with the razor, and told this man there was nothing cops could do about it. Just about then I buzzed you into the shop."

The man turned and stared at the three Brooklyn boys.

"So you think no one would do anything to you if you cut up Ronald with your blade. You think anyone will do something about this?" He swung his left elbow hard and caught the man with the razor right across the temple. The razor clattered onto the concrete floor, immediately followed by the young man's dazed body.

The woman swung her right hand and connected with the next punk. His nose shattered under her closed fist. She shifted slightly and punched the other man in the face with the same hand.

I stood and took in the show. It was like a boxing match without all the extraneous hoopla. Blood gushed out of the one man's nose. The second man had stumbled back and fallen onto the floor. The man who'd held the razor was desperately trying to stand.

As soon as he got to his feet, the woman shoved him back down to the ground.

He looked at me and whined, "You're a cop. You have to help us."

"You already told me the mayor said I can't do shit." I winked at the three people who'd just come in. The big man smiled. The woman tried to hide her smile but then started to giggle.

I told the one Brooklyn punk to leave the razor on the floor as he stood up. The three of them scurried to the door as a group.

I said, "I want you boys to go home and look up the word *karma*. If you have any brains at all, you'll realize you just had a master class in it."

I was still smiling after Ronald had buzzed them out and they ran away.

# CHAPTER 16

**AFTER MY ADVENTURE** at the pawnshop of Ronald Higdon, Esquire, I thought it might be a good time for a change of pace. It had been a very busy autumn. I missed seeing my grandfather. Like a lot of things, I was afraid I'd taken those off-the-cuff talks with the old priest for granted.

It wasn't just me who was busy. My grandfather had taken on an important new role for the church. He was working hard at using the resources available to him to help the entire community. He had set up a literacy program staffed by seniors at the school. He had set up a sports program at a nearby park and convinced the fire department to provide coaches twice a week. Seamus Bennett's vitality hadn't diminished with age.

Because both of our lives had sped up so drastically, my grandfather had missed dinner with the family for a record five nights in a row. We'd spoken on the phone briefly, but I hadn't seen him face-to-face since he came to dinner almost a week ago.

I walked to the administrative offices of Holy Name Catholic Church. The path that led to my grandfather's office was neatly maintained. Patio stones marked the route in a serpentine pattern instead of straight ahead. I tapped on the door before turning the knob.

Even though Seamus was into his eighties, there was no telling what I would find when I stepped past the door. Would he be drinking a hidden beer? Would he be playing cards with one of his buddies? Would he be yelling at some patron who hadn't come through with money for his community programs? It was always an interesting question.

Instead, I found my grandfather on the phone, discussing a proposal to provide free lunches to needy kids on the weekends. He had found a supplier who could provide simple meals and some city agency that would pay for it. I smiled as I listened to his "rational voice" while he finished his conversation.

As soon as he hung up, Seamus smiled at me. "I feel blessed by the Lord Almighty that you could find time in your busy schedule to come by and visit an elderly priest."

"Can it. You've been just as busy as me."

"And I'll bet you're really here to talk about your two sons and their encounter with some bullies yesterday."

I smiled. His Irish accent made everything sound pleasant and at the same time like an accusation. "I do want to talk about the incident. The boys seemed pretty open, but I wanted to make sure they didn't leave anything out."

My grandfather said, "They told you it happened down the street and not on school grounds, right?"

"I'm not looking to assign liability. Just wondering what happened."

My grandfather held up his hands like he was trying to keep me calm. "I know, I know. Didn't mean to come on so strong. I'm just so used to dealing with parents who're outraged about one thing or another. One father complained that we were talking about Jesus in class. Imagine that, a Catholic school that mentions Christ. God save us from stupidity."

I waved off his apology. "I haven't been mad at the school for anything since I got detention in sixth grade for horsing around with Matthew Callahan."

Seamus sighed. "All I know is what the boys told me. They were wearing their school shirts and I think that's what attracted the other boys. It's sort of a cool thing now to single out kids in any kind of a religious school. Maybe that's what they were trying to do."

"Any ideas on how to keep it from happening again?"

"If the boys stayed on school property, they'd be fine."

"I understand that. But I also don't want them to be afraid to walk down the street. There should be some kind of middle ground."

"That's the way it is with everything. Politics, sports, anything humans are involved in. There *should* be some middle ground, but usually no one looks for it. People stake out their positions and rarely want to listen to the other side." He leaned in and looked at me more closely. "Sweet Jesus but you look tired. Did you get any sleep last night?"

I just shrugged. A homicide detective's universal answer to that question. Then I heard the opening chords to the piano solo from "Layla" and reached for my phone. It was Terri Hernandez. I picked up immediately.

Terri said, "They just found a body in New Rochelle. It's Juliana's friend, Suzanne Morton."

I muttered, "Shit." I popped up and headed for the door, waving good-bye to my grandfather. He nodded back. How many times had this happened on the job over the years? Even before he was a priest and worked in the bar he owned. When the NYPD called, I went running. It rarely mattered who I was with or what I was doing.

At least my grandfather understood the meaning of the word *duty.*

# CHAPTER 17

**AS I NAVIGATED** the roads north, I was torn. Should I phone Mary Catherine and Juliana to break the news or wait until I had more information? It was always a tough call. I could hardly even contemplate what hearing words like that might mean to me. I let the idea wash through my brain and felt my anxiety rise.

The whole drive was just images of Suzanne Morton in my house, laughing and preparing for life after school.

About forty minutes north of the city, wedged in with half a dozen other towns in Westchester County, New Rochelle was not the kind of place accustomed to murder.

I pictured Suzanne's parents, David and Rachel. I didn't envy the poor New Rochelle police officer who would have to drive to notify her parents in Yonkers that their daughter had been found, and that she was dead.

Every cop remembers giving their first death notification. There's nothing in the academy and no training that can adequately prepare you to tell someone a family member is dead. It doesn't matter if the death is from a car accident, a drowning, or a homicide—it's difficult to look at a mother's face and tell her that her child won't be coming home.

My first notification was about eight days after I started with the NYPD. I was in the Bronx and my training officer got the call that we were to notify a family that their daughter had been struck by a truck and killed in East Harlem. My training officer said the best way to learn was to do it by myself. Later, I realized the veteran patrol officer hated to make notifications. Seeing people in grief tore him up.

He'd paused at the front of the building with me, saying, "Be honest, be direct, and try to be helpful. Those are the only rules. If helpful means you stand there and listen to them cry for ten minutes, that's what you do. If helpful means leaving them alone, then you exit immediately."

My right hand had trembled as I knocked on the second-floor apartment door not far from Yankee Stadium. A woman, about forty-five and dressed in surgical scrubs, answered the door. She was a nurse about to go on shift. As soon as she saw me, she blurted out, "Who is it? My husband? My son? My daughter?" Later I realized that nurses see as much death as cops do. They know the dangers out in the world.

I'd wanted to stick to the script and make sure I had everything perfect. Instead, I just looked at the ground and sort of mumbled, "I'm so sorry. Your daughter was hit by a garbage truck. She was pronounced dead at the scene." At the time it might've been one of the hardest things I'd ever said to someone. And the response was exactly what I thought it would be: the woman stumbled back, plopped onto a small, floral couch, and started to weep. *Wail* might be a more accurate term.

I had no idea what to do. I stepped into the apartment and eased onto the couch near the woman. I just sat there while she sobbed. I asked her if I could help in any way or perhaps make a phone call. She just shook her head.

About twenty-five minutes later, my training officer came up to the apartment to see what had happened. He said I did the right thing sitting with her. No death notification has ever been easy.

Now I found myself parked in the lot beside the bland tan building that housed the police department on North Avenue in New Rochelle. I raced up the sidewalk's low incline toward the front steps. Just as I made it through the set of glass doors, I saw Rachel and David Morton standing by the reception desk. My stomach tightened, and I tried to put on a calm face.

Rachel looked up as I was walking toward them. She immediately burst into tears. David took her in his arms and stroked her hair. He just stared at me silently.

"I am so sorry. I was hoping for the best. I don't know what to say."

David Morton had a distant look on his face as he said to me, "Someone stuffed our little girl in a cabinet behind an empty construction office. They think she's been there at least two weeks." His voice started to break, then he said in a louder voice, "Two fucking weeks."

Over the years, I've found that families of a missing person feel their loss twice when that missing person turns out to be a homicide victim. The pain can be unbearable. Families are ripped apart, and parents have even committed suicide over the death of a child. I know never to take the reactions of a grieving family personally. They have a lot to process. I stood with them in reception until a detective stepped out to meet them. She looked at me like I was a representative for the family.

I just badged her and said, "I was hoping to talk to the lead detective on the case."

We all awkwardly walked through the open door and down a long, sterile hallway. I saw a few cops I knew from joint cases or training.

New Rochelle had a dedicated homicide detective. Once that detective was overwhelmed, the department rotated the homicides that occurred within its city limits among three detectives who handled other crimes in addition to homicide.

Once I got the Mortons settled with a victim advocate, I headed off to find out who had been assigned the case. I saw a detective I'd known for years. She specialized in crimes against children, but I had to know who had caught this homicide.

I said, "Sandy, who got assigned the body they found this morning?"

She rolled her eyes and shrugged as she said, "Bill Stanton."

I muttered, "Shit, not 'Suicide' Stanton."

# CHAPTER 18

**I FOLLOWED SANDY** through the small building to the detective bureau. It was more hectic than I would've expected for a town of eighty thousand people. I scanned the room for Bill Stanton, the detective who'd caught the homicide, and saw the fifty-four-year-old, balding detective at a desk in the corner. As usual, he had a washcloth next to him, which he used to wipe the sweat from his forehead about every three minutes. No one had ever told me whether he had a medical condition. I wasn't about to ask.

He got his nickname, Suicide, as a joke. All nicknames cops give one another are jokes. Some are in poor taste. Some are extraordinarily clever. This one was somewhere in between. Stanton had an excellent clearance rate for death investigations. But an unusually large percentage of those clearances were classified as suicide. It seemed to be his working theory on every unnatural death. He created elaborate reconstructions to prove suicide, even if the theories worked only one in ten times. I'd never heard of anyone else doing that. I didn't know if it was because Stanton was competitive or lazy. But that was how he'd earned his name: clearing cases via suicide.

He glanced up at me and said in a fast clip, "You want to take one of my cases? I just got a new homicide. Tell me you think she was killed in the city and her body was moved up here. I'll be happy to give you everything I have on the case." He grabbed the washcloth and wiped his forehead.

"I wish it was that simple. She's a friend of my daughter. I've been keeping her parents informed on Suzanne's missing person's case."

"I'm sorry to hear there's a personal connection. But I gotta tell you, Bennett, all kinds of shit has been dropping around here. The burglary rate is off the charts. Armed robberies are up in all of the Westchester towns. And this homicide is our fifth since May. That may not cause a stir in Manhattan, but it's a big deal here."

"I'm here because of the Mortons, but I wanted to find out the circumstances of her death. We're wondering if this homicide could be linked to a couple of deaths we're looking at in the city. It's a possibility."

That caught Stanton's attention. "Are you talking serial killer?" He reached again for the washcloth.

"It's a possibility. But if it is, you won't be able to write this one off as a suicide."

Stanton scowled at me. "That shit's not funny. I don't even know how that nickname got started."

I held up my hands. "I retract my snarky comment."

"What do you want from me, Bennett?"

"Details about the body, method of death, everything."

"Look, Bennett, you're a good guy, I'd like to work with you. But right now, I'm getting screamed at for a briefing with our assistant chief, the mayor, and my captain. We've only had the body a couple of hours. I haven't even seen it yet. Let me get back to you tomorrow or the next day, when I have more information."

Reluctantly, I agreed to leave and call him the next day. I didn't want to say something I might regret. I didn't understand a homicide detective who hadn't gone out to the scene immediately. I didn't care if he had half a dozen other cases.

As I worked my way through the maze of hallways, I saw the Mortons sitting in a small but comfortable-looking room. Suzanne's mother dabbed her eyes with a Kleenex. Her father just stared at the victim advocate. I weighed the risk of stepping into the room. I didn't want to upset them any more than they already were. Or maybe I was just trying to justify avoiding something I didn't want to do.

Just then I glanced at my watch. It kicked me into gear. I was supposed to be at Holy Name coaching the first practice of the girls' basketball team in a little over half an hour.

# CHAPTER 19

**I WAS ALREADY** wearing an official blue Holy Name basketball coach's shirt. I didn't say anything about the mustard stain on the collar or the hole under the arm. The shirt had probably been around since I was a student here. The girls were already huddled in a group at the corner of the bleachers. A relatively new nun named Sister Elizabeth was checking uniforms and talking to the girls. When she noticed me, she stepped away from the group to talk to me in private.

She had a flat, midwestern accent. "Mr. Bennett, I'm thrilled you agreed to coach. Your height alone is going to give you credibility."

I laughed at that. Then I looked at the group and said, "Are there any assistant coaches?"

Sister Elizabeth looked stricken. Finally, she said, "I'm sorry. You're the only parent who answered the call to service.

But I can help. I played some ball in college. And I have a few ideas for the girls."

"If you played college basketball, you're eminently more qualified to coach these girls than I am."

"The problem is, I also coach volleyball and field hockey. I can't always be here just for basketball. Sister Sheilah said that you'd enjoy coaching and that you were good with the kids. I guess you'd have to be if you've got ten of your own."

I liked this young woman who said what was on her mind. "In your opinion, how are the girls' skills?"

She hesitated. "About what you would think they'd be. Except for your daughter Fiona. She's shown some real ability."

"Really? That's good to hear."

"Not only does she have a decent jumper, she also goes to the basket hard. She's fearless."

I smiled as I looked over at my beautiful daughter talking with her friends on the team. "She gets that from playing hoops with her brothers. They don't cut her any slack. She wouldn't survive if she didn't throw the occasional elbow or take a hit once in a while. If she wasn't tough and aggressive, she'd hardly see the ball."

I got the girls together and started some simple drills. First, they warmed up by dribbling all the way around the edges of the court three times. Then we did a few shooting drills. Sister Elizabeth was right. I was impressed at how Fiona confidently handled the ball. Then she started sinking everything from twelve to fifteen feet out. How had this slipped my notice until now? The boys always said she was okay. Not great. Just okay. Had she been holding out on them? She was smart.

Maybe she'd been trying to sandbag them for some big reveal down the road.

I enjoyed seeing the girls concentrate so hard. After a while, I noticed my grandfather at the very top of the bleachers, watching the practice. Even with ten great-grandchildren, the man managed to show up for almost every function.

I felt a wave of melancholy as I thought about poor Suzanne Morton. It can be easy to get sucked into an endless loop of despair and hopelessness with this job. Early on in my career, a senior homicide detective told me that no matter what I see on the job, life goes on. I was trying to honor that sentiment right now. But watching these girls laughing and playing made me think of how many things Suzanne would never again experience.

All I could do was prepare these girls to play as best they could. That's what "Life goes on" means.

# CHAPTER 20

**I WAS HAPPY** to get back to the apartment a little earlier than usual. Today hadn't been as long as yesterday, but it was still trying. Thank God I'd had the chance to spend some time with Fiona and the basketball team. I was still amazed at how good Fiona was. The whole team had some skills. Sister Elizabeth had done a great job teaching them the basics of the game.

I see rudderless kids on the street with no direction, no adult to encourage them, and no real interest in most activities. I learned when I was a kid that sports provide a place to have fun, get some exercise, and give some focus. I feel it's important for kids to keep busy. I'm lucky that I've never had to force any of my kids to join a club or try a new activity. They all seem pretty interested in a lot of different things.

From arts and crafts to cooking, each of the kids has

a serious interest. Juliana has her acting. Jane writes in her journals and is a phenomenal student. My oldest son, Brian, is working hard at straightening out his life and is enjoying his job at an air-conditioning repair company.

I found Mary Catherine in the kitchen. I was excited to tell her how well Fiona had played. I really felt like basketball could be Fiona's "thing."

I swept my wife up in a hug but instantly felt something wasn't right. I took a step back, looked at her, and asked, "What's wrong?"

She led me by the hand to the living room, where Ricky and Eddie were playing a video game. A video game during daylight hours? Usually that would be a rule infraction. But Mary Catherine eased up on the rules when the kids weren't feeling well or had had a bad day.

I didn't see any fresh cuts or bruises.

Mary Catherine said, "The same boys bothered them again today."

I looked to Eddie to tell me the whole story.

He started up instantly. "Dad, we weren't causing problems. We went down the street to the other basketball hoop. Trent was going to meet us after he put something in his locker. Before we even got to the court, I heard someone say, 'Look, the little Christians are back.' It was the same two boys, and they had another boy with them. When Trent wandered up and asked what was going on, one of the boys punched him right in the face."

I glanced around the apartment. "Where is Trent now?"

Mary Catherine said, "He's cleaning up in the hallway bathroom."

I broke off from our conversation and rushed to the bathroom. Trent was sitting on the edge of the tub, holding a washcloth to his nose. It wasn't a lot of blood, but any blood coming out of your kids is too much.

"You okay?" I tried to keep my voice calm. Inside I was burning up. *Someone punched my kid!*

"Feels like the time I fell off the skateboard and landed right on my face." He didn't sound mad. That was Trent. He tended to go with events rather than fight them.

I sat there with him for a couple of minutes. He said he hadn't seen the bullies until it was too late. I listened, then we both went back out to the other boys to hear the rest of the story.

As we walked into the living room, Mary Catherine said, "You haven't heard the worst of it yet." She turned to Ricky and said, "Tell your father what happened just before you went back to Holy Name."

Ricky said, "The guy who punched Trent lifted his shirt. He had a pistol stuffed in his waistband."

"What kind of pistol?"

"A black one."

The universal, unhelpful description from people unfamiliar with guns. I was able to piece together a few more questions to get a better picture of the situation.

I looked at the boys sternly and said, "For now, stay on the school grounds. Don't risk going down to that hoop. We'll figure out how to fix this. Is that understood?" I was satisfied as all three boys nodded.

# CHAPTER 21

**AFTER DINNER, I** was dragging and ready to turn in a little early.

Brian caught me in the hallway. He looked ready for bed too but said, "Hey, Dad, you got a second?"

"Of course."

"Eddie told me about the trouble they're having. I could go with them one day after work and hang out at the park where they keep seeing the bullies."

"You're a good big brother, Brian. And I certainly appreciate the offer. But it's better to just stay away from the park for now. I don't want any of you mixed up with boys who carry guns. Plus, if you did something to help your brothers, someone might try to turn it around on you. You don't want to mess with your parole. You've done everything right since you got released. You got a good job. You're even taking a class at City College. I wouldn't want to screw that up for anything in the world."

We didn't often talk about Brian's stint in prison. He knew he'd made a mistake. Trying to fit in by selling designer drugs. Making a few extra bucks. But he'd gotten swept up in the excitement. He was lucky he hadn't been killed.

I still didn't know if his release was directly related to influence from the mayor. The mayor had said he would help after I found his missing daughter. But the mayor of New York was not known for keeping his word. Regardless, not long after I found his daughter, I got a surprise call that Brian was being released. Now it felt like a hole in my life had been filled.

A few minutes later, I was easing my head down onto my hypoallergenic, memory foam, oversized pillow. And it felt like I was using a drug. My body instantly relaxed and started to sink into the mattress.

Mary Catherine had the thermostat turned low and the room was already dark. It was perfect. Then she slipped into the bed with me and slid close, draping her arm across my chest and resting her head on my shoulder.

She said in a low voice, "Tell me about the best part of your day."

I said, "Our first basketball practice went really well. Fiona has some serious skills. I think her talk about a scholarship isn't too far out of line. I also think Sister Elizabeth put some of it in her head. But I liked coaching."

Mary Catherine squeezed me.

I turned to hold her as well. "How about your day?"

"I was doing research on fertility treatments."

"Did you learn anything new?"

"Are you kidding me? I have about five hundred more questions since reading a few articles. I can't believe how complex the process can be. Or how it can wreck your body."

"I thought it was pregnancy that can wreck your body."

"So then it's a double wreck." She giggled then.

I lay there and held her, feeling her steady breathing and heartbeat against my body.

She propped herself up on her elbow and looked at me. "Be honest with me. How do you feel about the prospect of another child in this home?"

I considered the question as well as the tone in which it had been asked. All I wanted was to be supportive. "I think it would be great. But I need you in my life, healthy and happy. If this treatment is dangerous, then I want us to both think about it carefully."

"You say the sweetest things without letting me know how you really feel."

"What can I say? It's a tough question. But I'll think about it seriously."

"That's all I can ask."

"Would a new baby speak English or Irish?"

She laughed and punched my chest playfully.

Then we didn't go right to sleep.

# CHAPTER 22

**I WAS UP** and out of the house quickly the next day. I was going to visit one of my least favorite places: NYPD headquarters at One Police Plaza in lower Manhattan almost at the foot of the Brooklyn Bridge. No working detective enjoys time at One Police Plaza.

Today I had two people to talk to inside the building: Gary Avram, my main contact in the Missing Persons Squad, and Gary's wife, Kathy Figler, a sergeant in the juvenile unit. Kathy was used to dealing with kids who caused problems. I was hoping to get her opinion on how I should deal with the bullies bothering my boys near Holy Name.

I greeted half a dozen people as I walked through the lobby. But the place definitely lacks the camaraderie found in a regular precinct. In a neighborhood precinct, there is no question you are all in this together. Here, everyone is looking out for themselves or trying to climb the ladder.

I took the elevator to the seventh floor, then found the small squad bay that held the Missing Persons unit. Most people have no idea how many missing persons there are in the United States. And when I say *most people*, I'm including the police. There are so many ways a person might disappear. Most of the time there's very little to go on with a missing person.

I found Gary Avram at his standing desk, a real anomaly inside the old-fashioned NYPD. A serious power lifter, Gary was the kind of guy who told anyone who would listen that sitting was the new smoking.

He was in his usual monogrammed, long-sleeved white shirt with a blue tie, and nodded as I approached his desk. I waited in silence while he finished whatever he was working on.

After thirty seconds, he looked up at me. "This damn crossword gets harder every week."

Gary had a prankster streak, and I swear I didn't know if he was joking now or not. Then he put on a serious face and said, "Sorry to hear that your daughter's friend was found in New Rochelle. But that explains why we had zero good leads on her disappearance."

"That's why I'm here. I have an idea. She's the third college student found murdered in the last two months. We considered her a missing person. Do you think there might be similar victims we've listed as missing persons?"

Gary didn't hesitate to reach across his absurdly tall desk and grab three file folders. He let them drop in front of me.

"What's this?" I asked.

"I'm big, not dense. I saw the reports from your and Hernandez's homicides. I usually look through ECMS to see if I can clear any missing persons. I saw that both of your victims were similar. Just like Suzanne Morton. College students, beautiful, bright. These are the only three in the past two years that fully match your victims." He added, "We haven't done much with any of these cases. The reports are all in the files."

"Gary, this is great. I'm impressed."

"That means something coming from a homicide detective. I know you guys think you've got the toughest assignment."

I knew some homicide detectives could be openly dismissive of other units. I just thanked him and said, "Guess who I'm visiting next?"

"You must mean my wife. But if you came to our house, you'd be visiting us. If you come to the office, you're *bothering* us," Gary teased. "Kathy and I have a strict rule never to discuss work at home. We think it would adversely affect the boys."

"Smart."

"Even here, during the workday, she's *Sergeant* Figler and I'm *Detective* Avram."

"Then I won't tell you where I'm going from here."

"You can mention how I'm on top of things. That would be okay."

I laughed. Most men want to impress their spouses. I'd probably say the same thing.

# CHAPTER 23

**I TOOK THE** stairs down three floors from Missing Persons to the juvenile unit. There was less risk of running into command staff on the dingy stairs that few people used. The juvenile unit was housed with a few other specialty units. They didn't even have their own squad bay.

The juvenile unit worked at containing crime by people under eighteen. Even if some of the crimes were as horrendous as adult crimes, there were rules in place to protect the young suspects. No one really disagreed, but it made working in the unit more complicated.

I've always believed the best juvenile crime detectives also *liked* working with young people. They viewed their encounters with young offenders as opportunities for them to turn their lives around. This approach became much more important to me after my son Brian was arrested for drug dealing.

I considered Kathy Figler to be one of the best cops I

knew. I was glad the NYPD was putting her talents to use in something as important as the juvenile unit.

I said hello to a couple of other detectives I knew in the unit as I navigated to the sergeant's office in the back. You could see the turnaround for the Brooklyn Bridge and a hint of the East River from Kathy Figler's window—a prize status symbol among the inhabitants of One Police Plaza.

The petite blond woman smiled when she saw me and got up to give me a hug.

She said, "What on earth would convince a homicide detective from Manhattan North to visit the juvenile unit at headquarters?"

"Actually, or at least officially, I had to talk to your husband about some missing persons cases."

"Detective Avram does a great job. I hope he was able to help."

I smiled at her deadpan response. "More than anyone has helped me in months. Or, I should say, he provided me with the most efficient help I've had this year."

"I wish he showed some of that initiative around the house."

We chatted about our families for a moment, then I explained to her the problems my boys had been having down the street from Holy Name.

Kathy listened and made notes. One thing the couple shared was their intensity and devotion to their jobs. I liked that.

"I hate hearing that one of the bullies had a gun," she said. "Ever since the city cut out funding for the anti-crime unit, we've seen instances of gun crime increase. The city disbanded the unit but tells everyone to keep doing what they were doing. It's crazy."

"Do you have any advice or insight on what my boys should do?"

"Staying on the school grounds would be the first step. I get what you're saying about not wanting them to be afraid to walk the streets of New York. But keeping them out of the situation is smart. I'll ask around and see if any of our detectives have heard the same sort of complaints. Maybe we can even get a security video showing the instigators so we can try to identify them."

"I appreciate anything you can do. My boys are a little rattled."

"Who would've thought we'd long for the days when there were fistfights in the schoolyards. The anti-bullying initiatives have helped in some places, but it's still a serious issue. Everyone is focused on cyberbullying right now."

I said, "I guess it's easy to bully someone over the internet when you don't even have to show your face in person."

"And herd mentality tends to favor the bully. Sometimes whole classes start to harass a student."

"I don't envy you. I'll stick with homicide."

Sergeant Figler said, "And we're glad you will."

# CHAPTER 24

**I RACED DOWN** the front steps of One Police Plaza, already knowing what I was going to do. Detective Gary Avram had given me some great leads.

Conveniently, the first address he'd supplied was just on the other side of the Brooklyn Bridge. I looked at the file and saw that this girl was the right age, eighteen, but appeared to have run away from home last year.

Her mother answered the door and informed me that the young woman had sent her a text a month ago, telling her she was safe but that she never wanted contact with the family again. That was not an issue I needed to get involved in.

The second missing person's case was in lower Manhattan. Very nice three-story walk-up. Turned out, the missing girl answered the door herself. She explained that she had fallen in love and run off with another student from Barnard but came home last week. The family was so happy, they'd forgotten to let the NYPD know. Case closed.

The third missing person's case listed the missing person's residence as a single-family home in Queens, a few blocks from Astoria Park. I drove out there, then sat in my car for a moment to glance at the file again. If it was another wild-goose chase, at least I'd have cleared up all three leads in one morning.

Cheryl Savage was a junior at Columbia when she disappeared last fall. She had been a stellar high school athlete, playing basketball, softball, and lacrosse. Her photo showed a tall, striking young woman with neat auburn hair and a dazzling smile.

Her roommate at Columbia had said Cheryl went out one night and she never saw her again. A single security video from her dorm showed her leaving the building, dressed in a cocktail dress. No one had any idea where she'd gone, and there had been no activity on her phone since the night she disappeared.

I felt a little sad closing the file. Although I saw it all the time, I knew it would break my heart if any of my kids disappeared. I'm not sure I could ever function properly again.

A girl about seven was sitting on the home's steps. When she looked up, I saw a resemblance to Cheryl Savage. She had the same auburn hair, and there was something about her eyes that seemed similar to the girl in the photo.

I stood back on the sidewalk to keep from startling the little girl. I smiled and said, "Hi. I need to get past you to ring the bell. Is that okay?"

The girl's hazel eyes took me in. She looked like she was about to say something. I never heard it.

Something crashed into me on my left side. I saw a flicker of movement just before I felt the impact.

I hit a decorative light post, which sort of spun me and made me step off the curb. The cascading effect of the surprise blow and the loss of balance almost sent me into the street in front of a delivery truck.

The truck's tires screeched as the driver laid on his horn. In New York, the horn is the first option for all situations.

The truck skidded to a halt and I managed to jump a foot back so that the front fender missed me by an inch. I heard the driver scream something at me through the closed windows.

Finally, I looked back to see the threat. A wiry man in his mid-forties stood next to the stairs with his fists clenched. He didn't want a fight. He wanted to kick my ass.

# CHAPTER 25

**I TURNED TO** fully face the man, a little dazed as the truck pulled away slowly. The driver was still yelling curses at me from the cab of the truck. I kept my eyes on the man who'd so forcefully knocked into me. I wondered how a guy that small could generate such force.

I stepped back onto the sidewalk to the left of the man. He didn't say a word. His eyes were fixed on me.

Then he growled, "Get away from my daughter before I take your damn head off."

It all came into focus for me. I said, "Mr. Savage?"

He stared at me, then said, "Who are you?"

I reached into my pocket and pulled out my badge. "Mike Bennett, NYPD." Instantly, the look on the man's face told me he realized his mistake.

He took a step toward me, but I held up my hand and he froze in place. "I'm so sorry. I just saw you talking to my daughter and I snapped. Obviously, you know my oldest daughter is missing. I'm not about to lose another one."

I nodded and straightened up. Then I moved my shoulder to make sure everything was still in the proper socket.

His expression changed. "Are you here with new information on Cheryl?"

I shook my head. "I'm looking at some other crimes." I hesitated to use the word *homicides*. I didn't want to freak him out. "I was hoping to ask you a few questions about your daughter."

A few minutes later, I was sitting in the living room of the home. Chuck Savage and his wife, Regina, sat across from me and answered all of my questions about Cheryl.

She was a happy girl. Didn't have a crazy dating life. No ex-boyfriends who'd threatened her. And they had not heard one word from or about her since the September evening she disappeared last year.

Regina Savage had a melancholy tone to her voice. The sort of thing I heard from homicide victims' families. She may not have understood exactly why I was asking these questions, but she was no idiot.

Mrs. Savage said, "You're trying to figure out if my Cheryl is dead, aren't you?"

I hesitated as I searched for the right words. "I have no reason to think your daughter is dead. I have another case that might, and I can't say positively, have a victim similar to your daughter's description. I'm trying to run down every possible lead."

The tired-looking woman lowered her head and nodded it slightly.

As cold and calculating as it sounds, I looked at Cheryl's disappearance as a chance to gain more information. Maybe we could use it to stop this killer from claiming more victims.

# CHAPTER 26

**JUST AS I** was leaving Queens, I got a text from Bill Stanton, at the New Rochelle Police Department. He wanted to meet at the Starbucks on 145th Street near Jackie Robinson Park. I told him I'd be there in less than thirty minutes. This was not an opportunity I intended to pass up, though I wasn't looking forward to getting the rest of the information on Suzanne Morton.

A mere twenty-three minutes later, I stepped into the Starbucks. The place was moderately busy. I craned my neck and saw Bill "Suicide" Stanton sitting by himself in the corner. A hard-copy case file rested on the small table in front of him. An extra-large coffee cup scribbled with the name *Bill* sat next to the folder.

I eased onto the stool across from him. "What brings you all the way down to the city, Bill?"

"I had to talk to Suzanne Morton's parents." Sweat started to build on his brow.

"Ugh. I don't envy you at all."

"It was brutal. I swear, Bennett, I'd rather get shot at than talk to grieving parents. It sucks the life out of you. I'll have more nightmares about my conversation with them than I would if I had a car accident."

I knew Suicide Stanton hadn't come here to discuss his psychological hang-ups. I said, "What can I do for you, Bill?"

He looked down, removed a handkerchief from his jacket pocket, and wiped his face. He mumbled something and shoved the case file toward me.

"Bill, I have no idea what you just said."

He swallowed hard, sat up straight, and said, "If this case is related to a serial killer, I have to admit I'm in over my head. Way over my head. I can't tell you how many stories I've read in the *Daily News* about your cases involving serial killers over the years. I'm willing to transfer the entire case over to you."

I let out a laugh. "I bet you are. There are a couple of problems with that."

"Like what? My chief won't care. As far as he's concerned, it's another closed case. One less thing for New Rochelle to worry about."

I understood what Stanton was trying to do. I couldn't ever do it myself. The idea of handing a case of mine over to someone else just sounded weird. But I understood that if you had a caseload that included everything from burglaries to homicides, you might have to clear your plate any way you could.

I thought about it for a few moments. Finally, I said, "The

first thing we need to worry about is establishing that there is definitely a single killer. We're working on a theory based on two bodies we've recovered that were dressed in a similar manner and had similar backgrounds. I'm trying to piece together the rest. We don't even know for sure if we have a serial-killer case yet."

He looked at me hopefully. He raised his eyebrows and pushed the file folder a little closer.

I let out a sigh. "You realize the NYPD would frown on me investigating homicides in other cities, right?"

"We can at least work it together until you decide if the murders are related or not."

"Aside from Suzanne being a pretty college student, I don't know if any of the circumstances of her death match up. Like, how was she dressed, what was the cause of death, when did the death occur? We still have a lot of questions like that to answer."

Stanton's face lost its scowl. It was like I'd given him a glimmer of hope. He started talking quickly. "She was nude and wrapped in a painter's drop cloth. Cause of death was blunt trauma to the head. She was hit with something heavy with a round base. The killer was strong enough to leave an imprint of the weapon in the victim's skull."

"How long had she been in the cabinet before anyone found her?"

"The medical examiner and forensic people estimate about three weeks. Right around the date she disappeared."

I made a few notes, then leveled my eyes at the detective. "I'm not saying this will all work out, but let's keep in touch. It's better to be prepared than be surprised."

"I agree. I also agree to let you take this case whenever you want."

I chuckled. "Okay, Bill, if these do turn out to be related, there's nothing I want more than to find Suzanne Morton's killer."

Then I heard the opening piano chords to my ringtone.

Stanton let out a laugh and said, " 'Layla.' Love it."

The three-number exchange code made it clear it was someone from One Police Plaza. That was rarely good news.

# CHAPTER 27

**BILL STANTON WAS** annoyed I wouldn't take his homicide case yet. I left him at the table with just a final nod as I walked quickly out of the Starbucks to answer my phone. Someone speaking very quickly said their name and title, but I didn't catch any of it.

I said, "I'm sorry. Who is this?"

The woman slowed down like she was talking to a child. "This is Persephone Garland. I work in the office of public outreach. I think we might've found a lead on your case."

"A lead? On my most recent homicide? I'm not following how public relations uncovered a lead."

*"Public outreach."*

"What's the difference?"

"I'd get paid more if it was a public relations job."

I laughed. She'd already picked up a cop's sense of humor, even if she worked in a non-sworn position.

She said, "Can you stop by my office? I have the info from the tip all right here. It came from a post on social media I put up about the body you recovered from the Hudson River."

"I'll be there as quick as I can." I cut off the call before I started asking questions about the privacy of the victim's family or who had approved using an active homicide as part of community outreach. She better have some good answers or a hell of a lead. Otherwise, I was going to be annoyed. Loudly annoyed.

Two trips to One Police Plaza in one day was very unusual. I hoped to keep it that way. I marched into the public outreach office about thirty minutes after I got the call. I kept thinking about Estella Abreu's family and if they'd seen the social media post. I would've liked to have given them a heads-up before it came out.

The office was empty. For a moment I thought I'd walked into the wrong place. To be honest, I'd never been in the public outreach office. I knew they existed and occasionally interacted with the people who worked in the unit. Most of them were marketing and technical people. Their job was to get out the word about what the NYPD was doing and how the public could help.

I stood by the door to the office and called out, "Hello?"

A young woman stepped out from one of the rear cubicles. "Detective Bennett, right? I'm Persephone Garland."

Persephone was a very attractive Black woman in a professional blouse and skirt, but she looked impossibly young. Young enough to easily pass for one of my teen daughters.

As soon as she saw me, Persephone smiled and started walking toward me. But she must've seen the look on my face because she stopped, folded her arms, and said, "No, I'm not a kid. I'm twenty-four years old and a University of Maryland graduate."

"I'm not questioning your qualifications."

"I'm not offended at all, Detective. In fact, I'm an army brat. I'm not offended by anything. Except maybe extreme stupidity."

I laughed. She may have looked like a Girl Scout, but she talked more like a marine. I liked that.

"I know I look like I'm only twelve. I'll tell you what I tell every other detective I work with: Get over it. This is the best result I've gotten in my five months working for the NYPD. And I think it's something that could be useful."

Persephone led me back to a computer in another room. She brought up a simple Facebook post that had a picture of Estella Abreu and the facts surrounding her death. Any cop will tell you that if you open up a tip line, you'll get a lot of tips. Many will be from well-meaning citizens who have no relation to your case. Some of the tips come from people bent on disrupting the police department. They are tips designed to waste time. And some tips just come from crackpots who believe every conspiracy theory that floats down the internet.

The biggest thing I look for is someone willing to put their name to a tip. Anonymous tips are generally bullshit.

Persephone didn't disappoint me. She pulled out a single sheet of paper with two photographs printed on it and some biographical info.

I studied the upper photograph for a moment. "Is that Estella at a bar?"

Persephone nodded. "Almost three weeks before she was murdered. And the man to her left was her date."

The photo wasn't the highest definition. I wouldn't have been able to positively identify the man in court. But I could tell he was young and looked athletic. He was wearing a nice suit, and his hair was cut short.

Persephone kept going. "The name in the text box is the man who gave us the tip. He's willing to talk to a detective, and I have his contact information."

Today seemed to be the day for NYPD personnel to be at the top of their game. This was the second well-thought-out and well-presented lead I'd gotten from someone at One Police Plaza today.

Persephone leveled a stare at me. "Now you want to make any cracks about my age or experience?"

"Persephone, I believe you just made it into my investigative plans on every case I ever get."

"Then can you do me a favor?"

"Anything you want."

"Will you keep me in the loop? This is the most exciting this job has ever been. I was already looking on LinkedIn to see if there were any public relations jobs on Wall Street. Now I feel like I have to stay here to do my part."

"Spoken like the daughter of an army vet. Your dad should be proud of you."

"Mom."

"Excuse me."

"My dad is a deadbeat living somewhere in Los Angeles. My mom was a medic in the army."

"Your mom must be proud."

Persephone beamed. "She is."

# CHAPTER 28

**I BOLTED FROM** One Police Plaza again, already trying to reach the tipster by phone. I had called Walter Jackson, who did a quick profile for me. The tipster's name was Ivan Mirotic. He had graduated from Boston University six years ago and now worked for one of the big trading houses on Wall Street. No criminal record. And no obvious reason to provide a fake tip. Even *I* had to admit this looked pretty good.

I called the cell phone but got no response. I didn't want to barge into his office if he was just a good citizen providing information. People get funny when cops show up at their work. It doesn't matter if they're a suspect or not. No one wants to answer questions from their boss about a visit from a homicide detective.

About twenty minutes later, Ivan finally answered his phone and agreed to meet me at South Cove Park, overlooking the

Hudson. Not far from where we'd found Estella Abreu's body a few days ago.

The Hudson still had some wind chop, and the breeze whipped along the surface. Clouds floated across the afternoon sun. I was surprised how much it made the temperature dip. I wished I'd worn more than my North Face windbreaker.

I saw a man standing alone at the seawall, looking at the screen of his iPhone. I approached him slowly. He was about thirty and average height. But he was dressed like a guy trying to impress people. A dark Brooks Brothers suit with a dusky red tie. A similar look to a lot of the people in finance.

"Mr. Mirotic?"

He looked up from his phone, assessed me for a moment, then just nodded. If he was trying to show that he had little use for anyone who didn't work with him, he was doing a good job.

Why would a guy like this take time from his work, which he probably thought was the only job that mattered?

I went the whole official route. I pulled out my ID and badge and dispensed with any small talk I might've made to put him at ease.

I held up the info sheet with the photo he'd sent us. Walter Jackson had also texted me the original electronic photo, which had better definition.

"Tell me, what made you post the tip?" I asked.

"Hell, I don't know. Just trying to do the right thing, I guess."

"Where was the photo taken?"

"We were at a big Wall Street party at an after-hours club by The Battery. Everyone from all the big financial houses was there. I saw this hot girl, and she was fumbling with a contact lens. I wear contacts too, and had some rewetting solution in my pocket so I let her use it."

"Did you know the man she was with?"

"I've seen him around. I'm not sure who he works for. He might be an analyst for one of the smaller firms. He always seemed like a dick to me. Hair always perfect, always in a nice suit. Then I see him with this gorgeous girl and it just sort of annoyed me that night."

I said, "You've never talked to this guy?"

"Never."

"And you have no personal relationship with him?"

"If I've never spoken to him, how can I have a personal relationship with him?"

I let the comment slide. Besides, it was accurate. I was just trying to get as much information as I could.

I said, "You said the photo was from about three weeks ago. Is that correct?"

"Not quite three weeks. Friday night will make it three weeks."

"Do you guys get together like that often?"

"We usually do one big blowout in the fall and another in the spring. Plus, there are all the holiday parties, but the firms usually pay for those."

I made notes about the bar and exact date. We'd have to see if the bar had security video and look through credit card receipts for the night.

"You said you'd seen this guy around before. Can you recall where?"

Mirotic looked at me like I was a child asking him the same

question over and over. Then Mirotic said, "I've already told you; I just saw him at parties like this once in a while. Listen, I've got a lot to do. You got my cell phone number if you really need to reach me again."

I had been dismissed.

# CHAPTER 29

**NOW I HAD** a photo of a suspect and a rough time period he was with the victim. I racked my brain to figure out how to identify the man with Estella Abreu. I sent the photo to several different units at the NYPD, and Walter Jackson was running it past his contacts in all the federal agencies.

Was the man Estella's boyfriend? How did she know him? The questions were rolling into my head.

This was the first decent lead I'd had on this case. Actual physical evidence. It was frustrating to see what a potential suspect might look like but not be able to put a name to the photo.

I took the extra step of calling Ronald Higdon, Esquire.

He answered the phone talking. Before he said hello or anything else, all I heard was "I'm working on finding out about the dead girls, Bennett. I've got guys all over the city asking questions."

"That's good because I'm going to need you to use the same network to ID a man in a photo. I'm going to send it to your phone in a few minutes. He's standing next to the beautiful girl. He's in a dark suit and has short light-brown hair. I think he works on Wall Street somewhere."

Ronald said, "I've got good connects on Wall Street. Back from my days when I used to make deliveries down there."

No great surprise. But it showed how much Ronald trusted me to casually admit he used to deliver cocaine to people on Wall Street. Everyone knew the industry was a major consumer of cocaine as well as amphetamines. Financial people's personalities seemed to push them toward drugs that made them more hyper than they already were.

My next plan involved looking through the Financial Industry Regulatory Authority, or FINRA, files of every man registered in New York as a trader. But there were thousands and thousands of those. And if the picture on the respective man's driver's license or employee ID was even a year or two old, he might look quite different from the man in the bar photo.

I thought about Persephone Garland in the public outreach section. Maybe she could work some more magic. Problem was, if we put out the suspect's photo, he'd be just as likely to see it as anyone. He could flee. He could change his appearance. He could figure a way to cover his tracks and develop alibis.

I dismissed the idea. When I finally found this guy, I wanted to be able to surprise him. Instead, I sent the photo to four other informants. None of them nearly as good as Ronald Higdon, Esquire. But one of them operated in lower Manhattan and had been a trader himself until addiction knocked him all the way to the street. Now he was a financial advisor to people who couldn't afford one of the big firms. And he made extra cash by helping law enforcement with information.

I'd covered my bases. And I still had time to make it to Holy Name and teach some middle-school girls how to throw elbows and not be seen by the refs. Or at least understand others would be trying to do the same to them.

# CHAPTER 30

**THERE IS ALWAYS** something comforting about walking the grounds of Holy Name. Maybe because I essentially grew up on the campus, or perhaps it's the artistry of the architecture. I always breathe a little easier when I'm here.

I felt like I had wheels in motion on my investigation. I had informants trying to identify the man in the photo with Estella Abreu, I had Walter Jackson skimming through trader licenses, and Terri Hernandez was discreetly visiting some of the financial houses where she had contacts.

I was trying to make sure my kids had well-rounded childhoods so I could produce good citizens. At least that's how I justified taking an hour out of my day to go over to my kids' school on the Upper West Side and work on basic basketball skills.

The girls were already lined up when I arrived. I saw that

Fiona had taken charge during my three-minute absence. She was adjusting some of the other girls' stances for shooting free throws. And she was right on the money.

It was a good thing I had backup on the court. I may have been able to block the investigation out of my mind for a few minutes to spend some quality time with Fiona, but seeing Trent, Eddie, and Ricky all sitting at the end of the bleachers, waiting for a turn to play on the court, broke my heart. The bullies had accomplished just what they wanted: they had scared us. That's what bullies do.

I cut practice a little short. We played a quick scrimmage, with the first team to 11 points declared the winner. Fiona scored the first 7 and the last 2 points for her team, bringing home a victory of 11–4. Then I had them practice 3-pointers. It was a simple drill. You pass once and then shoot from wherever you are on the 3-point line. When each of them made a basket, they could get cleaned up. After a few minutes we adjusted it to lining up to shoot free throws instead of 3-pointers. I needed to be back at work today.

Then I walked past my boys and told them to follow me. On our way out of the gym I told Sister Elizabeth I'd be back with the boys in about ten minutes.

We walked out the front gate of Holy Name, then up the street toward the park where the boys had seen some trouble.

Trent was worried. "Are you sure this is a good idea, Dad?"

"No, son, I'm not. But I don't like to see your freedom restricted. And that's what these bullies are trying to do."

Ricky seemed ready to rumble. "With you on our side, Dad, we can settle this once and for all."

I looked at my son. "We're not members of the Crips. This is not a showdown. I just want to see if I can reason with the boys. Very simple." Then I looked at Eddie. "Is this about the time you usually see them?"

Eddie shrugged. "Usually a little later. It's been on afternoons when we have a free period at the end of the day."

When we arrived at the park, I realized we should've brought a basketball to blend in. There were a few kids in the park already.

I said to the boys, "Do you see them?"

Trent pointed to two boys at the far corner of the small park. "That might be them."

I couldn't get a good look from this distance. They were clearly older teenagers. I could see how they could intimidate the boys. I felt my face flush and my blood pressure rise. The idea of someone tormenting my kids was something I just couldn't live with.

I was still dressed in my blue Holy Name basketball coach's shirt. I had no ID. My comment to Brian came back to me. What could I do as an adult dealing with an aggressive adolescent? The answer was not much.

The boys Trent had pointed out were now walking our way. My sons turned to face the approaching teenagers. I liked how they acted as a team. Ricky was in the middle with Eddie and Trent flanking.

I stepped closer to the boys to stop anything from escalating. But my anxiety was high. I was just trying to straighten out a situation that might be better off left to the juvenile unit detectives. Or maybe social workers. Or teachers. Or their parents.

I had fallen into the classic trap of thinking other people's kids would listen to me. They wouldn't. Now we were all in a worse situation as the boys kept walking directly toward us.

Then Trent relaxed and said, "I was wrong. That's not them."

We looked around for another few minutes, then all walked back to Holy Name. It gave me a little insight into the anguish the boys felt being prey to a bully. Anxiety and fear can definitely color your judgment.

# CHAPTER 31

**AFTER A DECENT** night's sleep, I woke up alert and ready to find the suspect in the Estella Abreu case. I had a little extra time this morning, so I grabbed our extra-long Ford passenger van and chauffeured the kids to school a few blocks away. The remarkable thing was that we made it to the school ten minutes before the final bell. A new record. The kids cheered inside the van.

I looked up with a big, goofy grin on my face to see my lifelong nemesis: Sister Sheilah, the school principal. When I had started at Holy Name, it was also Sheilah's first year.

Now she stared directly at me. I didn't falter. I looked her right in the eye. That's what I was told to do if I ever had to face a dangerous animal one-on-one. Sister Sheilah made a show of looking at her wrist. Then she gave me a big smile and a thumbs-up.

I didn't mind being acknowledged for doing something well. I think her thumbs-up was more an indictment of how often I got the kids to school late. None of it really mattered. I knew she loved me. And I could tell she loved my kids.

I never want to lose sight of what's important. The NYPD will function without me. Homicides will be solved without me. But time with my family is precious.

My little adventure with the kids had put me in an exceptionally good mood. I switched from the van to my city-issued Chevy Impala in a matter of seconds. Before I even reached the garage's exit onto West End Avenue, my phone started to ring.

I pulled over and answered the call. It was Ronald Higdon, Esquire. The first words out of his mouth were "I got a name to go with your photo. I'm working on getting more stuff."

"I'll be at your shop in ten minutes."

I walked through the front door of Higdon's Pawn and Jewelry about nine minutes later. As the door shut behind me, I said, "I hope you're not wasting my time."

A grinning Ronald Higdon, Esquire, met me at the counter and slapped a sheet of paper on the glass. I picked it up and studied it for a moment. It was a registration form from FINRA's central depository for an investment advisor. It had a FINRA logo at the top. A copy of what looked like an employee ID photo was attached, and the man looked a lot like the man who'd been standing next to Estella Abreu.

His name was Kyle Banning. I read some of his identifying features. He was twenty-six years old and lived on the Upper East Side on Fifth Avenue, a couple of blocks from the Guggenheim. How the hell does a twenty-six-year-old, even one in finance, earn enough to live in an apartment with a direct view of Central Park?

I looked at Ronald. "How'd you find this so fast?"

"One of my people in lower Manhattan is hooked into all the financial houses. He recognized several of the people in your photo as being from one particular firm. He took a chance that your suspect was with that group. It worked out."

"This is really good work, Ronald. What's it going to cost me?"

"Get that detective from the First Precinct, Richard Matthews, off my back. He called me again yesterday just after you gave me the photo. He says I'm in deep shit for pretending to be a lawyer. Sounds like a big guy. I don't know why he's hassling me. Do you know him?"

I nodded. "I've met him over the years. He is kind of big. Your assessment just from his voice is accurate."

"His deep voice makes him sound deadly serious."

"What did you say to him?"

"What I always tell the cops: *I didn't do nothing. Why are you hassling me?* He didn't say much else. It's like he's too lazy to come up here and arrest me."

"So we'll be square if I can keep this Detective Matthews at the First Precinct from bothering you?"

Ronald made a show of wiping his hands together and holding them up. "We'll be even Steven. Seriously, Bennett, I'd appreciate that kind of support."

I just nodded and headed out the door. As I walked to my car, I pulled out my cell phone and called the First Precinct. More specifically, I called the cell phone assigned to Detective Richard Matthews.

He answered with his usual gruff baritone voice. "Detective Matthews."

"Rich, it's Mike Bennett. Thanks for scaring my informant. He bought the whole thing."

A deep chuckle came across the phone line. "I love to help when all I have to do is call a snitch and scare him a little bit. Is he doing everything you need him to?"

"With a good attitude."

Matthews laughed again. "Feel free to use me any time you want."

I was still smiling when I got to my car. I love having friends all over the department. I wish I could say I felt bad deceiving Ronald Higdon, Esquire, about the NYPD investigating him. I didn't feel much remorse.

And now I had a lead on a real suspect.

# CHAPTER 32

**WITH THE NAME** Ronald Higdon, Esquire, gave me in hand, I didn't want to wait one second without acting on the information. I was barely even settled in my car before I called Walter Jackson, asking him to find out everything he could about Kyle Banning. I knew it wouldn't take the criminal intelligence analyst very long before he called me back with some juicy info.

I texted Harry Grissom, but all I got back was: In a meeting at 1PP.

I sat in the car for a few minutes, making notes and a couple of phone calls. I called the Abreu house and spoke to Mrs. Abreu about whether she had ever heard the name Kyle Banning.

Mrs. Abreu said she had talked to all of Estella's cousins and friends. She'd even made notes. But Kyle Banning was not a name mentioned by any of the younger members of the Abreu family.

I knew the grieving mother just wanted to talk and feel like she was contributing to the investigation. It happens all the time. Just like when making death notifications, you never cut off a family member when they want to talk about the victim. This was one of the few times I felt antsy. I was ready to roll with this new suspect. But I let Mrs. Abreu release all her pent-up emotion and told her I'd talk to her again later in the week.

As soon as I hung up, Walter called me.

The big man's rumbling voice tested the limits of my iPhone's speaker. He said, "Sorry I didn't call you back quicker. I was having trouble with my reverse origami class. I'll let you know how things unfold." He couldn't help laughing at his own pun.

"Ugh. You owe your daughter another dollar in the pun jar," I said. "What do ya got for me?"

Walter jumped right into the meat of his information. "Your suspect, Kyle Banning, has one arrest, from January of this year. Guess what it was for?"

"Some kind of violence against women?"

"The universal indicator of a creep."

All I managed to say was "Go on."

"A patrol officer near Times Square heard a woman cry out just after midnight. The officer located the woman, who was with Kyle Banning. The woman was crying and had a red mark on her face. The cop believed Banning had struck her, so he was arrested but later released without bail. Investigators tried to talk to the woman, but she left a message on the detective's phone that she wasn't interested in pursuing charges. The case was dismissed."

The cynical side of me came out. "Let me guess: Banning comes from a wealthy family."

"His father is general counsel for one of the big insurance companies. Kyle still lives with his parents."

I wrote a few more notes. Walter gave me the address of the financial company where Kyle Banning worked and phone numbers that were connected to him.

Walter added, "There's one other thing I noticed. It looks like someone tried to remove the reports from ECMS."

"I didn't know that was even possible."

"It can be, like when someone has their record expunged or if a judge orders us to remove a report. In this case, it looks like whoever tried it didn't have official permission and wasn't able to remove the case file. There're only three reports. The arresting officer's report. The investigating detective's report. And the report by the detective closing the case after the victim refused to talk."

This concerned me. "Sounds like Kyle Banning's got someone inside the department."

"More likely his dad has someone inside the mayor's office."

I snapped my fingers as I saw the truth of what Walter Jackson was saying. My best choice was to jump on this lead fast and play everything close to the vest.

# CHAPTER 33

**WALTER JACKSON COULD** fit together information better than any computer. His profiles always prepared
me for interviews on sensitive subjects.

The victim in the case of Kyle Banning's arrest was named
Celia Cartwright. She lived in Newark. I groaned. It could
take me an hour or more just to get there. Thankfully, Walter
next dropped that she worked at the American Museum of
Natural History, right here in the city.

When I asked him what her job was at the museum, Walter
said, "The wage and hour report only tells me who pays her,
not what she does."

"Fair enough."

It didn't take me long to get to the impressive American
Museum of Natural History on the western edge of Central
Park. My kids had had little interest in the museum until they

watched the movie *Night at the Museum* with Ben Stiller. Now the place was a great family outing.

I went through the museum's main entrance. I badged an uninterested guard and asked if I could speak to the head of security. I smiled when the tall form of Steve Barborini strolled toward me. The former lieutenant had retired from the NYPD to become head of security here at the museum.

Barborini raised both hands and said, "Homicide? I swear I haven't murdered anyone."

As we shook hands, I said, "You're too lazy to murder anyone, Steve. Unless you shouted at them long enough that they just died."

The director of security laughed and patted me on the back. "Good to see you, Mike. I got no one to talk to around this place. And not all that much to do most of the time."

I gave him the name of the woman I needed to talk to and a brief rundown of why I wanted to talk to her.

Steve understood. He made a quick phone call, then told me, "Celia Cartwright works on the second subfloor in entomology."

"She works on the origins of words?"

He shook his head in disdain. "No, you idiot. That's etymology. She studies insects."

After what seemed like a miles-long trek, following Steve Barborini down two floors, through endless hallways, he led me to a sublevel office-lab without windows but with nice, soft light.

A very pretty young woman with dark hair looked up from a magnifying glass. She said, "May I help you?"

It was Celia Cartwright. Once Steve Barborini made sure

she was comfortable talking to me, he left us alone. I tried not to look at what she was working on currently, which appeared to be maggots swarming over some kind of rotted flesh.

She noticed my discomfort and placed a rag over the dish of maggots. I smiled and said, "How did you get into this line of work?"

"I've always been fascinated by insects. Did you know they make up over two-thirds of the life forms on Earth? They can work together on projects far beyond the scale of anything humans have ever built. And even these simple maggots digest waste matter and turn it into useful material, like fertilizer or feed for other animals, without us ever appreciating them."

Celia explained that she was on a fellowship and paid a small stipend. "That's why I live in Newark." She saw me wince at the name of the New Jersey city. She smiled. "I always get that reaction from New Yorkers. But I could never afford to live on my own in the city on what they pay me here. Anyway, I'm sure you're not here to talk about my salary."

"You are correct. I appreciate you getting to the point. I'm here to ask you a few questions about what happened to you in January."

"Why? No charges were ever even filed." She seemed upset but continued: "Using my deductive reasoning from watching *Law & Order*, I'm guessing Kyle's assaulted someone else and you're trying to figure it out."

"Impressive. You've expressed exactly why I'm here and what I'm interested in. Maybe I should start watching more TV."

Then she started to cry.

# CHAPTER 34

**I SAT SILENTLY** while Celia Cartwright sniffled, then blew her nose. When she looked up, her brown eyes had red rims around them. She managed to say, "I'm sorry. I don't know why I reacted like that."

"You're allowed to react any way you want. You were the victim of a crime. And nothing was done about it. That's a crime in itself."

She reached over and patted my arm like she appreciated my comments even if they didn't make her feel better. I heard a quiet "Thank you." After a moment she added, "I take responsibility for my part in not filing charges."

It is rare for a cop to hear anyone take responsibility. Everyone has an excuse for all kinds of stupid behavior. This was refreshing.

I gave it another minute and she started to talk without prompting.

Celia started slowly. "I met Kyle at a party in the financial district. I was there with one of my roommates. He invited me on a date, and a couple of weeks later, right after New Year's, I met him in Times Square. We ate from sidewalk vendors, had drinks at a couple of different Irish pubs, just had a nice evening. He was charming and so good-looking."

Celia paused, gathering her composure and fighting off more emotion. I didn't say anything. I just waited.

She swallowed hard and ran a finger under her eyes. "When I told him I had to catch my train back to Newark, he suggested we stay at a hotel. We were standing in front of the St. James. That's when everything changed. I told him I had to get home. But he kept insisting we go into the Hotel St. James.

"He grabbed me by the arm. That's when I jerked it away from him. Then he slapped me in the face with his other hand. I had never been hit in my whole life. Not even as a kid. What a shock.

"If that policeman hadn't stepped around the corner and taken control so quickly, God knows what would've happened. Kyle's whole face transformed. It was like a horror movie. I was terrified."

Now Celia looked more determined than scared. She said, "My mistake happened the next day, when a lawyer came to my apartment in Newark. He offered me money not to move forward with the case. I declined. Then he upped his offer to twenty thousand dollars. You have to understand, I have huge student loans. Working places like this isn't going to help me much. But twenty thousand dollars would. I agreed, then avoided the detective when he came to my building to interview me. I left a message on the detective's phone that I didn't want to pursue any charges. I wouldn't even tell him in a phone call. I left a message. How cowardly is that? I've had nightmares about it ever since. I made a mistake."

"Everyone makes mistakes. You explained your reasoning quite well. I was trying to solve the mystery of why no charges were filed and now you did that for me. There's nothing you did or said that was wrong. You don't need to feel bad or guilty about one thing."

"Will I get in trouble for accepting the money?"

"No."

"Will I have to testify against Kyle for paying me off?"

"I wouldn't want to put you in that position. I just needed to know the details."

We spoke for a few more minutes. I was impressed with her poise and intelligence. As she spoke, she reminded me of how Estella Abreu's family spoke about her. Smart, articulate, beautiful.

My biggest conclusion from talking with Celia Cartwright was that Kyle Banning's family must have some serious cash. Paying someone twenty thousand dollars not to file a misdemeanor battery seemed like overkill.

My other takeaway was that if Kyle Banning thought he could get away with anything, there was no telling what he would try to get away with.

# CHAPTER 35

**I HAVE, OVER** the years, been accused of rushing leads I like. I prefer to think of it as being efficient and not wasting time. I pride myself on being fair and impartial in my investigations. That doesn't mean I can't feel sorrow for the loss suffered by a family. It doesn't mean I don't feel anger at the way senseless violence can shatter families.

I needed to keep an open mind on this homicide. Just because I had a suspect fall into my lap for one victim, Estella Abreu, didn't mean he was good for her death, or that of Suzanne Morton or Emma Schrade. There was still a lot of information to gather and evidence to evaluate.

That's why it was tough to justify calling Terri Hernandez to see if she'd join me in a surveillance of Kyle Banning. This was a delicate situation. If I was too obvious, Banning could try to hide any evidence and come up with alibis. The family would no doubt hire big-time criminal defense attorneys who would tie up every element in court before we found out any information at all.

Terri answered on the first ring.

I used a cheerful voice to say, "How would you feel about doing some surveillance this afternoon and this evening on a suspect?"

"A suspect in *our* case?"

"Of course a suspect in our case." I explained to her everything I had learned so far about Banning.

"You just assumed I didn't have a date or anything going on tonight?"

"I'm sorry. Do you have plans?"

"No, but it would be nice if you assumed that I did."

I said, "Really, I can find someone else."

"Not unless you want your face to look like a Picasso painting."

An hour later, Terri met me in lower Manhattan. She got right to the point. "What's our plan of attack?"

"I was thinking we start at his office and see where he goes. The problem is, some of the financial people stay kind of late. This is a tough one. It's not like a surveillance where we can hide in a crowd. This guy lives at a different altitude than most people."

"I can see if I can get into the building. Maybe poke around a few places. At least see if he's definitely inside."

I thought about Terri's offer. Perhaps I should've figured this out before I'd bothered her. I just wasn't sure what else to do. We talked about it for a few more minutes. Then I got a text.

I looked down at my phone. It was from Ronald Higdon, Esquire, thanking me for squaring everything with Detective Matthews of the First Precinct. The end of the text had a key piece of information. It read: Someone told me your suspect hangs out at a bar in lower Manhattan called Rain.

I chuckled out loud.

Terri said, "What's so funny?"

"Informants. Mine just gave me an idea for a plan. But it shows he was holding information back the last time we talked."

Terri said, "They always hold something back to negotiate with later."

I nodded. "I don't know why that's so hard to remember."

"So what's our new plan?"

I looked at her, smiled, and said, "I don't think you're gonna like my idea."

Terri gave me one of her flat stares and said, "I rarely do."

# CHAPTER 36

**I THOUGHT MY** plan had flair and creativity. I explained it to Terri. From her expression, she didn't agree with my assessment.

She took a step back, put her hands on her hips, cocked her head, and stared at me. Then, after a couple of seconds, she said, "You think I can walk into a bar filled with super-slick, well-educated financial people and just fit in? Especially while I'm wearing cargo pants and a Yankees sweatshirt? Do I have that right, Mike?"

"Your problem is self-confidence. You can still be a badass cop *and* beautiful."

"You sound exactly like my father."

"Thank you. I've always found Ramon to be very intelligent."

"Seriously, those guys will be dressed in thousand-dollar suits. What can I do, put an NYPD raid jacket on to hide my sweatshirt?" Then she straightened up and held one finger in the air, telling me to hang on.

Terri slipped her phone out of her front pocket. She stepped away from me and made a quick call. After ending the call, she walked past me and said, "I'll meet you a block north of Rain in an hour. I want no funny comments or compliments about how I look. And you can tell no one that we tried this."

Terri and I were rarely serious with each other. I wasn't even sure about this moment. To be on the safe side, I silently nodded my assent and watched her pull away in her city-issued Ford Explorer.

One hour and three minutes later, I was standing on the corner of Fulton and Nassau Streets. I'd already walked past Rain. It had a healthy crowd that was growing by the minute. Terri had overestimated how well the clientele would be dressed. It was clearly a mix of financial people, but tourists and others were there as well. It looked like a high-end martini bar, with a sports bar element.

Like most cops, I notice people. I look at faces and pay attention to details. Today, I was probably more focused on the bar down the street. At least that's the excuse I'm using for not noticing Terri's approach until she walked right up to me.

It was tough not to say, *Wow.* Luckily, I remembered her admonishment to withhold all comments, and Terri kept a scowl on her face to ensure I didn't open my mouth. She wore a dark blue cocktail dress and carried a small black clutch with pearls around the clasp. Her hair was brushed straight down her back. Most surprising was the red lipstick and dark eyeliner. I wasn't sure I'd ever seen Terri wear makeup.

I carefully said, "How did you pull that off so quickly?"

"My cousin lives on Mulberry Street near the Fifth Precinct. We always share clothes when we go out. She works at a salon in Midtown. She's the one who did my makeup. She also insisted I brush out my hair and not leave it in a ponytail."

Terri bit her lower lip like she was thinking about something. Then she said, "You may make one comment and one comment only."

"You look fantastic."

"Good choice. Let's get this shit done."

I said, "How do you want to do it? Wait till we see him go in? Wait inside? Split up and I'll tell you if he's coming down the block?"

"This could be a couple of nights of surveillance unless we get lucky."

I thought about that. I said, "If it goes past tonight, I'll get us help in the form of a surveillance team."

"I'm not doing your crazy plan in front of a surveillance team."

I figured I'd worry about that when and if the time came. I was trying to seize the initiative.

Finally, I said, "Let's wait inside and give it a couple of hours. If he doesn't show, we'll make up another plan."

Terri had a little grin.

I said, "What is it?"

She quickly glanced down the block. "Isn't that our man?"

I stared as Kyle Banning approached the bar from the other end of the block. We were in business.

# CHAPTER 37

**I WALKED INTO** Rain a few minutes before Terri. She knew to come through the door and look for me. I intended to find a seat near Kyle Banning. Any kind of close surveillance like this had a boatload of things that could go wrong. I was hoping to identify and mitigate any of those problems.

I scanned the place. It was about what I expected. Kind of loud with a fraternity-house feel. A few tourists sprinkled in with a lot of young guys with too much money.

A long bar with high tops on the other wall. The whole place couldn't have been thirty feet wide. The narrow space gave it the feel of being popular when, in fact, it looked crowded because it just wasn't that big.

Behind the bar was a Tito's Vodka–branded mirror flanked by four TVs high on the wall. Two TVs were tuned to ESPN channels and two were on financial channels. I noticed closed-captioning on CNBC and the Fox Business Network. This place was definitely catering to their clientele.

I spotted Kyle Banning at the bar, talking to a pretty bartender with long blond hair she wore in a ponytail draped over her shoulder. It was clear he was a regular. I casually took a stool one seat away from him. It wasn't too close, and he didn't look in my direction.

Many of the stools at the bar were available. Most people gathered around the tables by the opposite wall. Maybe there were some tribal gatherings of the different financial houses. I wondered where Banning's buddies were.

I noticed a couple of the guys at the bar turn to stare at the front door for a moment. I followed their gaze and was not surprised to see Terri Hernandez. She looked even better in the soft light of the bar. She had a certain expression I'd never seen on her. It was hard to describe. Maybe because her usual expression was annoyance verging on violence. Now she had a pleasant smile, and her dark eyes scanned the room. She casually walked toward the bar and sat down on the stool to my right, between Banning and me.

At nearly the same time, a heavyset young man in a suit plopped down on the stool to the left of me. He looked in my direction but deduced I wasn't in the financial business, so he didn't bother to acknowledge me.

The bartender finally came over and I ordered a beer. After she slid my beer in front of me, I was surprised to hear Terri order Old Forester bourbon, straight up.

I didn't know if it was a ploy or if bourbon was Terri's usual drink of choice. Either way, it caught Kyle Banning's attention. If I concentrated, I could hear their conversation over the din of stockbrokers blowing off steam. Mostly small talk, but I could tell Banning had nice manners. He introduced himself and asked Terri a few questions about where she worked and lived.

Terri had a set backstory for short undercover roles like this. She worked in the hospitality industry for a website that recommended hotels in the city. It was a tough story to pin down or confirm. I noticed she didn't give a last name either. Even though Banning used his full name, she just said, "Hi, I'm Terri."

They seemed to be getting along, and I had full faith that Terri would ask all the right questions. Banning never looked past her or to his other side. A classic narcissistic move. No one else in the world existed.

Terri started slowly working the questions around to how many times Banning had come to this bar this week.

I looked up at the mirror with the Tito's logo and saw Banning flash a charming smile as he said, "I usually go out in lower Manhattan. I know a lot of the financial people. They're fun to hang out with."

Terri said, "I came in here Monday night. I don't remember seeing you."

Suddenly a commotion came up from the back of the bar. Everyone looked over their shoulders to see a group of well-dressed young men cheering a soccer match from England on the TV nearest them. It felt like soccer had replaced football among males under thirty these days—maybe because most of them played soccer growing up, not football.

I wanted to hear Banning's response to Terry's question.

Then someone slipped onto the stool on the other side

of the man to my left. I glanced up at the mirror again and froze.

I knew the man who'd just sat down. I also knew why he was here. My right hand instinctively slid off the bar and into my lap. Just in case I needed to draw my duty weapon.

# CHAPTER 38

**SOMETIMES YOU HAVE** to wonder about fate or coincidence or whatever you want to call it. Here I was, happy to be making some progress on a homicide case with an unusual investigative technique. Terri and I had the whole situation well in hand.

Then I looked up and saw Robert Hatcher sit down at the bar.

I tensed, recognizing him, then put my hand on my forehead and looked down like I was reading my phone. It had been a few years, but I was pretty sure Hatcher would recognize me. I'd helped on his arrest for aggravated assault with a deadly weapon. He was a low-level drug dealer with some kind of anger management issue. He'd shot at least four customers a few years ago, but we could only prove one case— a guy he'd shot in the face near the Fulton Street fish market.

The victim had been lucky, and the bullet passed through his cheek. He'd lost a few teeth and about a third of his tongue, but he'd survived.

It was clear that the sixteen months Hatcher had spent in Attica hadn't done much to rehabilitate him. In the mere seconds he'd been sitting to my left, he had already slipped the tubby guy next to him a small envelope. I watched with my peripheral vision as the man slid some cash back to Hatcher. He wasn't even subtle. He just shoved the cash across the varnished wooden bar.

I knew Hatcher would have a gun on him. What a great opportunity to get a dangerous criminal off the street. But I couldn't act. At least not at the moment. It would do nothing to help the homicide investigation I was actually working on. It may not have been *Sophie's Choice*, but it was still a difficult decision.

I was still trying to eavesdrop on Kyle Banning and Terry's conversation, but now I was also trying to watch the pair on my left. If nothing else, I could text someone about what I just saw. Maybe we could get some help here quickly.

When I glanced up in the mirror again, I locked eyes with Robert Hatcher. It was clear he recognized me.

I almost nudged Terri. No matter what happened, I couldn't let this situation get out of hand. We were in a crowded bar in Manhattan.

The tubby businessman sitting between me and Hatcher realized there was an issue. His hands started to shake. He used a napkin on the bar to wipe his face. Pieces of the napkin stuck to his cheeks and chin and made it look like he had whitehead acne. He scooted his stool backward and made a beeline for the front door.

That left Hatcher and me staring at each other across an open space. I felt like an Old West gunfighter in a showdown. I tried to read the emotions on his face. I got nothing.

My pulse increased and my hearing became sharper. At least that's how it feels while I'm under stress. This was going to be a close encounter no matter what happened.

Then Robert Hatcher turned on his stool to face me.

This was it.

# CHAPTER 39

**ROBERT HATCHER KEPT** both of his hands on the bar even as he faced me. He looked like every felon I'd ever pulled over as a patrol officer. They know to keep their hands on the steering wheel or stick them out the driver's window so the approaching cop can see their hands are empty.

Hatcher didn't say a word. He slowly took his hands off the bar and held them in front of him. He didn't put them in the air because that would attract attention and look like he was being robbed.

Then he carefully backed away from me. About halfway to the front door he turned, then walked quickly until he disappeared outside.

I considered calling someone, hoping to catch him with some dope and a gun on him. But I realized I couldn't solve all the city's problems in one evening. I was relieved things had played out the way they did.

I focused back on Terri and Kyle Banning to my right. It didn't sound like Banning had answered any questions. Terri was going in another direction now. She kept a playful voice, but I knew her well enough to realize she was coming up with a new question as she spoke. Maybe something that would get this guy talking.

Terri and I had discussed the possibility of having Banning follow her to a coffee shop on the corner. I'd reluctantly agreed that I could follow them by myself a few doors down to the mom-and-pop coffee shop called The Free-Trade Shop. I sort of liked the subtle dig at Starbucks.

Now Terri was using that option. I heard her say, "Want to go someplace a little quieter? Maybe the coffee shop down the street?"

There was a pause. I couldn't believe how interested I was in hearing his response.

Banning turned in his seat to face her. He had a sincere look on his face. He said, "Maybe we could meet at a hotel later. But I have a certain reputation among these guys. And no offense, but you are a couple of years older than the women they usually see me with. It may sound harsh, but reputation is everything in the financial industry."

It was one of the dumbest, rudest comments I think I had ever heard. I wasn't sure I'd heard him correctly until I glanced down and saw Terri flexing her hand into a fist. Part of me wanted to see that punch land right on this guy's smug face. Maybe knock a couple of those perfect teeth crooked.

Instead, Terri did a more elegant thing: she threw what was left of her bourbon into his face. It was the perfect move on several levels. It maintained her undercover persona very nicely and gave her a release. It was clear Banning wasn't going to say much more in the bar. She had nothing to lose. And it was less awkward than slugging this creep.

I tensed, waiting to see his reaction.

Banning casually pulled a handkerchief from his suit pocket. The white hanky even had his initials monogrammed on it. Classy. Banning calmly blotted his face and chest. He kept a very mild expression as he looked up and said, "Does that mean you won't meet me at the Holiday Inn Express on Water Street?"

Terri glared at him but didn't say a word.

Banning stood from his stool and said, "It was *mostly* nice chatting with you."

I watched as he joined a group of chattering young men in the corner. Several of them were laughing and one slapped Banning on the back.

Terri sat at the bar and stared straight ahead. She mumbled to me, "I'll meet you back on the corner. I don't want to give this guy the satisfaction of thinking he chased me out of here. I'm going to have another drink."

It looked like the direct approach was the only one I could take against Banning. This guy appeared pretty sharp. But first I wanted to gather more information. Unless I had everything nailed down when I talked to him, he might get more from an interview than I would.

# CHAPTER 40

**I WAS LATER** than usual getting home, yet much earlier than I'd told Mary Catherine to expect me. I liked the little wave of surprise that ran through the kids when I walked through the door just as everyone was starting to eat dinner. Those smiles would stick in my memory forever.

I smelled chicken cacciatore. That meant Ricky had probably made it. Mary Catherine liked more traditional meat-and-potatoes dishes. Ricky was a great cook who specialized in spicier Italian and even Cajun cuisine.

I took a moment to run around the table and greet each kid individually. Then I gave Mary Catherine a kiss on the lips, earning us groans from just about every kid under sixteen.

Then I made sure to give my grandfather a hug. I hoped his presence here meant that he was getting a handle on all the extra work he'd taken on around the parish.

My grandfather made the kids sit still while he said a second prayer before I could eat.

Seamus said, "Dear Father in heaven, please bless the food that my grandson is about to receive. Protect him during the day and bless him in the evening. Amen."

In prayer, my grandfather always knows exactly what to say. He had touched on something I feel strongly about: my blessings at home. No matter what happens during the day, when I come home to these beautiful, smiling faces, I always thank God for the wonderful blessing. It's nothing I've ever said specifically to my grandfather. But he knows. Everyone knows.

I listened intently to each kid as they talked about their day. Sure, Juliana and Brian had days that were more similar to mine than the younger kids. Juliana was taking an acting class as well as her academic classes at City College. Brian was working hard at the air-conditioning repair service. He was also taking a class at City College.

Chrissy told us about petting the class guinea pig until it fell asleep in her hand. Trent told us he'd aced a geometry exam and that Sister Mala had held up his test as an example for the other kids.

What I really wanted to hear about was whether the boys had been bullied today. I didn't want to ask about it. I didn't want to make it seem like the focus of the boys' lives. But it concerned me. It concerned me a great deal.

I looked over at Fiona and said, "Did you get a chance to practice free throws?"

She nodded excitedly. "Then I played Horse with Trent, Ricky, and Eddie. I beat all three of them and only had an *H*."

I couldn't help but smile as I looked at the boys. You would've thought they'd been caught stealing something the way they looked down at their plates and mumbled.

When Ricky looked up, I could still see the shade of the black eye he had from the run-in with the bullies a few days earlier. He said, "On the bright side, Fiona doesn't punch us while we're playing."

That earned a few snickers around the table.

That's when Shawna chimed in on the subject for the first time. "Boys think they have it so tough. Girls get bullied too. All the time. Especially online."

Ricky reached up and touched his black eye. He winced and said, "I don't think I'd mind getting bullied online as much as being bullied in person."

That opened an interesting conversation around the dinner table.

# CHAPTER 41

**THIS WAS THE** kind of dinner conversation that most parents don't get to hear. I had always taught the kids to be tolerant and respectful of other people's opinions. This would be a good test of how effective I had been at getting that message across.

We all started to discuss the problem of bullying. Almost immediately the lines were drawn. The boys all wanted to act tough. The girls used reasoning. A classic gender schism.

Eddie said, "If our bullies didn't carry guns, we'd have taught them a lesson."

Jane calmly pointed out, "The first time they bothered you, I don't remember hearing how super brave you were." Her maturity made her calm delivery that much more devastating to the boys. All three of them sputtered for an answer, but nothing came out.

Bridget, normally quiet during these kinds of discussions, said, "I don't understand why you didn't just talk to the boys."

Eddie groaned, then glared at his sister. "Believe me, they didn't want to listen."

Chrissy chimed in with "Why didn't you just run away?"

Eddie appeared to be the official spokesman. He said, "Then the bullies win."

"But you wouldn't get beat up." Shawna had offered it sincerely. "Who cares who wins?"

I got it. It was a tough situation. When I was their age, bullying had a different edge to it. There were rarely any weapons involved. Parents stepped in when things got out of hand. I remembered Matthew Callahan's parents finding out he was taking lunch money from kids a grade younger than him. Matthew couldn't sit comfortably for a day after his father paddled him for stealing and bullying. I'm not saying I agree with those kinds of parenting tactics. But there's no denying that they occasionally got results.

Chrissy turned to my grandfather. She said, "Grandpa Seamus, what did you do in the olden days if someone was bullying you?"

Seamus leaned back in his chair and patted his belly like some kind of medieval Irish chieftain who had just finished off a meal of his enemy's entrails. At least that's how I imagined he viewed his display. Then he leaned forward and put his elbows on the table.

Seamus said, "You mean way back in the forties and fifties? Back before science had been invented?"

Chrissy nodded her head vigorously. The older kids, Mary Catherine, and I all had to keep from laughing out loud. I was a little nervous about the answer because I'd heard a few stories about my grandfather's youth in Ireland. I wasn't sure they were the kind of stories I wanted my kids to hear. At least the ones still in elementary school.

"It was a different world back then. I went to a school attached to a Catholic church. I played soccer in the afternoons until someone introduced me to baseball. I remember one year I got a baseball bat for Christmas and I felt like someone had given me a ticket to a whole new life. It was nothing like today."

Eddie looked at my grandfather and said, "That sounds exactly like today."

Seamus laughed. "Every generation thinks they're facing new issues. Did I get bullied as a youngster? Sure I did. I don't even remember any specific incidents. I got into a few scrapes, and my mother used to paddle me when I got home, and tell me not to fight. One thing I learned: bullies hate to be confronted. I don't think I won many fights against bullies, but I must've done all right because I don't remember it happening too often. Bullies are cowards. The boys you described, who have to carry a gun to feel important, are the biggest cowards of all."

I loved seeing the twinkle in my grandfather's eye as he told these stories with incredible detail, enthralling the kids. I enjoyed seeing the kids follow every word and want to hear more. In this case, my grandfather even gave me an idea. What was Kyle Banning if not a bully? Wealthy, good-looking, and entitled. Maybe it was time I stopped nibbling around the edges and headed directly to the bully's stronghold. Not his house but his office.

# CHAPTER 42

**THE NEXT MORNING,** all I could think about was surprising Kyle Banning at his office. I did a little research on Banning's employer, Lancet Financial. It wasn't considered one of the big players, like Fidelity or Bain. It was exactly the kind of place an ambitious young man like Kyle Banning would use as a stepping-stone before moving on to one of the big hedge funds. I wasn't sure exactly what he did for the company. His degree in economics was from Princeton. I was not sure what that prepared you for, but it sounded impressive.

The company occupied the top three floors of a building in lower Manhattan on Canal Street. It used to be some sort of warehouse, and they'd kept the working-class facade on the outside, but the inside was quite trendy. Soft lighting and expensive prints on the walls. A terrarium covered the center of the big lobby. A small palm tree and other tropical plants filled the climate-controlled glass hut.

I walked directly into one of the elevators and hit the button for the eighth floor like I knew where I was going. No one in the lobby gave me a second look. Exactly why I'd dressed a little nicer today. I was wearing my favorite blue sport coat with some nice Pierre Cardin slacks. I thought a suit might be overdoing it.

The elevator opened to the reception area of Lancet Financial. An attractive young woman looked up from her computer and smiled as I approached the desk. I had debated whether I should identify myself or just ask to see Kyle Banning.

Just as the young woman asked if she could help me, I saw Kyle Banning walking down the hallway directly toward me. I smiled at the young woman and said, "Never mind. Here's the man I need to talk to real quick."

Banning looked up, and I stuck out my hand. I said, "Kyle Banning? I'm Michael Bennett. Can we talk in your office for a minute?"

I appreciated the confusion on Kyle Banning's face. I thought he recognized me but couldn't put his finger on why I seemed familiar. Exactly why I hadn't brought Terri Hernandez with me on this interview. He would definitely remember her.

"Do I know you, Mr. Bennett?"

"I don't believe we've ever met officially." I turned slightly, hoping to lure him away from the receptionist. He followed my lead, then started to walk with more purpose, so I followed him. A few doors down from the reception area we turned into a small but comfortable office with a view of Lafayette Street, where I could just make out the front of 11 Howard, a boutique hotel a block away.

I reached over and pushed the door shut so we were alone in the room. The movement seemed to startle Banning. I pulled out my badge and ID. I said in my best official voice, "I'm a homicide detective with the NYPD. I'd like to ask you a few questions."

Banning looked at me and said, "Am I under arrest?"

"No."

"Then I don't have to answer your questions. Is that correct?"

I didn't answer. It didn't sound like I needed to.

Banning said, "It's not my policy to talk to the police while I'm at work. I'm paid by the Lancet corporation to do my job while I am in this building. I'm paid quite well and I'm very effective at my job. What I am not paid for is to chat with public employees. I'm afraid I'm going to have to ask you to leave."

This was not turning out the way I'd expected. But I didn't move. Somewhere in the back of my mind I heard my grandfather's voice. Kyle Banning was a bully, and I was going to stand up to him.

Banning said, "Did you hear me? I'm asking you to leave. Right now you're trespassing. If you don't leave, I might even call the NYPD to escort you out of the building. I wonder how embarrassing that would be for you."

I didn't want to tip my hand or give him any ammunition to accuse me of harassment. I swallowed my anger and nodded but had to throw in, "Perhaps we'll meet again soon." I backed out of his office like I was expecting to be shot from behind if I turned.

Banning had a smug grin on his face as he said, "I doubt it," then slammed his office door in my face.

I endured a few stares as I marched out of the office.

# CHAPTER 43

**I LEFT LANCET** Financial and drove up the Henry Hudson, heading out of Manhattan. It wasn't a trip I particularly wanted to make. I was going to meet with Suzanne Morton's parents at their home in Yonkers.

I was trying not to let emotion dictate my actions. Sure, I was pretty hot about the way Kyle Banning had dismissed me. I needed some real evidence to confront him with. Something that would get his full attention.

On the flip side, I hadn't given up any details of the investigation or even the fact that he was a suspect.

I easily found the Mortons' lovely two-story brick home in the middle of Yonkers. Sometimes it's hard for me to wrap my head around a neighborhood so close to the city comprised of just houses. I couldn't see any high-rises in the distance. Visits like this make me question my reasons for still living in the city with so many children.

I saw David Morton's Saab in the driveway and knew he'd probably stayed home from work just to talk to me. I'd contacted them a few days before, asking if I could meet with them. After Banning cut our interview so short, I'd called to see if they could talk to me this morning. I had kept my reasoning vague. I even had made it sound like I was just checking on them as a friend. That's a shady thing to do. That's why I intended to check on them *while* I interviewed them.

Rachel Morton offered me coffee as we sat in the downstairs living room. There were pictures of the family all over the walls and on tables. Two parents, beautiful Suzanne, and her younger brother, Paul. Disney World, the Empire State Building, somewhere out west with mountains. They were smiling in all of them. I hoped they'd be able to find those smiles again someday. But I knew it wouldn't be anytime soon.

I checked for subtle signs of emotional distress while I spoke to David and Rachel Morton. Rachel's eyes were rimmed with red and David appeared to be under the influence of prescription pills. His speech was slurred, and sometimes he seemed to just stare straight ahead while Rachel answered my few questions.

Then she asked, "I thought Detective Stanton from New Rochelle was handling this case. Why are you asking questions?"

"I'm just helping Detective Stanton out." I didn't want to complicate matters or upset them further by suggesting their daughter might have been the victim of an active serial killer. Once I had proof, I could talk to them about it.

Suzanne had mainly lived in the NYU dorms, but I asked to see her room at home.

Rachel told me Detective Stanton had already looked through it, but it had taken him only about ten minutes.

That annoyed me. Ten minutes wasn't enough time to find anything.

It appeared to be a typical young person's room. Suzanne had a planner from last year on her wall. A rope chair hung from the ceiling. A couple of framed photos showed her with girlfriends at Coney Island and a few other places. One photo had Juliana in it. There was nothing at all unusual about her room.

Rachel Morton told me about their efforts to get into Suzanne's iCloud account, but so far they had had no luck. Apple essentially refused to deal with the police. Suzanne didn't appear to have written down her passwords anywhere. It was an awkward situation. Technically, I was not assigned to this homicide. It wasn't even within the NYPD. It wasn't like I could take Suzanne's computer back to my office and have our forensic people look through it. That would cause far too many questions. I was afraid Bill "Suicide" Stanton wasn't as dogged in the investigation as I would've liked him to be.

That's when I had an idea. "Were Suzanne and her brother close?"

Rachel Morton shrugged. "They're a little over three years apart. I never considered them close. But they didn't fight all the time like some siblings do."

Just then Paul padded out of his bedroom, probably for the first time today. I called his name, and he slowly walked backward till he was in the doorframe. He didn't appear to be surprised to see a stranger in his house. He just stared at me, waiting for my question. He wore a thick, terry-cloth Stony

Brook robe that hung open over shorts and a Green Day retro T-shirt.

I said, "Any idea how to get into your sister's iCloud account? You don't have her user name and password, do you?"

He mumbled, "Always *S-u-z-e-M*. And she used to use *cheer123* for most of her passwords. Try that." He couldn't have had less enthusiasm in his voice. He shuffled away from the door as soon as he'd answered.

I typed in the details and had instant access to Suzanne's voluminous iCloud account with all her photos. I was about to ask Rachel Morton if I could look through the account from my office. I wanted her to know exactly what I was doing. Then, about the twentieth photo in, I stopped and took a closer look. It was a picture of Suzanne at some kind of party.

And Kyle Banning was standing right next to her, smiling.

# CHAPTER 44

**THIS NEW PHOTO** of Kyle Banning with Suzanne Morton was a bombshell. I needed help. I emailed the photo to Walter Jackson as I raced back to my office from the Mortons' house in Yonkers.

Police work isn't a solitary activity. It's a team sport. That's why we have specialists. People like Walter, who know where to find any piece of information. Our Tech Unit can break down any computer or internet issue like it's magic. And sometimes you just need smart people to bounce some ideas off of.

That's why I called Terri Hernandez, Walter Jackson, and my lieutenant, Harry Grissom. Terri agreed to meet all of us at the Manhattan North Homicide office so everyone could listen to what I had so far on the case. We were still focusing on the two victims from the city. Suzanne Morton was in the mix, but we had plenty to do, and Suzanne was still a New Rochelle case.

We met in Walter's office, which was the largest. He'd earned it through his hard work. As I stepped inside, I was reminded how important it was for him to have some space. Files, books, and logs were in neat piles on shelves around the walls. The office was a testament to a working intelligence analyst.

Walter already had information on the case spread out over his desk, a long table, and even some stacks of paper on the floor. There were a few photographs on top of some papers and warrant requests. He had printed out the photo of Kyle Banning and Suzanne Morton that I'd emailed him.

Walter looked up and smiled. "I'm getting a good start on creating a timeline for this guy. I've already figured out where the photo you sent me was taken. You can see the sign in the corner. The Dead Rabbit down on Water Street in the financial district. It's kind of famous for hosting holiday parties where all the financial people mingle and show off their significant others."

Walter continued: "They hosted an early Halloween party for their regular customers, on the second Friday night in October. The owner said in a *Village Voice* article that he likes to beat the rush on Halloween parties. That means this photo is about four weeks old."

"Or just about the time Suzanne Morton went missing."

Walter nodded. "Exactly."

He walked us through a few more of his findings. Terri Hernandez stepped in a few minutes later, followed by Harry Grissom. I explained my disastrous initial contact with Kyle Banning. I could tell Terri was a little miffed I hadn't called her to come with me. Even after I explained my reasoning that Banning could identify her from the bar.

Walter had one more interesting piece of information. He held up a NCIC criminal history for Banning. It looked like the only arrest was for assault against Celia Cartwright. We knew that case had never been filed. I had to say, "I'm sorry, Walter. I don't see what you're talking about."

Walter held up the page and showed me an extra indent on the side where there should be information, but there wasn't. Walter said, "I've seen this before. It's something that was expunged when he was a minor. It must've been something pretty serious to have even made it onto the NCIC printout. Sometimes I've noticed this discrepancy when crimes have been expunged through the legal system. It's almost as if the FBI created a back door to warn law enforcement about a serious issue with an individual."

I said, "I guess it's one more thing I can ask Banning when I interview him."

"Probably the easiest way to figure out what happened. We could track it down. But it may not be that important."

Harry sat in a hard wooden chair flexing his left knee and right hand. That was a habit he had developed in the last couple of years because it made his arthritis feel a little better. When I finished going through everything I had on the case and Walter added the information he had developed, Harry looked off into the distance as he nodded his head.

Harry said, "I'm impressed with the information you've gathered already. But we're not about to get a conviction for homicide based on a couple of photographs. I agree it can't be a coincidence that this guy, Kyle Banning, knew two different murder victims. But that's not going to sway a judge when we try to get a warrant."

I said, "I'm going to take another shot at interviewing him."

"Did he ever ask for an attorney?"

"No. He said it was his policy not to talk to the police at work. So I intend to surprise him at home tomorrow."

Terri asked, "Do you want to do surveillance to figure out the best time to catch Banning at home?"

I smiled. I already had a plan.

# CHAPTER 45

**I EXPLAINED MY** idea to the three solemn faces sitting around the table. Harry Grissom and Terri Hernandez were a little skeptical. Basically, it just involved interviewing Kyle Banning at his house on a Saturday morning. *This* Saturday morning. Tomorrow.

I knew the building where Kyle Banning lived. It had a doorman and decent security. My first hurdle was figuring out how to get to Banning without giving him advance notice. If I identified myself to the doorman, he'd make a quick call up to the apartment. Banning would say he didn't want to see me at all. That was something I needed to avoid.

As soon as Harry Grissom reluctantly agreed to my plan, I went to my best source for finding out about the Bannings' doorman: Ronald Higdon, Esquire.

Ronald gave me a big smile when I stepped through the

pawnshop door. "Bennett, thank you again for getting that Detective Matthews off my back."

"You can thank me by saying you found a way to help me get in the building I told you about."

Ronald waved like it was no issue at all. "I called my boy Artie, who knows Midtown and the park. He got ahold of one of his delivery buddies named Soolie, who knows a lot of the doormen. Anyway, the doorman at the building owes a friend of Soolie's a fair amount of cash. That came from some bad business decisions involving the Jets and the Patriots. So Soolie worked out a deal where his buddy is giving the doorman an extra week to come up with the cash if he lets you slip into the building. Simple."

I appreciated the work Ronald had put in on this. It was too bad he always tried to go for the quick buck. He might've made a decent detective if he'd had some integrity. As it was, at least he was doing his part for law enforcement.

I said, "And what is this amazing feat of assistance going to cost me?"

Ronald was quiet for a moment. That was unusual. It made me nervous. He had already thought this through.

"Just a favor. Whenever I need it."

"What kind of favor? You know I can't do anything crazy. Unlike you, I have to follow a lot of rules."

Ronald shrugged. "I don't know yet what kind of favor. I just want to know you'll come if I call. I won't ask you to alter records or anything that would get you in trouble."

I agreed and we shook on it. He knew I'd never breach an agreement like this. I already felt a twinge of concern about what I had just agreed to.

Ronald gave me the information about the doorman at the Bannings' building. He even had the man's schedule. I quickly smiled to see he was working Saturday morning.

I was proud of the amount of progress my team had made today. I just hoped it paid off tomorrow morning.

# CHAPTER 46

**MY FRIDAY EVENING** was busy. I'll confess I was a little distracted while coaching the first girls' basketball game of the season for Holy Name, a game with a small Presbyterian school from Midtown. I tried to concentrate on my duties as a coach, but my mind wasn't focused on sports. All I could think about was tomorrow morning's interview with Kyle Banning.

The crowd was festive. Keeping in mind that about a quarter of the crowd on the Holy Name side of the bleachers was my family, it was a nice atmosphere. I noticed Bridget cheering loudly for her twin. It made me smile the way only a daughter can make a father smile.

I had to rein in Fiona a bit. I'd never seen her like this. She was trying to psych up her teammates but starting to sound a little like an NBA head coach screaming at his team. I stepped in and placed a hand on my daughter's shoulder.

"Hey, Pat Riley, back off a little bit. This is the first game. Just a chance for you guys to scrimmage against someone besides one another. Show good sportsmanship, use the skills you've learned in practice, and, most importantly, have some fun."

Fiona didn't look particularly happy with my goals. She wanted to crush our opponents. I was just looking for thirty-two minutes of fun for both teams.

In the bleachers, Mary Catherine tried to start a wave. It didn't even make it all the way through my family, but I smiled when I saw Sister Sheilah, sitting a few feet from my family, join in the wave.

Seamus sat directly behind the bench. He was my unofficial assistant coach along with Sister Elizabeth. His main job was to make sure the girls drank water and had clean towels. Sister Elizabeth's experience in college basketball dictated our lineup and strategy.

I noticed my son Brian come in and join the family just as the game started, still wearing his air-conditioning company shirt. That made me smile. Then Juliana came in behind him. She was in a form-fitting dress and looked like she was going out after the game. Her long dark hair was tied in a straight ponytail that hung down her back. I couldn't believe this was the little girl who used to like to jump in the mud in the park near our building.

Seeing Juliana made me think of Suzanne Morton. I wondered if Suzanne had gone to her brother's events. I thought about how the Mortons were handling Suzanne's death. I pictured them sitting in their nice home in Yonkers, fixating on what they had lost. I hoped it wouldn't be to the exclusion of their son, Paul. That happens more often than you'd think.

A family loses a child, then they drift away from the children still in the house. It's a tragedy piled on top of tragedy.

Then a basketball whizzed right past my head. It snapped me back to reality. Here I was thinking about parents ignoring children while I was ignoring my own child. I focused back on the game as Fiona leapt into the air and sank a basket. It wasn't exactly a dunk, but it was incredibly athletic. I couldn't believe it.

The crowd went wild. About a fourth of the crowd went extra wild. Chrissy held up a sign she'd been waiting to show. It was on white poster board with giant, colorful letters saying, "Fiona Shoots and Scores!"

Everything came together at once for me. My daughter Fiona excelling. My family here to support us. The kids making posters for their sister. Who could ask for anything more?

I guess I could. I badly wanted to have a good interview with Kyle Banning and charge him with murder.

# CHAPTER 47

**I WOKE UP** early Saturday morning. A tingle of anxiety ran through me at the prospect of interviewing Kyle Banning. That's right, I was excited to work. Show me a detective who doesn't get pumped about a good case, and I'll show you a detective who doesn't clear a lot of cases.

I drove past the building on Fifth Avenue where Banning lived with his parents. I was treating this like some sort of narcotics surveillance. I drove past it again. I wanted to know alleys and back entrances, foot traffic in front of the building, everything. I stashed the car a few blocks away and walked back past Madison to the building.

The building had a spectacular view of Central Park but especially the reservoir directly in front of it. This was one of the areas where old money lived. Or at least people who'd had money in the 1980s. Now you had to be some kind of ungodly celebrity or tech tycoon to have an apartment in a building like this.

The doorman Ronald Higdon, Esquire, had told me about stood in front of the building. His name was Dorian. He was tall, with an extra fifty pounds wrapped around his waist. He wore a traditional doorman's uniform and stood just outside the ornate entrance to the luxury apartment building. He looked a little on the nervous side. I wondered if it was because he knew I was coming. I'd told Ronald I'd be at the building between 10 and 12 on Saturday morning.

I approached the hulking man, who appeared to be in his mid-forties. The little rim of hair he had around a bald head was already graying. He noticed me almost immediately.

I approached him with a smile and wave. I said, "Are you Dorian?"

The immense man hustled down the five steps to meet me on the sidewalk. He had a Brooklyn accent and held out a hand with pudgy fingers to stop me. "You Ronald's friend?" He whispered it like someone inside the building might hear him.

I nodded.

"I left the back door open. I can't risk you being seen on a security video in the lobby. Just in case somebody complains. People pay a lot of money to have peace of mind in this place. But I needed the favor Ronald worked out for me. I'm just glad you're not here to collect from me."

"What do you mean, 'collect'?"

"Ronald said you were collecting a debt. That if I didn't let you in, maybe you'd be collecting from me."

"I'm not here to break anyone's fingers. I'm a cop. I'm just trying to do a surprise interview." This seemed to confound Dorian. He gave me an odd look and then glanced up at the building like he was trying to figure out who I might be talking to.

Dorian turned back to me and shook his head. "I don't know. I'm not sure I can let a cop in."

"Let me get this straight: you were okay with me if I was going to break someone's arm if they didn't pay, but you wouldn't let in a cop on official business? You've got some screwed-up values."

Clearly, Dorian realized his extension on his gambling debts was based on me getting into the building, not what I did for a living. Finally, he said again, "The back door is unlocked. Go back the way you came, turn left behind the building. The door's directly across from the back door to the building behind us."

I made sure to give the doorman a good stern glare before I left. To a guy like Dorian, it didn't matter if I was investigating a homicide, child molestation, or parking tickets. He didn't want to be seen helping the police.

I slipped through the unlocked metal door in the remarkably clean and orderly alley. Nothing littered the asphalt, and no graffiti scarred the walls. I took the service elevator to the top floor. It didn't say PENTHOUSE, but that's what it had to be. When I got off, I noticed there were only two doors. Each apartment must have a phenomenal view of the reservoir.

I knocked on the Bannings' door casually, hoping whoever was inside would think it was Dorian. A woman about fifty, wearing yoga pants and a loose T-shirt, opened the door wide and looked surprised to see me standing there in a coat and tie.

I said, "Mrs. Banning?"

She smiled and nodded. The bangs of her light hair almost hung to her eyes.

I kept my cheerful, used-car-salesman smile and said, "I talked with Kyle the other day. I just wanted to show him something." Vague and friendly gets you into a lot more places than stern and official. Both cops and vampires have to be invited into a home before they can enter, so I threw in, "May I come in?"

She motioned me inside and said, "Of course."

I knew her manners would kick in before her sense of caution. As I stepped across the threshold, I realized I'd cleared my first hurdle. I was inside the apartment.

# CHAPTER 48

**MY HANDS FELT** clammy as I took in my surroundings. There was a whole lot that could go wrong with this plan. Now that I was inside the Bannings' apartment, I knew I had only a few minutes. My goals were simple: find Kyle Banning and start talking. Who knew what could happen next?

Thanks to Walter Jackson, I had a fair amount of information about the family. A sixteen-year-old brother named Jaden also lived at the house. The mother, Joan Banning, had just let me in and was still in the friendly, chatty mode.

The father had been a wildly successful attorney and now seemed to be winding down his career as general counsel for a major insurance company. I had read an article about him that insinuated he got the job as part of a settlement with the same company. It didn't sound ethical, but I wasn't in a position to judge ethical behavior right now. I had just fooled my way past a trusting woman. Essentially, I was trespassing.

Then things broke my way. A shirtless Kyle Banning came out of a side bedroom, clearly having just woken up. He rubbed his eyes, then brushed his light-brown hair out of his face. I couldn't help but notice his ripped physique. He had an honest-to-God eight-pack for a stomach, with good biceps and broad shoulders.

His mother turned and looked at Banning. She still had a smile on her face. Until her son said to me, "What the hell? I thought I already told you to get lost."

I said in a friendly tone, "Actually, you said it was your policy not to speak to the police at work. I assumed that meant I could talk to you here."

His mother was obviously no stranger to dealing with police officers. She realized she'd made a serious error. But I was already in the apartment. I had nothing to lose.

I said to Banning, "Give me fifteen seconds. Let me show you two photographs and then if you think it's smart for me to leave, I will. Simple as that. No other obligation for you other than looking at two simple photographs."

Banning was frustrated but couldn't pass up a fair deal like that. Maybe it was the financial analyst in him. The easiest way to solve a problem was usually the most direct. I was a problem I was sure he wouldn't mind getting out of his life. That's why I wasn't surprised when Banning made a curt motion for me to follow him into a den.

I'll admit that when I walked into the room, the view took my breath away for a moment. I could see from one side of the reservoir to the other. I could even see people relaxing in the park on a Saturday morning.

I didn't waste any time. I reached into my pocket for the

two photographs Walter Jackson had printed out for me. I stepped over to a walnut desk with legs that were hand carved with decorative maple leaves. It made each leg of the desk look like a small tree.

Banning stepped over to me. He looked down at the two photos. In one he was posing with Suzanne Morton. In the other he was standing next to Estella Abreu. The young man studied the photos for a moment, then looked up at me and said, "So what? I'm in photos at parties. I didn't do anything wrong."

I took a moment to gather my thoughts and say exactly what I thought would hit home. "In both of these recent photos, you're in the company of women who subsequently became homicide victims. Do you know what the odds are of knowing two different murder victims? I was wondering if you could explain this."

Kyle Banning was clearly uncomfortable and fumbled for words. "What do you mean, homicide victims?"

"That sentence only has one meaning. These two women were both found dead not too long after you were seen with them at parties." Now I was starting to gear up to hit him with some questions about his whereabouts and how he knew the girls. I felt like my ploy had worked perfectly.

Then a shadow fell across the doorway. I turned that way to see a man in his late fifties, wearing slacks and an Izod shirt. His graying comb-over didn't do him any favors.

The man said, "Kyle, don't say another word." He pointed his right index finger at me. "You need to leave. Right now."

# CHAPTER 49

**MR. BANNING GLARED** at me from the doorway and used his excellent authoritarian voice to get his point across. A teen I assumed to be the little brother, Jaden, stood behind the father, trying to see what was going on.

Mr. Banning looked directly at me and said, "This interview and future interviews are over. Kyle wants an attorney."

Banning whined, "But, Dad, you don't understand. This is—"

His father cut him off with a raised hand before Banning could finish his sentence. I imagined he had done that a lot when the boys were young. The move clearly terrified them. I based that assumption on the fact that Banning shut his mouth the second the hand went into the air.

His father said, "No, Kyle, *you* don't understand. A cop like this doesn't care about rights or privacy. He just wants to clear a case."

That's when I spoke up. "Yes, sir, that's right. I'm trying to solve the murders of several young women. And your son is in photos with two of them not long before they were killed." I held up the photographs.

Now Jaden stepped closer to look at the photos. His green eyes grew wide. "Who got murdered?"

Mr. Banning focused on me and said, "Crime like that is not our concern."

Kyle looked at me and said, "It's not what you think. They were just arm candy. Hell, my little brother even took one to a dance."

I asked, "One what?"

Now Mr. Banning stepped between me and the boys. He wasn't big. In fact, the top of his head didn't quite come up to my nose. But he was imposing.

Jaden Banning said again, "Who was murdered?" He looked at the photos with the fascination of a kid about to get on a roller coaster.

His father snapped, "Jaden, get out of here." Then he turned to his older son and said, "Don't you ever learn? Keep your mouth shut. Tight." He turned to me. In a much lighter tone, he said, "Detective…" and held his arm out to usher me from the room.

"Joan, please show the detective out. I need to talk with Kyle," he said to Mrs. Banning.

I followed Mrs. Banning to the front door. She was clearly nervous. Maybe *scared* was a better word. I could imagine what she'd been through with Kyle.

Joan Banning said, "I'm sure this is all a misunderstanding, Detective. You know how boys will be boys. My boys are just a little more intense. Jaden is still recovering from an illness that kept him out of school a few days," she said.

"I know about Kyle's arrest for striking the woman near Times Square." Why not try that? I had nothing to lose.

"He was never officially charged."

"I even know about his arrest as a juvenile." Even though I didn't actually know shit about that arrest, the effect on Mrs. Banning was remarkable. She sputtered and fumbled for words.

Then she said, "We're not making the same mistakes with Jaden. We've been much stricter with him. In fact, that's why we have him in the Wolfson Academy up in Bronxville. He usually lives there during the week. I think it has really matured him."

Now we were standing just outside the door to their apartment in the wide hallway. I turned to face Mrs. Banning. "What do you know about your son's dating life?"

Now she looked really flustered. She looked over her shoulder to make sure her husband hadn't heard the question.

I found myself leaning forward, anticipating the answer.

Instead, Mrs. Banning took a step backward into the apartment and shut the door carefully.

# CHAPTER 50

**THANK GOODNESS BEING** around my kids chased away any regrets I had about my fumbled interview with Kyle Banning and his family.

Sunday is always family day in the Bennett household. Picnics, playing tourist in New York City by climbing to the top of the Empire State Building, or rowing boats across the lake in Central Park. Or, if the weather is bad, board games inside. It doesn't matter.

Today was definitely an outside day. You grab those when you can this time of year in New York City. Clear and in the mid-50s. Perfect for some sort of outdoor game.

I'd lain awake much of the night, replaying the interaction with the Banning clan. My quick assessment, without any background or context, was that Banning's father was an asshole. His comment about a homicide investigation being none of their concern told me everything I needed to know about Mr. Banning.

The mother was just trying to stay afloat. I'd seen it before. Stuck with a husband who had no idea what being involved with the family meant. Two entitled boys who thought they could get away with anything. And probably a conscience that kept her awake at night thinking about that.

Kyle Banning had actually sounded like he *wanted* to talk to me if his old man wasn't around. He'd looked both bothered and surprised to hear about the deaths of Estella Abreu and Suzanne Morton. I searched for any connections between Kyle Banning and Emma Schrade. I could find nothing linking the dead Juilliard student found in the Bronx with my suspect.

But it was Kyle Banning's younger brother, Jaden, who had worked his way into my subconscious. The way he'd looked at the photos of the girls. The fascination. I didn't want to think about a teenage serial killer, but something told me it was a possibility. Call it a hunch or instinct or whatever you want— it was Jaden Banning I felt I needed to look at more closely.

His mother had mentioned a place called the Wolfson Academy in Bronxville. I did some research after I left the Banning residence. The Wolfson Academy's motto was *We turn problems into success!* I knew the academy had to be expensive because there was no hint of prices on their website. There were photos of young men dressed in sharp, military-style uniforms. Everyone's hair was cut short. Each cadet appeared to be in perfect physical condition. To me, sending your kid away to a boarding school was the last possible resort. You didn't end up at a place like that without a solid reason.

I didn't want to think about the methods the Wolfson Academy used to "fix" young people.

As I lay in bed on Sunday morning, considering the day ahead of me, Mary Catherine turned and put her hand on my chest. "You were restless last night. Everything okay?"

I told her about my interaction with the Banning family. I also told her about the younger boy, Jaden. I didn't hold back anything.

Mary Catherine whistled. "It's scary to think that a young man could be hiding such a horrible secret. What causes behavior like that? It's not really video games, is it?"

"If anyone figured out what caused this kind of behavior, maybe we could act to curb it. I don't have any evidence this kid is a killer. It's just an idea that concerns me."

"Imagine a boy capable of such terrible things. If he picked up one of our girls on a date and we didn't know him…" Mary Catherine couldn't bring herself to finish the sentence. I was glad she didn't.

Mary Catherine cuddled up next to me. "Michael, sometimes I just get so worried. This is exactly what scares me about having another child. Hearing about a boy who could go so wrong. A boy capable of hurting people. The world is a scary place."

I squeezed her and kissed Mary Catherine on the top of her head. I had the same thoughts all the time.

# CHAPTER 51

**OUR SCHEDULE WAS** a little off for a Sunday. My grandfather had organized a spaghetti dinner at Holy Name tonight. We were going to the evening service so our Sunday game day could start earlier than usual.

The kids whipped through breakfast and helped with cleanup. It was nice not rushing out to church on a Sunday morning. I wondered why that never happened during the week when we were late for school. But it was still nice seeing smiles and everyone dressed in shorts and sweatshirts for a day of hard playing.

Brian suggested we go to Central Park, but I knew I'd be constantly turning to look at the Bannings' apartment building. It would just be a distraction for me.

Instead, before I said anything, Mary Catherine suggested the much more convenient Riverside Park. Chrissy jumped up and down, clapping her hands. She loved to look for birds in the bird sanctuary section of the park. I liked some of the park's wide-open fields.

We walked as a group the few blocks to the park. We no longer made each kid hold hands with the one in front of him or her. But there was an unwritten rule that the older kids keep track of the younger kids. Still, a mob of ten kids and two adults marching down the street could startle the unsuspecting. Usually, people just assumed we were some sort of school out on a field trip. That was fine with me.

Some of the older kids and I carried backpacks holding a dozen different balls and rackets and bats as well as a picnic. We have learned it's easier to just buy drinks from a street vendor than carry a cooler along with us. The logistics were not unlike moving an army across occupied territory. You need to know what supplies are available and what to bring with you.

Mary Catherine said, "What do you guys think? Maybe basketball?"

Trent and Ricky immediately said, "Football," in unison. I was sure it had to do more with them not wanting to be embarrassed by Fiona dropping fifteen-foot jumpers on them than any great love of football. It didn't matter, a quick voice vote approved the measure, and after a leisurely walk past the bird sanctuary to make Chrissy happy, we found ourselves on a field rimmed by a few shade trees.

We fell into natural teams of six on six. It wasn't always the exact same teams. There were four or five variations. Each of us had our advantage. I was tall enough to see over everyone if I was quarterback. That's why they made the rule I couldn't be quarterback anymore.

Trent was much faster than everyone else. He used it to his advantage to outrun the coverage. The problem with that was he couldn't catch particularly well. It was still fun to see the ball sail toward him so far down the field.

Even Chrissy had an advantage. She was so small and quick, she could dart between us before anyone could tag her. When she managed to bend almost to the ground to avoid a tag by Ricky, her brother yelled, "That's not a legal move. Her knee touched the ground. I'm calling for an official ruling."

It was my oldest daughter, Juliana, who set her brother straight. "Keep it to yourself, Belichick."

I laughed out loud. Anyone who was even remotely a Jets fan always had to take their shots at the New England Patriots.

The game ended when Fiona threw a pass to Trent. He bobbled it and Jane snatched it right out of the air, then ran almost the entire field to score. Admittedly, our field was only about thirty yards long, but it was still impressive.

We marched back to the apartment, cleaned up, went to the evening service at Holy Name, and then sat down to the church's spaghetti dinner. Ricky was critical of the store-bought tomato sauce but said the decent garlic bread made up for it. Brian said it reminded him of going to school here at the church and had three helpings of spaghetti.

I leaned back at the table where my entire family, including my grandfather, was seated. I listened to the jokes and laughter and wondered if life got much better than this.

I doubted it.

# CHAPTER 52

**MONDAY MORNING WAS** back to reality. Time to find answers to all the questions that had nagged me over the weekend. That required a drive for my first bit of business. Specifically, a drive north about fifteen miles to the Village of Bronxville, in Westchester County.

I wanted to get a good look at the Wolfson Academy and maybe even Jaden Banning. My intention was mainly to walk through the school. I figured if I showed up as a concerned parent of a troubled young man, I might get a quick tour. Places like that always need cash and rarely turn anyone away. Unless they can't pay.

Driving into the small, well-kept village, it was hard for me to believe this was one of the most expensive suburbs of a major city in the country. There was nothing to it.

I found the Wolfson Academy's six acres filled with aged

oak and pine trees next to a country club off White Plains Road. It looked like a small college campus. The main administrative building faced the street and rose three stories. Two buildings ran perpendicular to the admin building so the three buildings together formed a giant U.

I strolled straight up the long walkway, trying to give the impression that I was casually interested in the institution. Someone buzzed me through the front door, where a receptionist met me. I told her my name and that I was interested in a tour for my three sons.

I guess being dressed in a nice coat and wearing a tie conveyed some sort of gravitas. Plus, the prospect of three new students at once had to be appealing to a school like this. The next thing I knew I was meeting with the headmaster, Charles Tilton III. Or, as he asked to be called, "Trey."

Trey immediately asked me what I did for a living. I didn't lie. I said, "I work for the NYPD."

That gave the man in his mid-forties pause. He bit his lip and looked out the window. I knew what he was thinking: *No way this guy can afford our tuition.*

The headmaster said, "We have excellent academics. That's a reflection of the money we pour into the programs. Money that comes from tuition."

"So, you're saying you don't think I can afford this."

"No, no, not at all. Just offering a warning. I don't imagine the NYPD pays enough for the risks you have to take. And our tuition is high by other schools' standards. I don't mean to be rude or abrupt. I'm just trying to be honest."

This was his way of covering all his bases. He didn't want some cop going back to the city saying they were a bunch of snobs who wouldn't take a civil servant's child. If he showed me around and I came to the realization myself that the tuition was too high, he knew I wouldn't have much to complain about.

I said, "I have other sources of income."

He perked up like a lawyer who'd witnessed someone slip and fall at a McDonald's. He smoothed his perfect hair, then said, "Let me show you our athletic facilities. Then you can decide if you're interested."

He led me out of his office and down the hallway. We were passed by a number of young men in sharp uniforms. Each of them greeted us with a "Good morning, sir."

Trey asked what I was looking for in a school. "You said you had three sons. Are they giving you problems?"

"I can't even begin to tell you." I couldn't because there was nothing I could think of that my younger sons had done wrong. Trent, Ricky, and Eddie barely ever broke rules, let alone laws. Although, I have to admit, I'd thought the same thing about Brian until he was arrested for drug dealing.

In effect, I was walking through this place in an undercover role. The headmaster knew I was a cop, but he thought I was here on personal business. I'd let him keep believing that.

The headmaster was slim and walked at a fast pace. Even with my long legs, I struggled to keep up with him. Everything about him was manicured and polished, a lot like the academy itself. We slowed our pace a few times to look through windows into classrooms. Each class had twenty or so students.

I stayed on the lookout for Jaden Banning.

# CHAPTER 53

**I KEPT MY** eyes and ears open as we continued the tour. I was hoping to pick up some kind of information or even a reference to Jaden Banning. I had to admit that with all the cadets dressed the same and all with short haircuts, I might not recognize Jaden if I only caught a glimpse.

We swung back by the office on our way to the athletic fields. Just as we stepped inside, a professionally dressed woman came out of an office.

The headmaster said, "Jill, this is Mr. Bennett. He works for the NYPD."

"Is he here about the money?"

The headmaster quickly shook his head and said, "No, that's the local police, not the NYPD."

I didn't ask what she was talking about. I had my own investigation to conduct. As we cut through the rest of the main administrative offices, a woman sitting at a desk near the window looked up and smiled at me. Then she gave me a little wave. She was attractive and in her forties with dark hair to her shoulders.

I smiled and waved back as I followed the headmaster. She looked familiar, but I couldn't quite put my finger on where I knew her from.

Once outside, we turned the corner of the building. The view of the fields and surrounding woods was spectacular. Two baseball fields and an eight-lane, quarter-mile running track ringed a football field.

I watched some cadets run in formation around the track. The last one in the formation had to sprint to the front of the line. I remembered doing something similar at the Police Academy. Thank God I'd never had to do it as a student at Holy Name. I smiled to myself, picturing Sister Sheilah learning this new way to efficiently exercise. She'd love it.

We crossed the running track once the cadets were past us and headed toward a large man with blond hair, holding a tackling sled while two cadets in pads hit the sled.

The big man noticed the headmaster and stepped away from the sled. He seemed even larger as he walked toward us. At least six foot five and a solid 260, maybe in his mid-thirties.

The headmaster said, "Coach Martin, this is Mr. Bennett. He's looking at the school for his three teenage sons."

The coach stuck out his beefy hand. "Perry Martin. Nice to meet you."

I said, "You have to get this all the time, but did you play pro football?"

Coach Martin chuckled. "Technically, yes. Right guard at

Syracuse and an undrafted free agent for Baltimore. Spent a year on their practice squad, then realized I wasn't going anywhere in the NFL. Been here six years now and it feels like home."

The headmaster's phone rang and he said, "Excuse me just a second."

After Trey stepped away, the coach asked, "Do you live in Westchester County?"

"The city."

"I figured you had to live someplace like that if you could afford to send your kids here."

"Do you have kids here?"

Coach Martin laughed. "Even with the discount I get for working here, I could never afford to send a child here. Besides, mine are only three and five."

"Doesn't the school offer scholarships?"

"Generally, in some sports, especially football. We've been the regional champs five years in a row. But the scholarships are also designed to promote diversity. I doubt your kids would qualify."

I smiled but didn't give him any details about my family.

The headmaster finished his phone call and ambled back toward us. Coach Martin stuck out his hand again. "Hope you enjoy your tour, Mr. Bennett. And be careful down there in the city. It's not like up here in the suburbs where everything's quiet. You could get killed in the city."

"You can get killed anywhere. At least I know my way around the city."

# CHAPTER 54

**ON THE PLUS** side, my tour was finished and the headmaster hadn't suspected what I was really after. On the minus side, I really hadn't learned anything of value. I wasn't about to mention Jaden Banning's name. A place like this would immediately inform Mr. Banning, who would almost certainly claim some kind of harassment. That would make it much more difficult to determine if either of the Banning brothers was involved in the murder of Estella Abreu, Suzanne Morton, or Emma Schrade, who'd been found in the Bronx.

I was on my way to my car when I heard someone call my name. I turned to see the woman I'd vaguely recognized from inside the office. She hustled toward me as fast as her high heels could carry her.

"Hi, Detective Bennett. Do you remember me?"

I said, "I knew I recognized you." I hate to ever admit not remembering someone.

"Michelle Finnegan." She read my blank stare and added, "My daughter Alyssa went missing when she was ten years old, and you found her."

I snapped my fingers. "The little girl who liked to ride buses. I found her on a bus headed from the Upper West Side to Midtown."

She jumped up and gave me a hug. "I've been holding that in for eleven years. You were the only one who actually listened when we were telling you about Alyssa. You're the one who figured out the bus schedules and brought her home to me safe. I'll never forget that."

"What's Alyssa up to now?"

"She's a senior at Binghamton. She wants to work in transportation. Go figure." We both laughed together.

It's moments like these that make every hardship a cop faces worthwhile. It doesn't take many successes like this to make you forget about the failures.

We chatted for a few minutes. Michelle told me how much she'd enjoyed working at the school the past four years.

I took a chance. "Can I ask you a question just between the two of us?"

"Of course."

"Do you know a student named Jaden Banning?"

"I know all the students. Jaden a little better than the rest. He seems to find his way to the office frequently."

"He might be involved in something serious. That's why I'm really here. I was just seeing if I could pick up any information."

"Jaden is sort of famous around here. He brought an unbelievably beautiful girl as his date to a school dance some months ago. A little older. Really made an impression."

That caught my attention immediately. "Would the girl have had to sign a register or anything to go to the dance?"

Michelle Finnegan shook her head. She said, "Some of the boys were talking about the girl the next week. Apparently, when someone asked Jaden if she was his girlfriend, he said, 'No, my brother got me The Girlfriend Experience.'"

"The what?"

"Apparently she was an escort hired by Jaden's older brother. He's some kind of financial analyst in the city."

"She was a prostitute?"

"I don't think so. More of a date for hire. I asked Alyssa if she'd ever heard the term. She said she had but wasn't sure what it meant."

This felt big. Huge. But I needed more. "Is there any way, short of speaking to Jaden Banning or his brother, that I could identify this girl?"

Michelle pulled her phone from a pocket of the blue sweater she had on over her blouse. She started scrolling through her photos and said, "I may have a couple of photos of them. I took about fifty that night. Mostly of decorations but quite a few of the students as well."

I waited while she scrolled through her photos. When she held up the phone, I had to squint and lean closer to see the photo clearly.

Jaden Banning was smiling with his arm around Emma Schrade.

# CHAPTER 55

***THE GIRLFRIEND EXPERIENCE.*** The phrase pinged around in my head. It seemed familiar but alien at the same time. I used my phone to look it up and saw that it was a TV show and used on several adult sites to describe an escort pretending to be someone's girlfriend. Those kinds of general terms didn't seem like they would help me at the moment.

I went to the best possible source of underground phrases: Ronald Higdon, Esquire.

When I walked into Higdon's Pawn and Jewelry, I saw a young couple at the counter talking with Ronald. The way my informant looked up and said, "Good morning, *Detective* Bennett," told me he was warning the couple not to say anything they weren't supposed to in front of a cop.

I was anxious to talk to him. I turned and looked at the front door. He took the hint and told the couple to come back later to finish their business.

When we were alone, I asked Ronald, "What kind of conspiracy are you involved in with those two?"

"Conspiracy? They were just looking at rings. I'm offended you'd think I'd conduct any criminal activity in my business."

I said, "*I'm* offended you'd think I *didn't realize* you're constantly conducting criminal activity in your business."

Ronald put on a pleasant smile and said, "Sounds like we should agree to disagree." Wisely, he changed the subject. "I poked around a little bit after you texted me. I think I've got some information on your Girlfriend Experience."

I didn't say anything. Sometimes silence can be a great motivator. It clearly made Ronald a little uneasy.

"A-a lot of p-people" he stammered, "use the term. But it's also the name of a little group here in Manhattan. I don't know how little, but it's not widespread. A group of young ladies who make money renting themselves out as dates. Sex is not always on the table. I heard that's negotiable."

"It sounds a little like prostitution."

"It's not like the old days, Bennett. No pimps involved. Everything's online now. Very sophisticated. Sounds like these girls run it themselves." He looked on his phone, then said, "I'm texting you a link to the site. I also talked to some of my people on the street. They've heard it was going on, but no one knows any of the girls involved. It sounds like they're pretty smart."

I stood there for a moment, thinking about what Ronald had just told me.

Ronald said, "Think the girls who ended up dead were part of this Girlfriend Experience?"

I shook my head. "Don't know. Maybe. Easiest way to find

out would be to ask Kyle Banning directly. He's already said he won't talk to me. Or at least his father did."

"You probably don't want to involve one of your smart kids who know how to sail around the internet, do you?"

I looked at Ronald. "That's a good idea."

"Using one of your kids on a murder investigation?"

"What? No, of course not. But I know some pretty smart tech people who aren't related to me. I bet I know exactly which one would want to help." I turned on my heel and hustled for the door. Just as I opened it, I turned back and said, "Thanks, Ronald. Sometimes you're even helpful when you don't mean to be."

"For the purposes of payment from the NYPD, I *always* mean to be helpful."

# CHAPTER 56

**THE NYPD HEADQUARTERS** makes me uncomfortable. I have never liked being around One Police Plaza for very long. As far as I'm concerned, the place is a necessary evil only visited if I want to talk to someone in Special Investigations or Human Resources, or our forensic tech people. That's why I didn't appreciate the fact that I had visited the place so many times in the past few days.

I walked through the main door of the Tech Unit. It wasn't dark and dingy like TV shows often portray tech hubs. But I knew that some of the tech people preferred to work in a darkened room since it reduced glare.

A young man looked out from behind his desk and said, "May I help you?"

"Is William Patel here?"

The young man pointed to a partially closed door, then

went back to working on his computer without another word. William Patel had been a tremendous help when I was stuck in Washington, DC, trying to find out who had killed my friend FBI agent Emily Parker. Not only did William help me; he'd also done so without approval from the NYPD. He trusted that I needed help to find a killer instead of listening to people who were trying to chase me out of Washington.

The ten-by-twenty-foot room had four computers and the lights turned low. William was in the corner, studying a screen filled with computer code. When he looked up to see who'd come in, his eyes looked bleary and bloodshot.

It took a moment for him to recognize me. Then he perked up instantly.

"Detective! What brings you to our little high-tech kingdom? Have another big case you need help with?"

"You should be a psychic, William. That's exactly what I need."

He got a big, goofy grin on his face. He looked at me and said, "Put me in, Coach."

It was hard not to feel encouraged by an attitude like that. Especially since I knew a lot of the tech guys took shit from other detectives. Some detectives viewed them as nothing more than nerdy administrative assistants. They were constantly trying to get the tech guys to bypass safeguards on their NYPD laptops. Mainly software to keep them from downloading dangerous programs and viruses or to track their internet usage.

I took the seat next to William and started to tell him what I'd learned about The Girlfriend Experience. I handed him an information sheet on each of my three victims, Emma Schrade, Estella Abreu, and Suzanne Morton. Each sheet had just their personal information, like their date of birth and their cell phone number.

While I laid out the information as I knew it, William started to work on his computer. I told him what I knew about the case and my two suspects, Kyle and Jaden Banning. I pointed out to him that I had no evidence on either brother. Or anyone else, for that matter.

He kept typing while occasionally glancing up at me. When I finally finished talking, I leaned back in the chair.

"What do you think, William? Can you get me some kind of a line on this Girlfriend Experience? I know you're busy and it's tough to take time out of your day, but you told me you wanted to be involved in more interesting cases. When do you think you'd be able to help me?"

William looked at me with no expression. I noticed his dark hair was longer than the last time I had spoken to him and he wore a new pair of more fashionable glasses. "The stuff on the printer behind you has the best match I could find looking through some of the seedier parts of the internet," he said.

"What?"

"Reach behind you and take the sheets from the big laser printer."

I turned in my chair and plucked nine sheets of paper from a blocky printer.

The top sheet was a printout of a New York State driver's license photo for an extremely pretty girl with long blond hair. I didn't recognize her, but there was a list of several phone numbers below the photo, as well as a few addresses. I turned my eyes back to William but kept silent. I knew any question I asked would sound stupid.

William said, "I cross-referenced the phone numbers from the sheet you just gave me through a few sites the NYPD would not approve of. Anyway, it looks like your victims all used at least one phone number in common. It was probably some kind of a hub or a computer. The printouts I just gave you have all the information on the girl connected to that phone number. Her name is Allie Pritz. Looks like she used to go to NYU. She's got a lot of addresses attached to her name. All over the city. Maybe she can tell you what you need to know."

I was speechless. It actually scared me that someone could find out all that information in just a few minutes, while still engaging with me *and* probably playing a video game at the same time.

It also made me evaluate my past experiences at headquarters. Maybe I had expected too little. Between Gary Avram, Persephone Garland, and William Patel, I had been able to jump ahead with their quick assistance.

Finally, I said, "William, I could kiss you."

He held up both hands and said, "I'm really not interested in something like that, Detective. I'm not judging you or your choices. I'm just saying it's not for me."

I was so anxious to work with the new information that all I said was "Understood."

# CHAPTER 57

**I WENT OVER** the information William Patel had just given me. There wasn't much more here about Allie Pritz. She was twenty-two. Born in Philadelphia. Never been arrested. Attended NYU for two and a half years. Now it seemed she was coordinating some kind of dating service. Normally, something I couldn't have cared less about. But if the members of this service were being murdered, I needed to learn more.

Before I could plan my next move, I received a text from my grandfather, Seamus. One of the kids had told him texting was cooler than calling. Now he was a texting maniac.

All it said was Can you swing by my office or call me?

My grandfather appreciated people's time and effort. He hated to disrupt their normal day if they were working. So a casual message like this meant something different coming from him. It was the equivalent of someone else shouting, *Come here right now!*

I texted him, On my way.

Even I was surprised how quickly I got uptown. When I stepped into his office in the administrative building next to the church and school, I immediately knew what the problem was. Trent, Eddie, and Ricky were all sitting around a small table in the corner of Seamus's office doing their homework.

My grandfather didn't say anything. He didn't want to embarrass the boys.

The first thing I asked was "Is everyone okay?"

My sons all nodded at the same time.

Seamus said, "The boys had a run-in with the bullies again."

I turned toward the boys. "I thought we agreed you'd stay away from those courts until we worked this out."

My grandfather interceded before the boys could speak. "It didn't happen down the street. The boys were right in front of the church."

Trent blurted, "We were just across the street. Tommy Sosa said we were too chicken to leave the grounds and started running around with his hands under his arms, flapping his elbows and clucking like a chicken. What were we supposed to do?"

I glanced over at my grandfather. Clearly, he was concerned about the situation, but Trent's colorful explanation made him want to laugh. He was holding it in. And not doing a particularly good job of it. Even I'll admit I can remember being goaded into doing stupid things when I was a kid. I think boys are especially susceptible to taunting. Tommy Sosa had known exactly what buttons to push.

I looked back at Trent. "It's okay. You're not in trouble. Just tell me what happened."

There were a lot of starts and stops from all three boys. Basically, the same bullies who'd bothered them at the basketball courts had been walking down the street and saw them. The oldest boy shoved Trent to the ground. Then the one who had shown them the gun in his waistband pointed his fingers at Eddie like they were a pistol, and mimed shooting.

This was troubling on a number of levels. The threat of gun violence was the most alarming. I waited for the end of the story. What happened then? Where did the bullies go? Did any adults see it?

Ricky shrugged his shoulders. "We ran back inside the fence around the school. We didn't see where the other boys went. I don't think anyone noticed us."

Eddie appeared to be the most shell-shocked. He said, "Can I be homeschooled for a while? I'm tired of getting pushed around when I come to school." His tone said he was trying to joke, but I could tell he'd be happy to stay at home for a while.

Ricky was much more brash. He said, "Don't you think it's time we stood up to them? I want to get my own gun."

I held up my hands and said, "Don't say stupid things like that, Ricky. This is a problem that we can solve. But the first thing you need to do is stay on school property, as discussed."

Eddie said, "Is this why some people think the police don't help much?"

"The police have to follow certain rules. Even when our own family is involved." I looked at my grandfather and said, "Would we be able to get any footage from the security cameras at the front of the school?"

Seamus smiled. "I already have a video file saved for you. You can see all three bullies clearly. It's a little harder to see what they were doing."

"That'll do for a start."

I decided I needed to call it a day and drive the boys home in my city car.

# CHAPTER 58

**ONCE I GOT** home with the boys, I started getting texts from Walter Jackson. He'd found a few more possible addresses for Allie Pritz. Two of the addresses were in Midtown, one in the Bronx, one in Brooklyn. Plus, I had the addresses William Patel had given me. It looked like I had a long day of checking addresses tomorrow.

Just after dinner, I sat at the dining room table, helping Chrissy with her history homework. She was studying the Dark Ages. It was generally basic stuff, like how most of Europe was in chaos and diseases like the Black Plague added to the misery.

Chrissy looked at me with her big blue eyes and asked, "I don't understand what caused the Dark Ages."

I'd been looking through her textbook to see if it included any details, but there were no real explanations. I said, "One theory is that as Rome withdrew from its outlying provinces, including Europe, organization and infrastructure broke down. Some people say there were no decent roads built for more than five hundred years after the fall of Rome."

"Do you think that will be on the test?"

I smiled. I undoubtedly had asked the same question of my grandfather when I was Chrissy's age. They were probably teaching history the same way they did when I was at Holy Name as a kid. "No, sweetheart, I doubt that's anything you need to remember."

That seemed to satisfy my youngest daughter. My two oldest daughters, Juliana and Jane, were also studying, at the other end of the long dining room table. I'd learned over the last few years that my older children were on top of their academics. I had very little to add to most of their lessons. They were far beyond me in math, enrolled in Calculus II. They certainly didn't care about my opinions on historical questions. But I couldn't help one kid and then ignore two others at the table.

Chrissy jumped up from the table like a prisoner just released after nine years in Attica. She darted out of the room, leaving me alone with Jane and Juliana. I moved down until I was sitting next to Jane and across from Juliana.

I smiled and said, "What are we working on?"

Jane gave me her famous flat stare and said, "I don't know what *you're* working on, but I'm working on American lit. My essay is about how none of the great writers of the early twentieth century would be published today."

She added, "And how does that affect classics of the future? Are we, as a society, encouraging the arts? What impact would an artless society have on the future?"

Any dad will tell you he doesn't want to look stupid in front of his kids. I feared it was unavoidable in this case. All I could do was mumble, "Okay, you sound like you have a handle on this."

I wasn't cracking a joke, but it made both the girls laugh. We sat and chatted for a few minutes. The younger kids were always interested in telling me about their days and their projects. The older kids were more reticent. You had to hit them at just the right time.

Jane told me about some experiments in her biology class that she found really interesting. Juliana told me about the acting class she took at City College in the evenings. Right now, they were breaking down Eugene O'Neill's *Long Day's Journey into Night.*

I loved hearing about my girls' interests. Then Juliana turned serious and asked me, "Have you heard anything more about the investigation into Suzanne's murder?" Her voice got weak toward the end of the sentence and I felt like she might start to cry.

I looked into my daughter's beautiful face and realized I'd been searching everywhere for information when I had a potential source right in the apartment with me. She shared a lot of characteristics with Suzanne Morton. She might help.

I said, "Have either of you ever heard of The Girlfriend Experience?"

Juliana said, "You mean like the TV show?"

"No, I mean from your friends or anyone in real life."

Even with ten kids, you quickly learn each of their little idiosyncratic mannerisms. In this case, I saw how Juliana's eyes focused on the table and she folded her hands across her writing pad. Ever since she was a little kid, that was a sign that she was keeping some sort of secret.

After nibbling around the subject for a few minutes, I finally asked Juliana directly. "Juliana, sweetheart, I feel like you know something about this, but you don't want to talk about it. This is important. It may help us find Suzanne's killer."

A tear leaked out of Juliana's left eye. She lowered her head and nodded silently. After almost a full minute, she said, "I've heard of it a couple of times. I know The Girlfriend Experience has something to do with getting paid to pretend to be someone's date at fancy parties or events. Someone asked Suzanne if that's how she had so much spending money. Suzanne blew off the question and didn't answer. But I can put it all together now. She *did* have a lot of extra cash and was always paying for our meals and rides. It also explains why she was never free to go out on Friday or Saturday nights."

I nodded and made a few mental notes as my oldest daughter continued to talk.

"Suzanne used to tell me about her friend Allie, whom she worked with. I always thought that was a little odd since Suzanne had no official job."

The mention of Allie caught my attention. "Do you have any idea where Allie lives?"

"I think it's somewhere close to NYU. Suzanne once said she was going to get an apartment like Allie's. She hated living in the dorm."

My daughter had just told me which address I would look at first when I tried to find Allie Pritz.

# CHAPTER 59

**I WAS UP** early the next day. Juliana had given me an idea. I snuck out of the house before most of the kids were awake. As I suspected, I found Walter Jackson already in the office.

I said, "You really are an early riser."

The big man let out a laugh. "C'mon, this is the only time during my day that it's quiet. No little girls begging me for ice cream. No detectives asking me to find out about old girlfriends or boyfriends. No lieutenant loaning me out to other units. I live for these two hours of undisturbed peace."

"That I'm about to disturb."

"That's why I have to ask you a question about silence."

"What's that?"

Walter said, "Why can't you hear a pterodactyl when he goes to the bathroom?"

I groaned and was about to ask, *Why?* Then at the last moment it hit me. "Because the *p* is silent."

That made Walter's day. He clapped and rolled back in his chair, laughing out loud. "I knew you'd start catching on one day."

I told Walter about my conversation with Juliana the night before. "It seems that these girls were all involved in The Girlfriend Experience. If that's the case, then we might be able to make a connection to the Bannings or another client."

Walter started working his magic on the computer.

I texted Emma Schrade's mother one simple question. I was wondering if you found out anything unusual about Emma's finances?

Dr. Schrade called me less than a minute later. "Yes, as a matter of fact. I was surprised to find out recently that she had almost twelve thousand dollars in a checking account."

Her mother assured me Emma hadn't made that kind of money singing at weddings.

I texted David Morton next. He also called me right back, and I went over the same question with him.

"We found fifty-six hundred dollars in cash hidden in her closet." There was silence on the line for a minute. Then I heard David Morton blow his nose. He came back on the line and said, "We told Detective Stanton. Didn't he share it with you?"

"No." I kept the answer short. There was no telling what the New Rochelle detective thought was important.

I thanked David Morton, then checked back in with Walter. I told him what I'd found out. "It gives me some specific questions to ask Allie Pritz, once we talk to her."

Walter asked, "When do you think that will be?"

"I'm hoping in the next couple of hours."

# CHAPTER 60

**LESS THAN TWO** hours later, Terri Hernandez met me at a coffee shop near Washington Square Park. It was only a couple of blocks from the apartment where I believed Allie Pritz was living on Cornelia Street.

Terri said, "I went by NYU yesterday and talked to the registrar. The registrar tried to help, but the only solid information they had was that Suzanne Morton barely attended class and had a poor GPA as a result."

I nodded, then said, "Why would she stop worrying about classes?"

"Because she wanted to be an actress and didn't think she needed a degree?"

I shook my head. "Or she was making so much money with The Girlfriend Experience she didn't need to stay in college. I know she hadn't told her parents. They were clearly under the impression she was doing fine in school at the time she disappeared."

We walked two blocks over to Cornelia Street. The building was a five-story walk-up with a beautiful stone facade. The fire escape was along the side of the building, landing in an alley.

It was still early enough that there was a chance we'd catch Allie Pritz snug in bed and surprised to find two New York City detectives knocking at her door. That might lead to some *open discussion.* That was our favorite phrase for scaring someone into talking.

Terri walked up the eight steps to the entrance. She checked the door buzzers. "I don't see her name, but there are six slots that just have numbers and no names."

As I was considering what we should do, the door opened. A young man dressed in a sweatshirt looked at Terri and smiled. Then he held the door open for her. She just said, "Thanks," and stepped inside. The young man barely looked in my direction as he rushed down the steps and started to jog down the block.

A moment later, Terri opened the door and let me in. Each of the sixteen mailboxes had names on them. I saw the name PRITZ for apartment 504.

When I was a kid, Seamus used to tell me you can learn a lot about a building from the condition of its stairwell. If the stairwell is kept clean and in good order, the whole building usually is in the same shape.

This stairway had the original hardwood handrail and steps. Each stair I took made a pleasing, hollow thud that echoed in the stairwell. We took the stairs all the way to the top floor. We stepped out of the stairwell on the fifth floor into a wide corridor with an apartment on each side. Light streamed through a tall window with access to the fire escape.

Apartment 504 was the one on the right. Terri knocked and stood in front of the peephole. Everyone knows that people are more likely to answer the door if a woman is knocking.

A woman's scratchy voice asked, "Who is it?"

Terri pulled her ID from her purse. She held the badge up to the peephole and said, "NYPD. We need to speak to you for a moment, Ms. Pritz."

The voice replied, "Give me a second to get dressed."

In many ways, it was going better than I expected. It could've been the wrong address. Allie may not have been home. It could've been a mail drop. Instead, we got an immediate response. So why was I still uneasy?

After about forty-five seconds, I looked at Terri.

She just shrugged and knocked on the door again. Nothing from inside. Then I heard a metallic scraping noise. I immediately recognized the sound of a fire escape brushing against the side of the building.

I rushed to the window at the end of the hall. I saw a young woman in shorts and a T-shirt, holding running shoes she hadn't had time to put on, carefully making her way down the outside fire escape.

I unlatched the tall window and opened it. I looked out the window past the fire escape to the alley below. My fear of heights hit me like a sledgehammer. In an instant, I felt clammy sweat spring up on my face. My stomach twisted and I could taste my morning coffee in my throat. It was worse than I'd ever felt it in the past.

Somehow I managed to gasp over my shoulder to Terri, "She's trying to climb down the fire escape."

Terri didn't hesitate to sprint down the hallway and blast through the door to the stairwell.

I had to suck it up and stepped out onto the fire escape with shaky legs.

# CHAPTER 61

**I GULPED A** deep breath to follow Allie as she descended the fire escape. She moved quicker than I could. I could barely let go of the rungs as I tried to make my way from the fifth to the fourth floor. I should've felt better as I moved closer to the ground. Instead, my palms got slick with sweat. I fought nausea with every step. Why was my dislike of heights hitting me so hard this time?

Between the third and fourth floors I looked down and saw that Allie was nearly to the street level. My heart pounded as I tried to take each rung of the fire escape quickly but carefully. My foot slipped, and I had to freeze in place for a moment. Finally, I gathered my nerve, closed my eyes, and kept going.

As I cleared the second floor, I couldn't see anyone in the alley below me. Allie Pritz had hit the ground running whether she was wearing shoes or not. I got to the end of the fire escape and dropped the few feet to the asphalt alley.

I suppressed the urge to vomit, then turned and sprinted toward Cornelia Street. I skidded to a stop as soon as I turned the corner.

Terri Hernandez was standing on the sidewalk with her arms folded in front of her and a stern look on her face. On a foot-high planter near the building's entrance, Allie Pritz sat sheepishly, slowly putting on her Nike running shoes.

Terri took one look at me and said, "You okay?"

I couldn't speak. I just nodded my head.

Terri said, "Oh, my God. I'm so sorry. I forgot about your acrophobia. I just acted on instinct and ran for the stairs."

I waved her off. This was not exactly the first impression I wanted to make with a potential homicide witness.

I looked at Allie Pritz still sitting on the edge of the planter. From this angle she seemed incredibly young. I wondered if she knew what she had gotten herself into. I said, "Why'd you run? We only want to talk to you."

She looked down at the sidewalk and mumbled, "I'm sorry. I just panicked."

Terri said, "Do you know what we want to talk to you about?"

"I can guess."

Terri said, "You're not in any trouble. Go ahead and guess. We won't hold it against you."

In a weak voice, Allie said, "You want to talk about The Girlfriend Experience, right?"

That's when I said, "Actually, we'd like to talk to you about a series of homicides."

That immediately got all of Allie Pritz's attention.

# CHAPTER 62

**A FEW MINUTES** after our short chase, we found ourselves back in Allie Pritz's apartment, sitting around her breakfast counter. Allie had poured us each a glass of some kind of green antioxidant drink. Apparently, the healthy Gen Z's version of coffee.

All my vital signs had returned to approximately normal, although I knew I'd have visions of the fire escape as I was trying to fall asleep tonight. Allie had been badly shaken when we told her about the deaths of Emma Schrade, Estella Abreu, and Suzanne Morton.

We gave Allie a chance to mourn. She cried, but I wasn't sure if it was stress or actual grief. I didn't know how well she knew the other girls. When Allie asked to use the bathroom, Terri said she'd stand by the door and that Allie couldn't lock it.

Technically, we didn't have the authority to do something

like that to someone who was not under arrest. But neither of us wanted to risk having to chase her down the fire escape again. Even if it seemed like Allie wanted to talk to us, there was no telling if she'd change her mind.

For her part, Allie took not locking the door in stride.

I looked at some framed photographs on the wall next to the breakfast counter. Allie with her mom at a play. With her dad at a shooting range, holding a Beretta 9mm. A photo of her playing soccer in high school, her blond hair flowing behind her as she streaked down a field.

When we were all sitting around the breakfast counter again, Allie said, "I can't believe any of this. I've always been worried about my parents finding out. That's one of the major reasons we've kept everything so secret. We make sure that none of the girls know one another. Well, most of them don't know one another. We use burner phones, and all the calls come through this phone." She held up an older Samsung. "It's prepaid and untraceable."

Terri said, "You didn't hear about the homicides on the news or in the paper?"

"Who's got time to read the paper? I might've heard something about a murder on TV, but I didn't make the connection to any of our girls. Like I said, most of the girls are just trying to get through college and don't want their parents to find out. I rarely speak to them more than once. Usually just texts. I make it a point not to track someone down if they don't answer a text.

"I spoke with Suzanne more than most of the girls. She was always wanting to meet for lunch or a drink." Allie thought about it for a moment, then added, "I guess she hasn't called in at least a month."

I chimed in. "Do you know who her clients were?"

Allie shook her head. "I'd have no way to know unless it was a first-time client who called the main, burner phone. Then all I'd have is a cell number."

Terri asked, "How much do you make per event?"

Allie shrugged. "I'm booked almost every Friday and Saturday evening, and I usually bring home about ten to twelve thousand dollars a month."

"And you don't even have sex with your clients?"

She shrugged. "Some of the girls negotiate for it as an extra. Not many, but the whole idea is that we're each responsible for ourselves."

Now I asked the question. "Have any of the girls ever mentioned being threatened by a client?"

"No, never. If I ever hear about a problem client, we cut them off and never deal with them again. We simply block their number. Once I had to tell a guy I was calling the cops if he didn't leave us alone. Our clients aren't drug dealers, they're businessmen and professionals. Since none of the clients knows where we live, we're safe. At least, we thought we were."

"Do the clients know you aren't working for an agency? They know you're all on your own?"

"That's one of the things I tell every client before any of us will meet them. They don't have to worry about anyone bothering them, the money has to be paid up front, and if one of the girls says no, it means no. I swear, in two years we've never had a problem."

I asked, "Are you still in school?" I knew the answer already but wanted to see her reaction.

She looked down and away from me. After a moment she said, "I dropped out of NYU last year when I had two twenty-thousand-dollar months back-to-back. My parents have no clue."

I said, "Most parents have no clue. About anything."

# CHAPTER 63

**THE LONGER WE** talked, the more Allie Pritz started to trust us. Terri Hernandez was the main reason. She was certainly more relatable to a young woman than I was.

The story Allie told us was similar to a lot of stories I'd heard about getting started in the escort business. When she was a sophomore at NYU, a girl Allie knew asked her if she wanted to make some extra cash. She explained that Allie would act as a young man's date to a wedding, and that sex was not required. Allie attended the wedding, had a good time, and couldn't believe she got paid nine hundred dollars. The girl who had told her about the job took a pretty hefty cut.

After that, Allie was in the rotation in The Girlfriend Experience. Eventually, she sort of took it over as other girls moved on or graduated.

Allie said, "All the girls who work in The Girlfriend

Experience are terrified their parents will find out or the cops will decide to bust us. Either way, we keep a low profile."

I repeated, "So none of the girls interact with one another."

"Not that I know of. If I can't take a job, I have one or two girls I can call, and I keep half of the fee. The other girls in The Girlfriend Experience do it the same way. It's not like we're a bricks-and-mortar business. It's a loose alliance."

"How many girls are involved?"

"I hand off assignments to about six girls. Sometimes there are as many as ten in the rotation. If a client asks for someone by name, I always send that tip directly to the girl. Otherwise, I sort of cherry-pick the better assignments."

Terri Hernandez said in a low voice, "I'm not judging, and you're not in trouble for it, but I was wondering if you, personally, ever have sex with your clients?"

Allie hesitated for a moment. "I've had sex with two clients. I didn't charge them extra. It was mutual and consensual. I don't know how any of the other girls do it. There was a girl in Midtown who made it a routine. She made so much money she moved to Florida and retired. At least that's what she told us."

Allie looked at me and said, "The main reason we limit contact with one another is that if someone gets arrested, they can't expose everyone else. With a string of burner phones and a couple of shaky email addresses, I doubted we'd ever be caught."

I said, "You might be overestimating your anonymity."

Allie smiled for the first time during our interview. I could see why men wanted to be seen with her at events. She had a beautiful smile that caused her cheekbones to pop. Even in shorts and a T-shirt, she had a certain elegance about her.

I said, "Allie, we're going to have to look at your burner phone to get some numbers off of it."

She nodded, then said, "I also have them in a Word document. I keep all the numbers along with notes. You know, if someone was rude or rough. Maybe they tried to short me on the money. These are calls into the main burner phone. I don't know what numbers the other girls might keep."

I had her email me the numbers list as Terri took the burner phone. It wasn't that we didn't believe her. But it's not a particularly professional cop who doesn't verify information.

I opened up the list on my phone. This list was going to keep Walter Jackson busy as he tried to find who belonged to each number. Somewhere in this list, I was sure, was a killer.

I said, "Have you ever heard the name Kyle Banning?"

She shook her head. Allie seemed surprised this was all we wanted from her.

Terri said, "There's something else you need to do."

"Anything. Anything at all. I feel sick to my stomach that someone's dead from our job. I feel responsible. I'll do anything you want to help find this creep."

Terri placed her hand gently on Allie's shoulder. She said, "The first thing you need to do is call your parents. Be honest with them, at least about the fact that you're not in college anymore."

Allie nodded and looked away.

# CHAPTER 64

**AS SOON AS** we were done interviewing Allie Pritz, and certain she wasn't going to run, I told Terri I'd catch up with her later. I had an appointment I didn't intend to miss. I braved the Midtown traffic and cringed when I found a lot that charged me fifty dollars to park. Since I wasn't on city business, I had to pay out of my pocket.

I walked two blocks to the building I was looking for. I took the elevator up to the nineteenth floor. The elevator doors opened into a hallway that led to the reception area for the Galt Fertility Clinic.

Sitting by herself in the corner was my beautiful wife, Mary Catherine. The smile that popped up on her face when she saw me made any traffic or parking hassles more than worth it. She hugged me even as I was sitting down in the comfortable, padded chair next to her.

Mary Catherine said, "Oh, Michael, I'm so happy you came. Forget what I said about wanting to do this on my own."

"Why would you do this on your own? We're a team. We tackle all of our problems together."

She kissed me on the cheek. The only other people in the waiting room were a couple in their forties. The man nervously bounced his leg while the woman absently thumbed through a *People* magazine.

I was surprised how nervous I was. The idea of Mary Catherine going through fertility treatments to have a baby had been an abstract thought before coming here. This place made it seem real and immediate.

The clinic was immaculate and well decorated. There were photos of mothers with newborns. Magazines about babies and child-rearing filled every table. I noticed the medical office had more plants than most and less of that usual smell of chemical cleaning products.

I'd already been through initial screenings during which I had to give sperm samples and receive instruction on the numerous treatment methods for infertility. For some reason Mary Catherine had it in her head that these appointments were a drain on my time. I didn't care if I was on the biggest, roughest serial-killer case of all time; there was nothing more important than the health of my family.

Maybe that was just my maturity finally kicking in. But a lot of it had to do with the death of my first wife, Maeve. She'd had cancer, and all treatment options had failed. We knew the prognosis was terminal. Even my NYPD bosses were sympathetic, and for eight months the family took the time we needed, essentially huddled together.

Then there was a crisis. A big-deal hostage situation in St. Patrick's Cathedral. At the time, I was still an active hostage negotiator. The men holding the captives created several odd incidents and I was pivotal in dealing with them.

And the whole time I was needed on the job, Maeve lay in a hospital bed. She had needed me more. I should've stayed with my wife. And to this day I regret it.

I like to think I can admit when I make mistakes. You don't make a mistake like that, then take lightly any kind of medical appointments of any kind.

A young man in scrubs came out and met us. He told us his name was Lyle and that he was assigned to us for the rest of our visit. I prayed this kind of personalized service was covered by insurance.

Lyle led us down the hallway to an examination room. He said, "Dr. Pilar will be in shortly." Lyle looked at me and said, "Today, Dr. Pilar will be performing a sonohysterogram. It's basically an ultrasound used to evaluate the uterus." He kept looking at me like he was expecting a response.

I nodded and felt Mary Catherine's grip on my hand tighten even as she kept a smile on her face. I resisted the urge to ask her if she was sure this was what she wanted to do. Mary Catherine had struggled with the decision for months. She had done her research and I respected her decision. But when I looked over at Mary Catherine, I felt like a coward compared to her. I took a deep breath, turned, and kissed my wife on the lips. It was about the only thing I could think to do.

# CHAPTER 65

**AFTER THE VISIT** to the clinic and a coffee with Mary Catherine, I set about the rest of my workday. One of the things I managed to accomplish was to send Sergeant Kathy Figler, my friend in juvenile crimes, a copy of the security video that showed the bullies' faces.

The sergeant said, "We're doing what we can, Mike. But with the violent crime rate moving up so quickly, the mayor's office is panicked. They got us out all over the city trying to figure out how to stem the violence."

"I completely understand, Kathy. And I appreciate your compassion. Every cop I know is overprotective of their children. I guess it's just because of what we see every day."

"Don't sweat it, Mike. You're doing everything right. We'll work it out eventually."

It was with that vague, optimistic statement in my head that

I settled down to a spectacular-looking dinner of enchiladas. Eddie and Mary Catherine had worked together to make an unusual and healthy version of the Mexican dish.

Even Seamus had made it to dinner tonight. We said a prayer, thanking God for all our many blessings. My grandfather added, "And let the youth of this city find love and compassion for one another."

Jane quietly added, "And stop beating up my brothers."

That smart remark earned a few snickers from her end of the table. It also garnered a glare from Seamus.

Then everyone dug in. Chrissy blurted out, "These don't taste like the enchiladas from Taco Heaven."

I was gratified to see Juliana step in and say, "That's because they're much better than anything Taco Heaven ever thought about making." She looked at the beaming Eddie, then at Mary Catherine, and said, "You guys work so well together, you should open your own restaurant."

I sat back and listened to the chatter. No one brought up any problems. No politics. Some sports talk among the boys. Brian told us about maintaining the air conditioners at a renovated office building in Midtown. I was pleased to see how enthusiastic he was about his job.

I decided I'd even have a glass of the Pinot Noir my grandfather had opened. Then my phone rang from the kitchen counter, where it sat charging. I glanced up sheepishly as every head at the table turned toward me. Mary Catherine looked sad that I had to answer the phone. My grandfather looked at me like I was breaking every possible social rule.

I was already angry at whoever was calling me now. It was like being awakened from a very pleasant dream. But any investigator will tell you that part of their job is being tied to their phone. At least a good investigator. Unless I am officially on vacation, and even then, probably out of the country, I always try to answer my phone. Or at the very least see who is calling.

I quickly excused myself and hustled over to check the name on the screen. Ronald Higdon. This time I would not add the Esquire. *Great.* I hesitated as it hit its fifth ring, highlighting the piano solo from "Layla."

Then guilt overtook me and I snatched up the phone. I said in a clipped, low tone, "What do you need, Ronald?"

"Bennett!" Ronald shouted into the phone.

I could hear loud banging on the line. I said, "What's that noise? Ronald, what's going on?"

"I didn't mean to cash it in so quick, but I need that favor you promised me."

"Why? What's happening?" Now I felt like *I* was shouting into the phone. Some of the kids turned and looked into the kitchen from the dining room table. I gave them a wave like everything was okay.

Ronald Higdon, Esquire, came back on the phone. "I need you to come to the shop. Two of the turds from Brooklyn are back. I don't think they realize I'm inside. They're trying to figure out how to break in. I have a padlock on the outside rear door. Just something extra. It's stopped them for now."

I could hear the panic in his voice. That was unusual for Ronald. He was the kind of guy who took advantage of panic, not one who displayed it.

Then he yelled in the phone, "Are you coming over to help or not?"

# CHAPTER 66

**AS SOON AS** I hung up with Ronald Higdon, Esquire, I left my apartment and drove uptown much faster than I should have. It would've made more sense to hand this off to a patrol officer, who could be there in two minutes instead of my ten-minute ride. But Ronald was right: I'd made a promise that if he asked a favor, I'd deliver. In the big scheme of things, this wasn't that tough of a favor.

Except for the fact that I was leaving my family. By the time I got back, the kitchen would be clean and there wouldn't be an enchilada left. I don't care how much food was made at any meal, with four adolescent boys, there was never anything left. Chrissy even had said she was worried she wouldn't grow to her proper height because the boys never left enough food for her to eat. It wasn't true, but I appreciated her sense of drama.

My tires squealed as I took the corner in Harlem and came to a stop directly in front of Higdon's Pawn and Jewelry. The place was dark. I started to worry that I was too late. I had a vision of Ronald sprawled on the floor with his head cracked open.

I called him.

He answered with alarm in his harsh whisper. "Bennett, where the hell are you? The guys got bolt cutters from somewhere. They're about to cut the outside padlock on my rear door."

"I'm out front. Sit tight. I'll check out the rear of the building."

Ronald sounded scared. Who wouldn't be? I jogged around the corner of the building and down to the rear alley, where I noticed a blue Cadillac XT5 parked. I could hear voices.

I peeked around the corner. A security light cast an eerie yellow haze across the alley. I saw three men huddled near the rear door to Higdon's Pawn and Jewelry and recognized two of them from our earlier encounter at the pawnshop. The third man was older, in his early fifties. He was short and stout, with graying hair, and held a pair of bolt cutters. There was a baseball bat leaning against the wall of the building, but no one appeared to have any other weapon on them. That was good news for me. Guns led to hassles. Maybe the older guy with them had a calming effect.

If I'd had any common sense, I would've called for backup. I certainly would've felt more comfortable with a couple of uniformed patrol officers behind me. But sometimes you have to play the hand you're dealt.

I stepped around the corner of the building. I purposely

left my gun in its holster on my right hip, where my dark red, all-weather jacket covered it. I stood there for a full thirty seconds and still no one looked up to notice me. I decided they weren't particularly effective burglars.

Finally, I cleared my throat and said in a loud voice, "Business hours are from nine to six."

All three men's heads twisted toward me. The two younger men recognized me instantly. Then I looked at the third man, his face now fully illuminated by the security light. I swallowed hard.

I recognized him too.

# CHAPTER 67

**I SAID, "YOU'RE** Sal Ventri, aren't you?"

The older man stood up straight. He brushed off his jacket like he was about to meet a fan asking for an autograph. Sal Ventri was hardly any sort of organized crime kingpin. He was well known and didn't mind the publicity, but for the most part he was a low-level member of a peripheral organized crime family.

Then he said with a thick Brooklyn accent, "This ain't none of your business. Who the hell are you?"

One of the punks said, "He's a cop. He's a friend of Ronald's. We saw him the other day when the gang attacked us."

I laughed out loud at that. "Is that what you told people? That a gang attacked you?" One of the younger men still had a black eye and a couple of cuts on his face. "I was there. It was mostly a woman who didn't like their manners."

Sal looked at me. "What kind of cop are you?"

"I like to think a pretty good cop."

Sal was not in a bantering mood. "Like I said, this ain't none of your business, smart guy."

I cocked my head and didn't say a word.

Sal looked irked. "What the hell you staring at?"

"I'm sorry. I've read articles about you. I like the one in *Esquire* when they called you the 'Ivy League Don.' What I'm saying is, you're supposed to be educated. You went to Dartmouth, for God's sake. Why do you talk like you dropped out of school in tenth grade and hang out on the street in Flatbush?"

Sal took a couple of steps toward me and lowered his voice. "Okay, we'll play it your way. Please explain to me why you care if we solve our differences with Ronald privately."

"Because privately doesn't mean *legally*. You're still burglarizing a structure. I'm sure if you found Ronald somewhere, you'd assault him. So, if you prefer, I can call a couple of patrol cars and let them deal with you."

The younger men looked ready to bolt, but Sal had been threatened too many times. It had absolutely no effect on him. "We're just collecting a debt. Trying to avoid clogging up the court system." He took a few steps closer to me.

I started to tense for a fight.

Sal looked at me and said, "What's your name?"

"Michael Bennett."

He stopped in his tracks. Sal said, "The homicide detective?"

I just nodded.

He gave me a strange look but stayed in place. "You arrested Joe Paltrice for the hit on Jimmy Vale."

"I did." I turned my body slightly so I could draw and aim if I needed to. These guys held grudges that went on forever. They treated revenge like other people celebrated birthdays. They loved it. I wondered how Sal was related to Joe Paltrice. Without thinking, my hand ended up on the butt of my duty pistol.

Sal took another step closer. His eyes narrowed. "Jimmy Vale was my godson. I was going crazy until you grabbed that animal, Paltrice. Too bad no one has the balls to use the chair anymore."

It was like I was looking at an entirely different man. His posture had changed and he was using his hands to talk. I said, "I remember the case. It was about six years ago. Paltrice tricked Jimmy into following him into an empty store. Then he strangled him."

Sal shook his head. "He even knew Jimmy was protected. No respect. No common sense. Now there's three kids without a dad and a grieving widow."

It was like chatting with an old colleague. I said, "I broke the case because of a simple fingerprint on the door. Then I got a warrant for a DNA sample from Paltrice. I still remember the look on his face the day I arrested him."

Sal chuckled and said, "You're okay with me. We all decided not to do that kind of business in upper Manhattan anymore. It was all because of you. A newspaper article called you 'dogged.'"

One of the Brooklyn brats heard him say that. The young man whined, "Sal, what the hell? We need our money."

Sal called over his shoulder, "Not today, boys. I owe this guy."

It's nice to be surprised this way once in a while. I liked how Sal scolded his young comrades as he ushered them toward his Cadillac.

Sal looked at me and said, "This was sort of chickenshit. I was just showing the boys the old-school way of handling problems. You have my word that they won't bother this pawnbroker again. But tell him he needs to know who he's dealing with in the future."

We nodded our good-byes. I needed to have a good, stern talk with Ronald Higdon.

# CHAPTER 68

**FIRST THING IN** the morning, I was sitting in Manhattan North Homicide's conference room. I was still a little groggy after my evening entertaining a local organized crime figure. I could've charged the punks from Brooklyn with attempted burglary or some kind of destruction of personal property, but they wouldn't have spent ten minutes in jail. I hate to quote Sal Ventri, but it didn't seem worth clogging up the court system with petty bullshit.

Now Walter Jackson, Terri Hernandez, and my lieutenant, Harry Grissom, sat around a pressboard table that had seen better days. We had a lot of information from different sources that we needed to turn into an actual investigation. Something that led us toward the identity of whoever had killed Estella Abreu, Suzanne Morton, and Emma Schrade. I was convinced they were all connected whether we had the evidence to link them or not. I was trying not to get tunnel vision and just focus on one suspect. That's why it was good to sit down and talk things through with other people familiar with the case.

One thing about my lieutenant: he doesn't need to run every meeting. Harry likes to listen. Don't get me wrong. He offers advice and insights, but he isn't so insecure that he feels like he needs to prove he's in charge.

That left me to turn to Walter and say, "You're the one with all the information from The Girlfriend Experience burner phone. Was Allie Pritz right when she said she thought most of the calls came from other burner phones?"

The big man nodded. "Whoever set up this whole enterprise was very bright. You said this girl, Allie, also seemed sharp. There's no way we would've known about it if someone hadn't talked. The use of burner phones and keeping their profile low means they were able to operate without any concern about the police. You told me Allie was worried about her parents finding out? I think that was more likely than the police finding out."

Walter had a slightly different demeanor whenever a supervisor was in the room. More monotone and less outgoing. I noticed he held back his urge to make puns on everything. I greatly preferred talking to my gregarious friend and listening to his puns in the privacy of his office at the side of the squad bay.

He picked up several sheets of paper with printouts of numbers and addresses. "Almost all the calls to this main burner phone were also from throwaway phones or phones that can't be traced easily." Walter slid a single sheet of paper to each of us. We each looked down at our sheets. Walter's narration picked up again. "There are six names I was able to come up with so far."

Terri looked up from her sheet and said, "Even a doctor was calling the line."

"Not really. He's just a veterinarian." Walter sounded dismissive.

I threw in, "Still, they have to go through a lot of medical training."

"But they also solve problems by euthanizing their patients. That is nowhere close to what a medical doctor does. Certainly they don't adhere to the Hippocratic oath."

I didn't know what Walter's problem with veterinarians was, but now wasn't the time to explore it. I looked down the list of the other names and no one jumped out at me.

Harry Grissom looked directly at me and said, "How do you feel about this suspect, Kyle Banning?"

"Certainly he's smart enough to use a burner phone. And the fact that he knew two of the three victims is a pretty good indicator. But his sixteen-year-old brother, Jaden, is also a decent suspect. And he can be connected to the third victim." I shook my head. "If I could've just had another two or three minutes to talk with Kyle Banning before their father shut me down…There's no way to check out an alibi unless someone tells you they *have* an alibi."

Terri said, "I like the timeline Walter drew up for us. He gives us something definite to look at with each suspect. We know, within twelve hours, when Estella Abreu was murdered. I have a two-day window when Emma Schrade could have been murdered. The wild card is Suzanne Morton. The best the medical examiner could give us about a time of death was a one-week window. I say we focus on Estella and see if we can figure out where either of the Bannings were during that window."

As usual, Terri Hernandez had expressed a practical and intelligent way of going about investigating these murders. The good news was that there were no new bodies. That made sense if our suspect knew we were looking at him.

And with the new names and numbers Walter had provided, we had plenty of work ahead of us.

# CHAPTER 69

**TERRI HERNANDEZ AND** I split up the names for interviewing. It was the fastest, most efficient way to narrow down our suspects. Despite my belief that I was avoiding tunnel vision by looking at more suspects, I had to admit I really wanted to clear any doubt so we could indict one of the Bannings. That's one of the first issues always raised in homicide trials: had we ever considered other suspects? Defense attorneys don't care who actually committed the crime. Their only goal is to convince jurors their client did *not*. Or, more accurately, to plant enough doubt in the jury's minds to avoid a conviction.

I'd quickly cleared one of the names from the list. A guy who ran a bar in Midtown had hired a girl named Carly from The Girlfriend Experience three times to hang out at his bar and attract customers. He said she did a great job. Even had her personal phone number. He also had video surveillance of his bar that showed him at work during the time Estella Abreu was murdered.

I called Carly, who answered the phone, "Hey, this is Carly. Who's this?" Her tone was flirtatious and friendly. I could see why men would want to talk with her.

I said, "My name is Michael Bennett. I'm a detective with the NYPD. I—"

Carly cut me off. She was not nearly as cooperative as Allie Pritz. "I have nothing to say to the police. I'm represented by Jonathan Berg. I'm going to call him now and tell him you called me. Please don't call me again without going through my attorney."

It didn't faze me. People say things like that all the time. I made a note of the attorney's name and figured I'd call him in a day or two. At the very least, Carly might give us some more insights into how The Girlfriend Experience worked. I had other things to worry about now.

Before I headed to the next name on the list—ironically a lawyer in Midtown—Walter Jackson texted me three more names he'd been able to figure out from the numbers on The Girlfriend Experience's phone.

I was completely aboveboard during my next call. When the attorney answered his cell phone, I told him who I was and that it involved a homicide investigation. The lawyer, William Dexter, didn't ask any questions. I thought about the old saying that a good lawyer never asks a question he doesn't already know the answer to.

Even though he worked at one of the big corporate law firms in Midtown, Dexter told me to come on over to the office so we could talk. Killers usually aren't that accommodating. Unless they think they're much, much smarter than anyone else.

I could see why these big firms with an international presence charged so much money for everything. The firm had fourteen floors of a building overlooking Sixth Avenue. The lobby had dark hardwood paneling and marble floors.

The receptionist, a balding man about forty, had a neatly trimmed goatee that came to a sharp point under his chin. He looked up with his rimless glasses but didn't bother to give me a smile as I stepped into the lobby. He said, "How may I help you?"

His tone made it clear he really wanted to say, *You walked into the wrong office, moron.* But I played the game and said, "My name's Michael Bennett. William Dexter is expecting me."

The man looked surprised that I had the name of one of his attorneys ready to spit out when needed. He called Dexter from his desk phone. Then he looked up at me and said, "William will meet you on the fourteenth floor. He'll be waiting at the elevator." The man went back to looking at something on his computer screen and completely ignoring me.

The elevator was a step down after the plush lobby of the law firm. Not that it was a terrible elevator. It's just that in the two minutes I was in the reception area I'd sort of gotten used to marble floors and live plants.

William Dexter was indeed standing just outside the elevator on the fourteenth floor. He was a lean, good-looking guy somewhere in his mid-thirties. His longish brown hair was styled to look like he didn't care about his appearance. His monogrammed shirt and silk tie told me otherwise.

We shook hands, and he led me down the hallway. The fourteenth floor didn't have marble but was still a high-end office. It felt like every other room was some sort of conference room with a spectacular view and filled with real plants.

I said to Dexter, "You guys must have a great view of the parade."

"Like any of us have time to watch the Macy's Thanksgiving Day Parade." He finally turned into a lovely office with a view of a side street. He sat in a chair opposite me in front of his desk. He put on an earnest expression and said, "I appreciated you calling, but I'm not sure how I can help a homicide investigation."

I said, "I don't want to bring up anything that's sensitive or awkward. But you called a phone number that's used by a group of young women who act as dates or escorts."

That question got a reaction. He calmly stood up and walked to the door. He closed it quietly, then came back to the chair.

Now I was really interested in hearing his response.

# CHAPTER 70

**WILLIAM DEXTER BRUSHED** a stray hair from his face, then looked at me calmly. His expression didn't change as he said, "The Girlfriend Experience, right?"

"Exactly."

"I didn't violate any laws. I never had sex with the young woman who met me. I just needed a date for corporate functions. I think I used her six or seven times."

"Always the same girl?"

"Stacy. Yes. That's the only name I have. A name and a phone number. Which you obviously have. Stacy wasn't a homicide victim, was she?"

I shook my head. "We're gathering background on people using the service. I also was hoping we could keep this conversation confidential until we make an arrest."

"I'm sorry, Detective Bennett, but I never make a commitment like that unless I'm retained as a lawyer. I will say I have no reason to discuss this with anyone else."

"I guess that'll have to do." I looked around the office. There were a couple of framed photos of Dexter running marathons. Clearly, the guy was athletic, educated, and had a good job. He also appeared to have decent social skills. I looked at him and said, "You seem pretty squared away. I'd think a lot of people would want to date you. Without charging you a fee."

That earned a chuckle. William Dexter had an easy smile. "I work seventy hours a week. I train for marathons about ten hours a week. If you factor in sleep and eating, that gives me eight to fifteen minutes a day to chat with people. A former colleague gave me the number of The Girlfriend Experience. It was easy. I'd make a call. Stacy would meet me wherever I told her. She looked fabulous. And it cost me less than maintaining a girlfriend in Manhattan." He gave a little shrug.

That answer had an important element in it. I said, "You met Stacy from a referral? Do you know if that was common?"

"Stacy told me it was the only way she got clients. It was a tight circle of people. That's why I felt comfortable with her."

I nodded as I wrote a couple of notes in my pad. "Did Stacy say anything else about The Girlfriend Experience?"

"She said something about one girl kinda running the whole thing. But each girl developed her own client list."

Sounded like Allie Pritz had been completely open with us. I took a moment before I hit Dexter with a tougher question. I said, "Can you tell me where you were on the first or second of this month?"

"Ahh, so I *am* a suspect. Or at least a person of interest."

"C'mon, as a lawyer, you must know we need to clear up a lot of things before we can charge the right person." I was about to go into more explanation when he held up his hands.

"I get it. And I'm not interested in screwing up a homicide investigation. I can't imagine anyone who would."

"Then you might be surprised."

He started rifling through his side desk drawers. After a few seconds, Dexter plopped a folder onto the desk. When he opened it, I could see printouts of airline tickets, a hotel bill, and some taxi receipts. Everything checked out.

Dexter said, "I was in Dallas at an arbitration hearing from the first to the fifth of the month. Ever been to Dallas?"

"Once, on a case. I do kinda like the Cowboys."

That made him groan. "I'm a Giants fan. It's tough lately. At least it's not as bad as being a Jets fan."

I was ready to give him a zinger about his Jets comment when I heard a piano. It took me a moment to realize it was my ringtone. I looked up at the attorney, who nodded for me to take a call, which was from a number I didn't recognize. I said, "Mike Bennett."

"Detective, it's Michelle Finnegan."

I knew the secretary from the Wolfson Academy wouldn't be calling me just to chat. I turned slightly, like it would keep the attorney from hearing anything, and said, "What's up, Michelle?"

"I wanted to give you a heads-up that we just heard Jaden Banning overdosed. He's done it a few times before. He left the academy without telling anyone last night and took an Uber back to his parents' apartment in the city. They found him this morning, unresponsive. The family's at Glendale General."

"Thanks, Michelle. I appreciate it. Call me if you hear anything else. This could be important." I excused myself with William Dexter. It seemed like it was okay with him that I was leaving. He was already studying documents.

# CHAPTER 71

**I CALLED TERRI** Hernandez to meet me at the hospital. I felt a little creepy rushing to a hospital to see if a family was distraught enough to talk to me. I didn't really want to impose myself on anyone during a stressful time like this. But I intended to be available in case someone *wanted* to talk.

As I made my way uptown, Michelle Finnegan rang again.

She said, "Okay, I have a little more information. Jaden Banning told one of his dorm mates he needed to get away for a little while. He found some OxyContin at his parents' apartment. They didn't even realize he was at home until the morning, when they found him unconscious on the couch."

"Why did they go all the way up to Glendale? There are several hospitals closer to their apartment." Glendale General was on Amsterdam Avenue in Manhattanville, near West Harlem.

Michelle said, "I overheard the headmaster talking with one of the administrators. Apparently, the Bannings have been to the same hospital for the same reason a couple of times before. He said they use Glendale because it's easier to keep things quiet. And they're known to offer personalized service."

I had to think about that for a moment. What kind of parent is so concerned about the family's reputation and social standing that they would drive past hospitals with an unconscious child in the car? I would say it made me revise my view of Mr. Banning, but my impression was already pretty negative.

I asked Michelle, "Is Jaden in trouble for sneaking out? Will they kick him out of the academy?"

"I sincerely doubt that. Parents pay a premium for the school to put up with this kind of foolishness. I see it all the time. And it doesn't help the students in any way. Like Jaden. He was sort of a known druggie. I think this was just a cry for help. He's troubled."

I believed her. Jaden Banning *was* troubled. That's what was bothering me. I thanked Michelle and concentrated on driving. I picked up speed and cut over to Amsterdam Avenue. I used my blue light and siren, rare for me.

I had to slow down a little bit because of traffic as I approached Holy Name on my left. At almost any other time I wouldn't have thought twice about pulling over and going in to talk with my grandfather or check on the kids. Today was no ordinary day. I had to get to that hospital fast.

As I passed Holy Name, I glanced to the right. Then I did a double take. I mashed the brakes, barely avoiding a rear-end collision. I looked over my right shoulder to verify what I'd seen. There, standing on the corner opposite the church, were the bullies who'd been terrorizing my sons. I recognized them from the video surveillance footage. One of them was even wearing the same jacket he had on in the video.

I couldn't believe it. What were the chances I'd just run across them on the street? Yet there they were, standing in front of our dry cleaner. I started to drift to the right and look for a spot to park.

Then I thought of Estella Abreu and Suzanne Morton. I recalled the anguish on their parents' faces.

I muttered, "Shit," aloud to no one. The goddamn bullies could wait. I took one last glance in my rearview mirror and hit the gas.

# CHAPTER 72

**TERRI MET ME** on the street in front of the emergency room. We paused just inside the door, where she grabbed hold of my arm and said, "How do we navigate this? We don't want to screw up the case by giving the family a reason to say we were harassing them."

"Since when do we need to give someone a reason to make a false accusation?"

"Still, let's figure this out now instead of winging it when we run into the family."

This was why I liked working with Terri Hernandez. Not only was she intelligent, she was also practical. Where I might just blunder into a situation, she thought things through.

I said, "We could go to the desk and find out what room Jaden is in." I could tell by the hesitant look on Terry's face she didn't necessarily agree with my plan of action.

"Let me try something first," Terri said. She pulled me down the hallway until we reached an intersection. From here we could see almost everyone coming or going from the emergency room. Terri looked at me. "ER nurses always know what's going on."

"Aren't there all kinds of HIPAA restrictions? I can never get medical people to talk to me without a warrant or patient permission."

Terri smiled. "It's all in how you ask."

We stood at the crossroads of the hallway for about three or four minutes. We nodded hello to a couple of doctors, a janitor, and a family who looked like they had just gotten good news. A rare sight in a hospital.

Finally, a friendly-looking nurse in scrubs patterned with colorful frolicking cats and dogs walked by.

Terri nodded at her and said, "How are you today?"

The nurse stopped and smiled, revealing braces. She might've been a few years younger than Terri. Her hair was cut short. Practical for any medical professional.

The nurse said, "So far, not too busy today. A car accident and an OD were our big adventures."

Terri nodded again. She leaned in toward the nurse. "I know about the OD. We're here for our friend's son, Jaden."

The nurse said, "Oh, you know Jaden? He always has a lot of support. His family stays right in the room with them."

I blurted out, "Even his dad?"

The nurse gave us a sly smile. "You really do know them." She looked up and down the hallway for a moment. "I like that his brother stays with him at night. It's sweet. I know he works at some high-pressure finance firm all day. I admire the fact that he still sits with his little brother every evening."

Little off-the-cuff comments like these always give me

better insight. I knew Kyle Banning was a good-looking guy, but I was starting to see his charming side. Of course, some serial killers seem to have the same trait. I'm not sure if that's what makes them effective serial killers or if they develop it to become better serial killers.

The nurse continued. "Last time they brought Jaden here was at the beginning of the month. I was impressed that the family was with him for three straight days and nights."

Terri and I both perked up at that comment.

Terri ran with it. "We missed visiting for that one. Just last week? I think it was on the second of the month, right?"

The nurse shook her head. "No, it was the first day of my rotation. I remember it started exactly on the first of the month. Jaden was released on the afternoon of the fourth."

Terri and I looked at each other. That was the night before Terri tried the undercover in the bar called Rain in the financial district. Kyle Banning must have gone out the next night after his brother got home. This kid hadn't gone a full week without relapsing.

I realized the duration of the stay had something to do with some kind of psychiatric hold. My guess was that Jaden's father had arranged to keep the incident quiet and out of a judge's docket. He probably had to promise the doctor that he would leave Jaden secure in the hospital for three days. That was the standard court-ordered observation period.

The hospital can bill for extra days. It doesn't get put on his permanent record. Jaden appears to be getting better. And the family can say they did the right thing. Everyone wins.

Terri chatted more with the nurse while I wandered away to figure this out. Of course, I'd have to get a warrant to see the exact days Jaden was in the hospital. But the story sounded legit.

# CHAPTER 73

**IT HURT TO** be knocked back to square one on the investigation. I'd been confident one of the Banning brothers was a good suspect. Now I felt like we were struggling to stay afloat. That didn't mean I could just give up. I had to confirm what the nurse had told us.

I located the head of security for the hospital. She was a pleasant woman who had retired as a captain from the Newark Police Department. She assigned a young man to help me search through the video surveillance of the hospital from the beginning of the month. She didn't even make me tell her what I was looking for. It was perfect. I didn't have to worry about anyone saying something to the Bannings later.

It didn't take long to find Kyle Banning. I was even able to figure out what room Jaden had stayed in from the video. And I saw Kyle often enough to establish that he hadn't left the hospital at night to murder Estella Abreu. He'd arrived every night at about seven, presumably after work.

After I texted Terri an update about the security footage, I left the hospital and got back on Amsterdam Avenue, driving slowly and scanning both sides of the street. I didn't see the bullies again.

I pulled up to Holy Name and found Seamus outside, directing some workers as they planted new shrubs. His face lit up when he saw me.

"Michael, my boy. What are you doing here this time of day? Lately, I only see you around here after the boys get beat up."

I had to chuckle at that. I told him about seeing the bullies on my way to an urgent interview. As always, he made me feel better about my decision.

My grandfather said, "I find myself taking my midday walk off the church grounds, just hoping to catch a glimpse of the bullies. It's a problem, to be sure. But the world is full of problems. You're one of the few people I know trying to solve them."

I nodded, feeling better already.

"Sometimes you forget how important your job is. You're trying to catch people who have *killed* other people. In the big scheme of things, some punk kids harassing the boys isn't that big of a deal. You need to show your profession more respect."

Seamus turned to admire the shrubs as they were settled into the ground. Then he looked back at me and said, "Was your interview fruitful?"

"Not really. I had to eliminate my two best suspects from the case."

"How can avoiding arresting the wrong person not be fruitful? It sounds like you hit a home run."

Just looking at it from a different perspective made me feel better.

My grandfather continued: "I'm going to keep taking my walks in the neighborhood. Those boys have to live around here somewhere. None of us had ever seen those bullies until this foolishness started, but why would they travel to bully someone? There are plenty of targets all over the city. I wouldn't worry about it, Michael. These things tend to work out. We'll either catch the bullies or they'll get tired of hanging out near the church. The boys won't have any problem."

Talking to my grandfather usually cheered me up. This was starting to feel like a full-on pep talk. And it was working.

# CHAPTER 74

**BY EVENING, I** barely had any energy left as I trudged through the lobby of our building, giving a weak wave to the doorman. In my left hand, I carried three giant bags: the family dinner. I'd picked up three buckets of fried chicken with enough sides to satisfy a small army. Which is essentially what we fed every night.

Food and my family revived me to a degree. Everyone's schedule had been hectic. We all chatted about our day. I left out most of what I'd done. Except that I'd visited my grandfather at the church.

Mary Catherine also skimped on details about her day. I knew she'd taken one of the prescriptions her fertility doctor had written. It had knocked the stuffing out of her. She put on a brave front for the children, but I was worried, although she seemed back to her old self once we finished eating.

I waited till the younger kids were in bed and the older kids were all doing their own thing. I even let the boys play a video game so they didn't care if I was around or not. Then I did something I almost never do at home: I worked on my case.

I sat at the small desk in our bedroom and looked through all the information Walter Jackson had sent me. He had come up with half a dozen more names. He'd also taken the time to attach criminal histories, work histories, and anything else he thought might give me an insight for each interview. Name after name seemed similar. All relatively wealthy young men who had decent jobs. None of them had any criminal history. There was nothing that pointed to one name more than another.

Until I reached the name Thomas Sloan. He was the veterinarian Walter had been unimpressed by. More importantly, Walter had found two incidents in which the NYPD had been called to Dr. Sloan's house. Both times on suspicion of domestic abuse.

That caught my attention. My personal belief is that someone who can commit domestic violence can commit any kind of violence. It isn't something I'd bring up in court, but it influences me when I interview people.

The next document Walter had sent me via email made me freeze in place. Dr. Sloan's son, Lewis, had attended the Wolfson Academy. What were the chances of that? Slim enough for me to put Thomas Sloan as my first appointment in the morning.

It looked like he had a veterinary clinic here on the Upper West Side. I immediately texted Terri Hernandez and told her I had a possible suspect. She agreed to meet me in the morning a block away from the veterinary clinic.

I tried not to be obvious, shutting down my computer when Mary Catherine walked in the room.

She laughed. "You don't think I know you're working on a case? I never set down the rule that you couldn't."

"I know. I just like to be engaged with the family when I'm at home."

"Aren't you able to do a few personal errands during your workday?"

"You know I try to be efficient."

"Then there's no problem working on a case at home once in a while. There's no need to look like a teenage boy caught looking at porn on his computer."

I stood up and took my beautiful wife in my arms. I didn't deserve someone as understanding as her. We embraced and kissed.

As things became more heated, we eased over to the bed. I paused for a moment to listen for kids.

As if she was reading my mind, Mary Catherine said, "Everyone but Brian and Juliana are asleep. They're watching TV in the living room. And I locked the door when I came in."

I smiled. "So, this wasn't spontaneous."

Mary Catherine snuggled in close to me on the bed. "The doctor said trying to have a baby by the natural method wouldn't interfere with any treatments I might get."

I kissed her and said, "I'm definitely on board with the method that both is fun and doesn't have a deductible."

For the first time today, something took my mind completely off our investigation.

# CHAPTER 75

**AT ALMOST EXACTLY** 8:30 the next morning, I met Terri Hernandez at a place on Columbus Avenue called Birch Coffee. Harry Grissom had planned to meet us too but had backed out when he realized he'd double-booked with a doctor's appointment. It occurred to me that Harry was going to more and more medical professionals. I hoped it was just routine.

We sat at a round high-top table and looked out the glass window onto Columbus Avenue. Thomas Sloan's veterinary office was a few blocks down, at about 100th Street. There was a Starbucks on the corner of that block, but whenever possible, I preferred to frequent local businesses that showed more interest in the neighborhood and its people beyond gouging them for extra-large lattes.

Terri looked across the table at me and said, "You look nice."

I shrugged. "Lately, I've noticed people are more open to talking with me if I'm wearing a sport coat and tie. Maybe it's just the professional look." I ran my hand down the tie to straighten it. Mainly to emphasize said professional look.

Terri giggled. Or as close to a giggle as she ever came. "This is Manhattan. Men wear five-thousand-dollar suits. If anything, they look at you and feel sorry. *That's* probably why they've been talking to you."

I had to smile. The trash talk between cops, even when it's directed at me, is generally pretty high quality. Probably a notch higher than you'd hear from NFL or NBA players. Part of it is because we know how to launch missiles at one another's very specific idiosyncrasies. I tried to think of a dig to shoot back at Terri. Preferably one focusing on fashion. I couldn't find one. She looked great as always.

Sharp as ever, Terri picked up on my failed effort to retaliate. She smiled and said, "Can't say shit about this blouse and slacks. Can you?"

I shrugged. I didn't have anything else to say.

Now Terri looked a little concerned. She reached across the table and put a hand on my forearm. "What's wrong?"

I could've said, *Nothing,* and moved on. But she was my partner—at least on this case. I also knew she was a damn good friend. I said, "We spent a lot of energy on Kyle Banning and his brother. It feels like we have to start all over again. Sometimes it's the same record that just keeps repeating."

"Not to rain on your pity party, but no one has listened to records in over a decade. You need to update your references. The fact is, we *are* sort of starting over. But that's okay. What's the alternative? Ignore three homicides?"

"No, of course not."

Clearly, Terri was trying to get my mind off my troubles. She said, "Tell me about this veterinarian."

I opened up my notebook and looked down at the sheet Walter Jackson had given me. "You saw his photo. Pretty average-looking. Graduated from SUNY Buffalo, then got his veterinary degree from some place in the Caribbean I'd never heard of before."

"Must be nice."

I skimmed more of the sheet and said, "He's divorced. His ex-wife called the cops on him for battery. That was somewhere in Westchester County. Two years later, a live-in girlfriend called again for the same reason. Both times the women wouldn't cooperate once the cops got there."

"Typical. But he sounds like a creep. How big is he?"

"Low end of average. Five foot eight and about 165 pounds." I showed her the photo again.

Terri said, "I'd beat his ass if he raised a hand to me."

I laughed. "I hope you'd stop at just an ass whipping."

She gave me an evil grin.

"I'd like to keep this low-key. At least at first. You know, not overwhelm him or anything. Just ask a few questions."

Terri said, "I feel like you're trying to tell me something."

"Don't threaten or intimidate him."

"Until you need me to?"

I gave her a smile and said, "Yeah. Exactly."

We finished our coffees and started to walk the two blocks to the veterinary clinic.

# CHAPTER 76

**THE VETERINARY CLINIC** was in the corner of an office building. The small white sign with faded blue letters was nondescript and had seen better days. It didn't look like Sloan had much room at all in the corner of the building.

I took a moment to scan the block. Nothing unusual for the Upper West Side. I took a deep breath. I didn't want comfortable, familiar surroundings to make me less vigilant. Technically, we were interviewing a potential homicide suspect.

Terri's phone rang. She looked at the screen, then cut her eyes up to me. She took the call with a curt, "Detective Hernandez." Then she started to speak Spanish. I heard the "*Sí, sí, sí*" and realized someone was speaking rapidly on the other end of the phone line.

Terri lowered the phone, looked at me, and said, "This is important. It'll take a few minutes."

I waved her off and said in a low voice, "I'll just go in and introduce myself. Come in when you're ready."

Terri nodded, pulled a small pad and pen out of her purse, and turned to write something, propping the pad on top of a box holding discount coupons bolted to the side of the building.

As soon as I stepped in the front door, I could hear a *ding* in the back of the office. The place was open with two chairs facing a reception area without a receptionist.

I waited about ten seconds. Then I knocked on the counter in front of the reception area and called out, "Hello, Dr. Sloan?"

I heard someone say, "Back here. I'll be a couple of minutes."

I decided to surprise him. I pushed through the swinging door into the polished tile hallway, past a minuscule office with only room for a desk and small chair. Then I saw a fit man of about forty holding a French bulldog on an examination table.

I pulled an old trick out of my back pocket and said, "I'm sorry. I couldn't understand you from up front."

Thomas Sloan looked up from the French bulldog. He was annoyed, but he swallowed it. He said, "My assistant called in sick today."

It was at that moment I realized the bulldog was here for some sort of bowel issue. The stench was overwhelming. I tried to hide it but waved my notebook in front of my face and took a step back.

Sloan chuckled and said, "Pierre here ate something that disagreed with him. He's been here since last night." Then the vet straightened, looked at me, and said, "What can I do for you?" He left his hand on the bulldog to keep the dog calm, slowly stroking the dog's back.

I pulled out my ID. "Michael Bennett, NYPD."

"Look, Officer, I support the PBA. But right now is not a particularly good time."

This time I heard the dog actually pass gas. It sounded like a tiny trumpet. The smell was hardly as cute as the image.

"I'm actually here on an investigation."

"How could *I* help you on an investigation?"

"You called a phone number connected to a business called The Girlfriend Experience." I held my smile as I saw the color drain from his face.

Now he snapped, "I've learned from past experience not to talk to the cops. Sorry, not for any reason at all."

"Seriously? That's your move? I thought you went to college. The best you can come up with is that you don't talk to cops?"

"Yeah. I need you to leave. Right now."

I nodded and said, "Of course." Then I laid down a warrant request form on the table next to the dog.

"What's that?"

I said, "A copy of the search warrant request we'll be filing for all your phone records covering the past two years. We'll be compelling your telecommunications supplier to turn them over, or you can come talk to us formally at Manhattan North Homicide next week. That way you can also talk to the media at the same time." I paused to let that sink in. I'll admit I enjoyed the expression on his face. Then I hit him with "This is a homicide investigation. You don't get to play the idealist who doesn't stoop to talking to the police. You're a damn wife beater. You've talked to the cops plenty of times." Then I turned and started to march out of the examination room.

Before I was completely out of the room, Sloan said, "C'mon, wait a second. I can take a break and talk to you."

I had to keep facing away from him so he wouldn't see the broad smile on my face.

# CHAPTER 77

**I LINGERED IN** the doorway with my back to the veterinarian. Suddenly I understood why Al Pacino overacted in everything. It was fun. I could see where an audience would've made it even more entertaining for me.

I spun on my heel. Sloan tried to act cool and nonchalant by continuing to treat the bulldog. Finally, he looked up from the dog and said, "No need to let this get out of hand. I'll talk to you."

The vet kept petting the dog's head and said, "Do you want to tell me what homicide you're investigating?"

"In fact, it's three homicides."

"I have no idea how I could help you with your investigation. I don't think I've ever even known anyone who was murdered."

"Most people don't. Then again, most people don't call

The Girlfriend Experience." That had the effect I wanted. I noticed Sloan gripped the bulldog's collar with his right hand. The bulldog twisted slightly, trying to look at the vet.

The veterinarian started to get nervous. I could see it from the sweat on his forehead to the tremor in his hands. He mumbled, "The what?"

"You just tried to kick me out of here for mentioning it. The Girlfriend Experience. You know, you called the number from your cell phone several times over the last two years."

It looked like the dog was starting to pick up on the veterinarian's nervousness as well. I heard a little whimper as Sloan stared in the dog's ear with a light. It felt a lot more like he was pretending to examine the dog rather than actually examining him.

Then the vet looked up and said, "Oh, yeah, the dating number."

"I'd like to dance around with you all day if I had time. But I have things to accomplish. You know as well as I do how many times you've called that *dating* number." Then I added, "Another reason we want to talk to you is that your son attends the Wolfson Academy. One of the girls who went to a dance some months ago at the academy also ended up dead. It seems like two pretty big coincidences, Dr. Sloan."

"Tommy graduated from Wolfson last year. I wouldn't know anything about a girl who went to a dance there." The veterinarian dropped the light onto the hard, tile floor. I could hear the lens crack. Sloan muttered, "Damn," as he picked it up. Then he fumbled with the lock to a cabinet and started looking at tiny vials of medicine, preparing a syringe with the contents of one of them. He continued to avoid looking at me.

I wondered if I should keep going or wait until Terri Hernandez finished her phone call. It felt like I was on a roll, so I went with it.

"Where's your son now, Dr. Sloan?"

"Philadelphia."

"Is that where he's attending college?"

Even with just a side view of his face, I could see the veterinarian looked absolutely crestfallen. "No, I'm afraid not. He's actually in jail." He looked back like he expected me to ask more questions. When I didn't, he said, "Tommy, um, had a misunderstanding with a girl."

"I wonder where he learned that."

"It's a bullshit rape charge. Typical police shenanigans." He was definitely getting worked up. He knocked over an empty coffee cup sitting on the counter and ignored it as he returned to the dog's side, once again taking hold of his collar.

I noticed him start to glance toward the door. I'd seen that look before. I asked him my next question. "Did you ever call The Girlfriend Experience from a different phone?"

The veterinarian spluttered and mumbled so badly I couldn't understand him. He was working himself into a nervous breakdown. Or at least a pretty good imitation of one. I liked it.

# CHAPTER 78

**I ASSESSED DR.** Sloan to judge how far I should take this. Talking to someone when they're this agitated can either produce great rewards or cause a lot of problems. I decided to push the envelope and see what happened.

I said, "Dr. Sloan, can I ask you about your previous domestic violence issues?"

"What domestic violence issues? I get along with my ex-wife and now I'm happily remarried." His voice had raised not only in pitch but also in volume. He didn't appear to notice at all.

I said, "I can bring up the reports on my phone if you'd like. But I'm specifically talking about when your ex-wife called the police and then two years later when your girl-friend at the time called the police. Now do you know what I'm talking about?"

"I was never charged. That has nothing to do with my life today."

"Tell me about your life today."

"Like I said, I'm remarried and we have a six-month-old baby. It'd be tough to explain any of this to my new wife." The bulldog started to whine again. I wasn't sure if the veterinarian's grip on his collar was too tight or if it was something else.

I stepped forward to comfort the dog. I started to pet his head to keep him calm as Sloan seemed to prep a spot on his hind leg for the syringe. I'd gotten enough used to the smell that it wasn't pushing me out the door anymore. The move to the dog also put me closer to Sloan. Almost inside his personal space. Just to give him one more thing to think about instead of lying to me.

I said, "You never told your new wife about your encounters with the police?"

"Why would I do that? It was just a big misunderstanding."

"Exactly like your son?"

The French bulldog was becoming more and more agitated. I leaned down as I petted him and started to talk softly, hoping it would have an effect on the dog.

Sloan closed his eyes and took a deep breath. I glanced toward the door, wondering when Terri Hernandez was going to come in so I could really turn up the heat on this guy.

I said, "Can you see why we need to talk to you? There's a lot to clear up. If you had nothing to do with the homicides, we're not interested at all in the dating service."

"But can you guarantee me it wouldn't make it into the media? A weird allegation like I called a dating service could kill my business."

"I can't make that guarantee. Any reports I write are eventually released to the public. But we have to talk or you'll have this hanging over your head forever."

I looked up from the bulldog, wondering when he was going to give the dog the shot. Just as I raised my head, I realized the veterinarian was right next to me. Then I felt the stinging pain in my neck. I shoved Sloan hard. He knocked over a small table. The clanging of the instruments as they hit the tile floor sounded like an untalented orchestra warming up. The noise was tremendous. He stumbled past the fallen table and caught himself on a counter.

I reached up and felt the syringe still in my neck. Then I noticed my vision starting to double. I could barely read Sloan's expression of terror. I'm not sure he knew what he was doing.

Sloan said something, then bolted out the door of the examination room. I tried to keep a grip on the bulldog's collar as he squirmed to leap off the examination table. I fought the feeling of panic rising in my stomach.

# CHAPTER 79

**I STRUGGLED TO** stay upright as I urged the dog into a sitting position on the table. Still gripping his collar, I yanked out the syringe and tried to focus enough to spot the tiny vial Sloan had left on the counter. I made my way around the table toward it. I needed to show it to whoever found me. Unless it was some kind of fatal concoction. Then they'd find the vial in my pocket.

It was much harder to pick up the vial as my head started to spin. Then the bulldog started to wail. It sounded like something out of a horror movie. It was wildly disconcerting in my altered state.

I needed to chase the veterinarian. I finally managed to corral the vial and stick it into my pocket. I even took a second to lift the dog off the examination table and set him gently on the floor. I couldn't risk him trying to jump the four feet to the hard floor and injuring himself.

I bumped into the doorframe as I tried to scoot out of the examination room, closing the dog inside. I bounced off the walls in the hallway like a pinball as I headed toward the front door. Now I felt a little nausea, but I wasn't sure if it was from the injection or my anxiety over what I had been injected with.

I finally made it to the front reception area. Now my vision seemed to be dimming. I fumbled with the doorknob on the front door. Even something as simple as that taxed my dexterity. Finally, I stepped outside and looked up and down the street. Nothing seemed to make sense. I thought I saw a figure running away.

Terri was at the corner of the building, still speaking on the phone. I tried to call her name but wasn't able to form a word. She finally looked up and saw me.

Terri said, "Oh, my God." She dropped the phone into her purse and rushed toward me. I pointed in the direction of the running figure.

I somehow managed to say, "Catch Sloan." Terri eased me onto the step in front of the veterinary clinic. She pulled an NYPD radio from her purse.

I could feel my consciousness slipping away. I heard Terri almost shout into the radio, "Columbus Avenue and 100th, Columbus Avenue and 100th, 10-13. Ambulance required."

The sharp dispatcher picked up on the urgency in Terri's voice. I could hear her say, "We have a 10-13 at Columbus Avenue and West 100th Street. Clear the air."

Even in my current state, I knew cops would start racing to us from all over Manhattan. Suddenly, I couldn't feel my legs. I drifted in a dream. I heard Terri giving Sloan's description.

"White male, running south on Columbus Avenue. His name is Thomas Sloan."

Next thing I knew, I thought I was holding Mary Catherine's hand as she was undergoing some sort of medical procedure. I heard singing. Or maybe it was sirens.

Then everything went dark.

# CHAPTER 80

**MY SENSES CAME** back to me piecemeal. I could hear a little, then the darkness became a little lighter. I could feel activity around me. I could even sense that I was in a well-lit room. I had snatches of consciousness and knew I'd ridden in an ambulance. I'd also heard a lot of radio traffic. That's a little unusual for a homicide detective. We're not typically in the thick of things. But I guessed somehow I'd managed to get right in the middle of everyone's day.

I opened my eyes and blinked. It felt like I had sand on my eyeballs, they were so dry. The same thing with my throat. I tried to swallow, but I had nothing to swallow. Everything in the room was just haze and shadow.

Someone gave me an ice chip, which felt like heaven in my mouth. A woman's voice said, "Can you sip some water?"

My eyes fluttered, and I took an involuntary deep breath. It just sort of got sucked in like I was in a deep sleep and snoring. I nodded my head, hoping that whoever had asked me about the sip of water understood I was ready. I felt a cup at my lips, and the few sips of water that entered my mouth ran straight down my throat like a waterfall.

I heard another female voice. She had an accent I couldn't identify immediately. She repeated my name. "Mr. Bennett, Mr. Bennett, Mr. Bennett, can you hear me?"

I nodded. The room was starting to come into focus quickly now. There was a young woman with light hair and in blue surgical scrubs. She was holding a cup of water. Another woman stood right next to my bed. She wore a white coat and had black hair.

The woman in the white coat said, "You're going to be okay. You're in the emergency room of Mount Sinai."

I was able to cough out, "Mount Sinai Morningside?" I don't know why it mattered. That's just what popped into my scrambled brain.

She shook her head and her dark hair swayed. "No, Mount Sinai on Madison. They decided it was faster to bring you here because of traffic. I'm Dr. Hoang. Do you know what happened?"

I nodded. "Suspect stabbed me with a syringe."

"We found the vial in your pocket. That was very smart. It was ketamine, a strong animal tranquilizer. You're very lucky."

I tried to sit up in the bed. "If this is lucky, I'd rather be good." Neither of my attendants got the reference to the old adage *Better to be lucky than good.* Then I managed to say, "Did they catch Sloan?" I was starting to feel better by the second.

The doctor wasn't sure what I was talking about. She asked

me if I was feeling up to seeing visitors. Once I nodded, she opened the door, and I was glad to see Terri Hernandez and Harry Grissom rush into the room.

Terri didn't need to be asked. She said, "A patrol officer picked up Sloan three blocks away from his clinic. He's being booked now."

Harry spoke up. "He's being charged with attempted murder. He had no way of knowing how you'd react. There'll be all kinds of assault charges as well."

Then the door to my room burst open again. Mary Catherine appeared with the light from the hallway framing her blond hair and freckled face. In my current state, she looked a lot like an angel.

Mary Catherine didn't exactly sound like an angel as she marched in, though. She pointed directly at Harry Grissom and Terri Hernandez. "You two need to leave right now. Michael needs his rest. He needs his family."

Harry started to say something, but Mary Catherine cut him off.

She said in a sterner voice, "Sorry, Harry. That's the way it's going to be today. You can talk work when Michael's feeling better."

All I could think about was Sloan attacking me. The needle piercing the skin of my neck. It might take me a while to get over this one.

I was conscious enough to see Terri realize it was time to go. She gave Mary Catherine a quick kiss on both cheeks and Harry a slight shove toward the door.

Then Mary Catherine rushed to my side and started covering me with kisses.

# CHAPTER 81

**THE DAY AFTER** my encounter with the sleazy veterinarian, I found myself in my apartment. My doctor had said I needed a minimum of two days' at-home rest to make sure I had no adverse reactions. Mary Catherine had ordered me to comply whether I needed it or not. I may not always do what the NYPD or doctors want me to, but I rarely defy one of my wife's commands. I have seen firsthand what happens to people who ignore Mary Catherine's will.

My boss, Harry Grissom, had spent his career in the NYPD. During the course of that career, he'd been shot, stabbed, and run over by a drunk in a Lincoln Continental, he'd sat on a ledge for almost nine hours to stop a suicidal stockbroker, and he'd delivered two babies. I had never seen him show even a flicker of fear or hesitation.

Until he dared defy Mary Catherine when he showed up at our door with coffee and donuts.

My wife welcomed Harry into the apartment, but as soon as he asked me a few questions about what happened and where the case was going, Mary Catherine sprang into action like a club bouncer.

Harry not only listened to Mary Catherine's command to stop talking about work but also jumped to his feet like he needed to stand at attention as she said, "We have to let Michael get his rest. He'll call you tomorrow if he's feeling up to it." There were no questions in her voice. These were commands. They couldn't be any more solid if they were chiseled into granite tablets. Her sweet Irish accent did nothing to soften them.

Mary Catherine led Harry out of the apartment in a friendly manner, but he had no chance to resist. There was something comical about the whole situation. That's why I was laughing to myself when Mary Catherine came back and made me lie down on the couch.

"I feel fine. In fact, I slept really well last night."

"And you're going to sleep really well today. You're going to let your mind clear and your body rest." She looked at me like she expected me to argue. When I remained silent, she gave me a stern look and just added, "Or else."

It was just about the first time I could remember not working on an open case in some capacity for more than a day. Incredibly, I had allowed Mary Catherine to shut off my phone. That meant calls had to come through the apartment. Mary Catherine could monitor those. She would've made a good prison guard.

The first conversation I heard was at about ten in the morning. Terri Hernandez was worried about me and couldn't reach me on my cell phone. Mary Catherine and Terri chatted like old friends. Terri completely understood when Mary Catherine said she wasn't letting anyone talk to me today. Instead, they talked about my quirks and snickered like two ex-wives comparing notes.

I could hear only Mary Catherine's side of the conversation. But she giggled and said, "I know. It's like sports had an actual impact on his everyday life. If he followed the stock market as closely, we'd be rich."

I tried to tune out the rest of the conversation to avoid being insulted.

She let me change into regular clothes at about noon and move from the bedroom into the living room, so I didn't look like I was recovering from some sort of plague. Once the kids got home, I started to feel like being ordered out of work wasn't such a bad thing. I'd expected the younger kids like Shawna or Chrissy to make a fuss over me, but I was touched that my whole brood made an effort to entertain me.

Chrissy told me a story she'd written for class. It involved chickens who lived at a farm and started to realize they needed to escape. I didn't point out that it was essentially the plot to the animated movie *Chicken Run*. Chrissy seemed too pleased with herself for me to spoil it.

Jane tried to improve my chess-playing skills. I'd always thought I was pretty good until my third-eldest child proved to be something of a prodigy. She'd backed away from chess as she got into high school, but she was still damn talented. So much so, it wasn't particularly fun to play her. Even after her hour-long lesson.

I noticed the boys, Ricky, Eddie, and Trent, had come straight home from school. Usually, they stayed and played basketball or some other activity. I worried that the bully situation was really having an impact on their lives. No parent ever wants to see their kids affected like that. It hurt. I made a mental note to call Sergeant Figler and see if she'd made any progress finding the bullies.

The boys got me to play a video game that involved building a fortress to protect against attacking rival tribes.

Most of my questions were left only partially answered as the boys concentrated on the screen.

All in all, it was quite the satisfying day. Apparently, Mary Catherine agreed with me. Just before dinner she eased onto the couch next to me.

She said, "Having you home all day has been a lot of fun. Did you see the look on the kids' faces when they ran to you right after school?"

"Not so bad, huh?"

"Maybe it doesn't have to be a one-day deal."

I turned so I could look into Mary Catherine's eyes. "Are you suggesting I retire on the basis of a pleasant day at home on the couch? We've got ten kids. If half of them decide to go to college, it could bankrupt us."

"You know we could sell this place and move somewhere cheaper than New York. We could live very comfortable lives."

"Mary Catherine, is that what you really want?"

She thought about it for a full thirty seconds. Then she looked at me and said, "I'll let you know when I find out where we're going with my fertility treatments."

Like a lot of New Yorkers, I could hardly imagine living anywhere else.

# CHAPTER 82

**IT DIDN'T TAKE** long for my life to get back on track. After almost three days spent on my couch, I found myself with Terri Hernandez. Sitting in an interview room. At Rikers Island. Staring across at the veterinarian Thomas Sloan and his attorney, Linda Beam.

A few days in New York City's holding cells had already affected Sloan's appearance. His hair was lank and hung, un-combed, across his ears and forehead. His tan jail scrubs had some kind of food crusted on the chest. I'd be lying if I said it wasn't gratifying to see him in this state.

While I was recovering, Terri Hernandez had been busy. She'd kept the pressure on Sloan and wasn't taking any shit at all from his attorney. We both knew Linda Beam from her days as an assistant district attorney here in the city. A graduate of Howard University, she was one of the sharpest lawyers I'd ever met. And even though I was a few years younger than her, Linda looked a decade younger. Now she was able to use her insight as well as her relationships as one of the city's most effective criminal defense attorneys.

Linda had an edge to her voice when she said, "C'mon, guys, you don't think an attempted murder charge is a little over the top?"

Before I could answer, Terri jumped in. "You don't think jabbing a needle into someone's neck isn't dangerous? You've worked with cops long enough to know how much shit we put up with. Now you want us to give a pass to your dirtbag client after he stabbed Mike"—her voice raised to almost a shout—"in the goddamn neck with a needle?"

I could tell Terri's outburst made Linda Beam uncomfortable. Her client could be facing some serious time.

Terri gained control of herself and said, "Your client didn't know if Mike had some kind of allergy to ketamine. There's no telling how he could've reacted."

The lawyer took a breath and tried to keep her tone more conversational. "As I said earlier, Dr. Sloan is a trained professional. He knew it was just a small dose."

Usually, I'd think that was bullshit. Just a lawyer lying on behalf of a client. A very common occurrence. But I knew Linda Beam and I believed her. At least a little bit.

I said, "Linda, are you arguing that stabbing people in the neck with a needle and injecting them against their will should be a misdemeanor?"

"Of course not. I'm just wondering if we could come to some sort of arrangement."

Terri said, "We can arrange for your client to spend the

next three to five years in prison. Unless we can pin a homicide charge on him, in which case he'll spend a lot longer there."

Sloan blurted out, "I swear to God I didn't kill anyone. I just panicked when Detective Bennett was talking to me. I don't know what I was thinking. I just…"

His attorney couldn't shut him up. The lawyer barked, "That's enough." She followed it with a nasty look. It felt like if they were alone, she might have slapped him. I was on board with that.

Linda looked at us both and said, "Dr. Sloan would be willing to talk to you without any reservation. He'll tell you everything you want to know about The Girlfriend Experience and anyone he knows connected to it. In return, we find a suitable assault charge instead of attempted murder."

I leaned in and said, "And what can he tell us about The Girlfriend Experience?"

"Does that mean we have a deal?"

I remained silent while Terri gave the stink eye to Sloan. This was more enjoyable than watching TV in the evening. At least it was more compelling.

# CHAPTER 83

**AFTER SOME NEGOTIATION** over the phone between Linda Beam and an assistant district attorney, we were
all set to interview the veterinarian Thomas Sloan. Linda
had done a good job of preparing him to answer quickly and
honestly. She probably had to tell him a hundred times that
nothing he said would get him in more trouble than he was
already in. That was a hard concept for most people to com-
prehend. Especially one who'd never faced serious criminal
charges before.

I established pretty quickly that Sloan didn't know Allie
Pritz. He didn't know about how The Girlfriend Experience
had been created or was administrated. And he didn't know
any of the three girls who had been murdered. He studied
each photograph and was adamant that he had no knowledge
about what happened to them.

Terri said, "How did you find out about The Girlfriend Experience in the first place? Where did you get a phone number to call?"

Sloan tried to brush his dirty hair out of his eyes. He was fidgety and seemed to have a hard time focusing. He gathered his thoughts and said, "A guy named Perry Martin used the service and gave me the phone number to call."

I blurted, "Perry Martin, the football coach at the Wolfson Academy?"

Sloan gave me an odd look and said, "You know him?"

"I've met him."

"He was my son's football coach. He's a fun guy. He went into great detail about how he tried to see one of the girls every few weeks during this time of the year. He said it helped focus him on Friday nights when he had to call plays."

I groaned inside. How had we come to another possible suspect so quickly? It was starting to feel like an unending parade. I took a moment, then said, "When did the coach tell you this?"

Sloan shrugged. "I don't know. The first time would've been over a year ago. Several of the fathers at the school talked about the service."

I wrote down a few names Sloan gave us. I wasn't sure how useful it would be but would have Walter Jackson run backgrounds on them.

"Did you ever use the service or just call it?"

His hesitation told me what the answer would be. I just wanted to hear the details.

Sloan said, "Yeah, I met a girl who went to a party with me thrown by a pet supply company. All the vets in northern

New Jersey and New York were there. I think her name was Nicole."

"What happened?"

"Nothing, really. She was a beautiful girl. Had long dark hair and a striking face. She was charming and stood by my side for three and a half hours."

"Did you sleep with her?"

"I, um..."

All I did was give a look at his attorney. She immediately gave him the standard speech that he had to be completely cooperative or there was no deal. She said no one cared about his personal life.

Finally, Sloan looked at me and said, "I tried to negotiate a price to sleep with her, but she claimed she never did that. I'm not sure I believed her."

He told us a few more things he'd learned, but all I could do was sigh. We didn't seem much closer to solving this case.

I was so wrapped up in my thoughts I barely noticed Thomas Sloan start to cry.

Terri snapped, "What are you crying about?" She sounded like a mother who'd broken up too many fights between siblings.

Sloan shook his head and said, "I'm sorry. It's just everything catching up to me."

Terri didn't hesitate. "You mean like stabbing people with syringes? You brought all this on yourself. Crying is for when you're sad, not for when you're just stupid."

I thought that was a good place to end the interview.

# CHAPTER 84

**THOMAS SLOAN HAD** given us three more names as part of his cooperation agreement. They were all fathers of students from the Wolfson Academy who had used The Girlfriend Experience. Walter Jackson worked on backgrounds for everyone. I was surprised to see one of the fathers from the Wolfson Academy, Charles Tassick, had a conviction for dealing cocaine from more than twenty years ago. Maybe that's how he made enough money to get his son into the academy and to blow on The Girlfriend Experience.

I was gun-shy. I'd been wrong on this case too many times, and I didn't want it to happen again. I wanted to learn as much as I could about each suspect quietly. That's why I'd arranged to meet Michelle Finnegan, the secretary at the Wolfson Academy, at a McDonald's on Adam Clayton Powell Jr. Boulevard and 139th Street.

McDonald's could be a cop's best friend. An office when needed. A quick meal if necessary. Whether with a witness, informant, or suspect, a McDonald's is the right place to meet. The coffee is actually quite good. And no one bothers you if you're sitting at a corner table in a McDonald's.

Michelle Finnegan was already waiting for me as I walked into the McDonald's. After I sat down with a couple of coffees, we chatted for a minute, then I showed her the names Sloan had given me. I appreciated how she studied the list so carefully instead of just giving me a quick answer.

I didn't want to seem like an officious jerk, even if I was anxious to move on to questions related to my investigation. People say patience can't be learned, but I've developed my patient streak over many years of hard work.

Michelle said, "I know the names, but I've never interacted with any of them. Though I think everyone on this list has a son on the football team."

That eased me into my next line of questioning. I said, "How well do you know the football coach, Perry Martin?"

Her eyes darted up to meet mine. "He's not calling that crazy phone line too, is he?"

I don't like to give out information on a case no matter who I'm talking to. All I said was "I like to be thorough. He knows all these men personally. I only met the coach once, briefly. What do you think of him?"

Michelle smiled and said, "He is a genuinely nice man. And his wife is a sweetheart. They have two darling little blond kids. I think the boy is five and the girl is three."

"Do you have any idea how much Coach Martin is paid?"

Michelle shrugged. "Even though the tuition is outrageous

and we receive several donations from families, they don't tend to pay employees that much. I like it because they work around my schedule. I can't imagine the coach makes much more than me."

As I made a note of that, Michelle said, "I'm not sure it means anything, but I know Coach Martin has been trying to get an assistant's job in college football."

"Really? Which school?"

"He applied to Syracuse and the University at Buffalo. I think it would be good for his family."

We finished up and I was closing my notebook, getting ready to leave.

Michelle said, "I know it's not any of my business, but I'm curious. Does this mean Jaden Banning isn't a suspect anymore? I heard he's being moved to a drug rehab facility. I never thought he was dangerous. Just confused and troubled."

"Confused and troubled can often lead to violence. But I don't think Jaden has anything to do with what I'm investigating. He was in the hospital at the beginning of the month and has an alibi."

"I remember him missing a week at the beginning of the month. I think his father believes that by keeping him on a routine and at a strict school it will keep him out of trouble. I can't tell you how many times I've seen that philosophy fail."

I was surprised when Michelle gave me a quick hug before she headed out the door and up to her job in Bronxville.

# CHAPTER 85

**MY FIRST STOP** after speaking with Michelle Finnegan was the Bronxville Police Department. The building might not have been as imposing as One Police Plaza, but it was convenient for the entire Village of Bronxville and therefore practical.

The reception area was about how I imagined it: quiet, clean, and empty. A middle-aged man with salt-and-pepper hair sat behind the glass partition. As I stepped forward, he looked up and said, "May I help you?"

I flashed my badge and held open the ID so he could read it through the glass. At the same time, I said, "I was hoping I might talk to the detective who handles your intelligence files."

The man laughed out loud. He sounded a little like a duck that someone had stepped on. Then he looked at me through the glass and said, "We can't all be the NYPD or FBI. We don't have an Intel unit. We have a detective sergeant and a detective. Between them, they try to keep track of everything."

"Then can I speak to either of them?"

The man behind the glass smiled and said, "You already are. I'm Ed Horvath. I'm the detective. Our receptionist is also our evidence tech, and I'm just covering the desk for her for a few minutes." He buzzed the door next to the reception area, and I stepped through. A moment later a tall Black woman marched into the back of reception and said, "Thanks, Ed."

Detective Ed Horvath gave me a quick tour of the tiny station as we walked back to his cubicle. There were files and papers stacked on every possible surface. The way Horvath collapsed onto his chair told me he was a little overwhelmed.

Horvath sighed and said, "I should've been a gastroenterologist like my brother. Now he lives in Florida and can play golf year-round. I guess we both deal with our share of assholes. Still, Florida sounds nice."

"Then who would keep the citizens of Bronxville safe?" I gave him a smile to let him know I was joking. He didn't seem to care.

Horvath looked at me and said, "Every time a detective comes up from the city it means more work for me. Let's cut through all the BS and you tell me what new assignment is going to spring from this visit."

Police work employs all kinds of people. Smart, not so smart. Tough and gentle people. Ambitious people and people who regret getting into the profession in the first place. Every indication was that Ed Horvath had some regrets. But I couldn't let that affect my case.

I handed him my list of four names and asked if he'd ever heard of any of them or if any were suspects in cases they were working.

I watched his bloodshot brown eyes scan the page. Then he jerked his head up and said, "Isn't Perry Martin the football coach over at the Wolfson Academy?"

"Yeah, he is. Do you know him?"

Horvath shrugged. "I don't think I ever met him. He's got that team playing at a high level. Feels like he's in the local paper every week in the fall. But we certainly don't have any cases involving him. Is he a suspect in whatever you're investigating?"

"You know how in big cases everyone is a suspect. I'm just trying to gather as much information as I can about any name that pops up."

His eyes drifted back to the list of names. After another few seconds he said, "I know this one, William Tassick. I haven't heard the name in years."

"How do you know him?"

"We had a joint narcotics task force with the county and the smaller towns in the area. He was like the biggest dealer we all knew. None of us ever made a case on him. But the DEA snagged him for bringing a couple of kilos a week into Newark. I heard he supplied all of northern Jersey. I thought he was still in prison."

I said, "Been out a long time. He lives north of here in Mount Vernon."

"That surprises me. He was a big hitter with big tastes. I figured him for Miami or LA."

"You know if he ever committed any serious violence? Was he suspected of any homicides?"

"I heard the Newark PD thought he was good for a double murder of some local dealers down there. Each dealer was shot in the face once. It eliminated anyone in competition with Tassick."

"So it was all business?"

"I guess you could look at it that way. Why would that matter? A homicide is a homicide."

I gave him a quick outline of my case.

Then Horvath gave me an insight I hadn't even considered. He said, "Maybe he missed the thrill. Maybe this is how he gets his kicks now. The only way he can cope."

# CHAPTER 86

**MY DAY WENT** by in a blur.

Sitting at the dinner table with everyone, including my grandfather, Seamus, took my mind off the case for a little while. Listening to the chatter among the kids never failed to entertain me.

Eddie said, "I beat Fiona playing Horse on the basketball court at Holy Name."

That surprised me. I stole a glance at Fiona but couldn't read her expression. Maybe it did happen.

That's where Eddie, like many teenage boys, made his mistake. He kept running his mouth. "I sank one from the top of the key and I even did an old-school skyhook like Kareem Abdul-Jabbar. She just couldn't close it out." He had a broad smile as he looked across the dinner table.

It must've been too much for Fiona to take. She blurted

out, "I spotted him *H-o-r-s.* And I made the shot from the top of the key too."

Eddie was quick to say, "Part of our bet was that if I won, you couldn't tell anyone about spotting me four letters."

Fiona hung her head and said, "You're right, I did. I'm sorry."

In an instant, Fiona displayed the biggest difference between boys and girls around that age. She was mature enough to accept responsibility and admit she was wrong. I was happy her basketball skills were so solid that she was confident enough to give her brother such a competitive advantage.

After all the dinner plates were cleared, I approached Jane as she sat at the end of the table, working on calculus. I slid into the seat next to her. In a classic, smart teenage girl move, she simply turned her head and said, "What?" in a flat tone.

"I was wondering if you could help me navigate Facebook."

Jane set down her pen and looked at me. "I'm sixteen, Dad. I don't use Facebook. That's for elderly people."

I guess I hadn't realized the change in technology. Then I heard Seamus clear his throat. I looked at him, standing in the kitchen doorway. I said, "Don't tell me. You're a Facebook expert."

"And I'm elderly. Just what you're looking for." My grandfather stepped over to the table and sat down next to me. I noticed Jane used that as an excuse to gather her book and slip away. Seamus said, "The word *expert* implies study and schooling. I just use Facebook to promote the church and keep up with friends and parishioners. Why do you need help?"

I told him what I was trying to do.

My grandfather looked shocked. He said, "You'd have your *daughter* work on a homicide?"

I wasn't sure, but I thought he was kidding. I said, "This is basic. I'm looking for connections. That's all."

Twenty minutes later, we'd looked through the profiles of my suspects. William Tassick had an old profile with no activity in the past year. As we looked back, I realized he had started his account just after he was released from prison. It looked like he was married with a young son. A cute boy about seven or eight years old, who would be a teenager now.

We looked at the profile of Coach Perry Martin. Michelle Finnegan was right. He had a beautiful family. Super-cute kids and a pretty wife. But most of his posts were about football or exercise. Nothing remotely negative or related to the case.

Seamus looked further back on the coach's timeline and then followed a couple of links. He said, "Looks like this guy was engaged to a different woman before he married this one." He showed me a link to an announcement of the engagement. Sure enough, it was a different girl. I wondered what had happened.

Seamus navigated to the woman's profile. She worked as the sports director at a youth center. And it was in the Bronx. How convenient.

# CHAPTER 87

**I WANTED TO** talk to Coach Perry Martin's former fiancée to gather some background. Cindy McCallister's profile showed her employment as a *youth specialist* and listed the youth center where she worked, located off Rosedale Avenue in the Bronx.

The place had a good reputation for serving local underprivileged neighborhoods. If kids had more role models and safe spaces like this and YMCAs, the country would need way fewer cops. I think everybody would be on board with that.

I pressed the button at the main gate. A stout metal fence ran around the entire perimeter to keep people not involved with the youth center out. That was a good idea. The door to the small administration building opened and an extremely heavyset African American man about fifty ambled down the path to meet me.

He didn't say anything. He just waited for me to speak.

"I'm looking for Cindy McCallister."

The man looked over his shoulder at the administration building, then back at me. Something about his facial expression and eyes made me think he was asking me, *Why?*

I pulled out my badge and ID. "I need to ask her a couple of questions about something unrelated to the center."

The man unlocked the gate and tilted his head for me to follow him. We walked around the administration building. The man's pace never changed. He waved to a half dozen different kids and they waved back. Three young men slapped him high fives as they passed. The kids obviously respected this guy. After a little trek past groups getting tutoring for schoolwork at some picnic tables, the silent man pointed to a woman in her mid-thirties with brown hair tied in a ponytail. She was showing some young men how to box someone out under a basketball net. Then she stepped back and hit a perfect jumper. This was someone Fiona would like to meet.

The silent man who had led me back here didn't speak to Cindy either. He just pointed at me and she nodded.

Cindy McCallister greeted me with a smile that would cheer anyone up. I could tell this was a young woman who spent most of her days involved in physical activity. There was no fat on her.

I nodded toward the man who'd let me through the gate. "He doesn't say a whole lot, does he?"

She said, "As a result, when he does speak, everyone listens. It's magical when he can draw order out of chaos on the basketball courts. He's a retired firefighter."

I explained to her that I had a case I was investigating with a number of people I had to eliminate as suspects. I left out the details. Then I mentioned Coach Perry Martin's name.

"Perry's not in trouble, is he? I couldn't see him doing anything too bad."

"Like I said, I'm trying to *eliminate* people from my suspect list. You answered my main question: what kind of guy he is. Why did you two break off the engagement?"

"He's a good guy. He's a good fifteen-year-old. Trapped in an adult body. Basically, I broke off the engagement because he was just so tough to pin down on things. All he cared about was football. Anything he thought would give him an edge, he'd try it. Whether it was ankle weights to strengthen his knees or eating foods he'd read might give him more energy. If he saw something that interested him, he'd drop whatever he was doing and move on. He once disappeared for three days to take up fly-fishing in the Adirondacks."

"So you're saying he was immature?"

"*Impulsive* is a better word. Either way, he's ancient history. I heard he's married with a couple of kids now. Maybe that's forced him to focus a little more."

Even though Cindy McCallister hadn't revealed anything earth-shattering, she had helped me. I decided I needed to knock Perry Martin off my list as quickly as possible to focus on William Tassick. Maybe I should just stop doing interviews altogether. It felt like every time I did one, I was further away from solving this case.

# CHAPTER 88

**WALTER JACKSON HAD** given me a carload of information on William Tassick. Even though he had entered the case late as a suspect, his criminal history was remarkable. Born in San Diego, he had been arrested by age twenty-one for selling cocaine, assault on a police officer, unlawful display of a firearm, and disorderly conduct four separate times. It looked like for all of those infractions, the most Tassick ever received as far as punishment was two years' probation. Later, when he hit the big time, he finally saw the inside of a prison cell.

Before I could focus my attention on William Tassick, I waited on hold with the Syracuse Police Department. I recalled Martin saying he had played at Syracuse. I'd already called the Syracuse University police, and they had nothing on Perry Martin. For some reason, the sergeant I talked to suggested that I call the Syracuse city police.

After going through three different detectives, I was waiting to speak to a sergeant who'd been in the department for more than twenty years. Just as I was about to hang up in frustration, a woman came on the line.

"This is Sergeant Pagan. Someone said you're asking about a case from sixteen years ago. I'm afraid unless it was a capital case or had some extenuating circumstances, the record has almost certainly been purged."

I said, "That's what I've been told. Apparently an officer at the university police thought you guys might know a name connected to a case I'm working."

She spent a few moments making sure I was actually a detective with the NYPD. We knew some of the same people, and she seemed satisfied. Finally, I was able to say, "Does the name Perry Martin ring a bell with you?"

She hesitated, then said, "What's this about?"

I gave her a quick rundown on the case and told her I was trying to clear Perry Martin to focus on other suspects.

Sergeant Pagan said, "Can we talk off the record for a moment?"

That wasn't something you heard when talking with another cop. Usually that was reserved for a reporter. And even then, it had to be a reporter you trusted. I said, "Yeah, sure."

She started slowly. I could hear the stress in her voice. Sergeant Pagan said, "I remember the case pretty clearly. It was just so odd. Your man, Martin, was a lineman for the Syracuse team. It was in the early fall, and we had a report of an assault. I was brand-new in the D Bureau. It involved a pretty freshman who'd been punched hard in the face. Her shirt was ripped, and she was inconsolable. Anyway, she said she went on a date with a blond Syracuse football player. When she wouldn't agree to have sex with him, he got rough with her. She managed to get away. She took a cab directly to the police department. She told me exactly what happened. She wasn't confused on her facts or in shock. I thought she was extremely credible. And she identified Perry Martin as her attacker. We sent a patrol officer to talk to Martin at his dorm. He confirmed he'd been on a date. He didn't say much else."

I was stunned. I confirmed with the sergeant Martin's date of birth. We were talking about the same man. I said, "No arrests show up in his criminal history."

"That's why I'm talking to you off the record. It was a weird sequence of events. I was getting ready to file the case when the victim's brother took a shot at Perry Martin with a .38 revolver. He didn't think we would file a case for the assault because Martin was a football player.

"The state attorney hated the idea of charging the brother, and everyone came to an agreement to drop all of the investigations. No one was ever charged with any crimes. I wasn't even allowed to talk to the Syracuse administration about the incident. They would've flipped out and kicked him off the team. I'm a little bothered by the whole situation even all these years later."

I thanked the sergeant and sat at my desk for a moment as I considered everything she'd said.

I immediately called Terri Hernandez and asked her to meet here at my office. We had to look at Perry Martin much more seriously.

# CHAPTER 89

**I CONTINUED TO** sit at my desk, considering what Sergeant Pagan had told me. Perry Martin had been a danger to women during college. Did that mean he was a murderer too? That could be a leap. I needed to fill in a lot of gaps in the case.

I spent an hour figuring out what I needed to verify about Perry Martin. Then I had my team with me. Terri Hernandez, Walter Jackson, and Harry Grissom all sat around a table in our squad bay. It took me about ten minutes to bring them completely up to speed.

Harry Grissom said, "This is all good info we could use to put together a case, but not nearly enough to charge a man with murder. I'm not dismissing the assault on a woman more than fifteen years ago. I'm saying that a defense attorney would eat us alive if we tried to introduce this information in court."

Terri Hernandez chimed in. "And we'd have to really cover this from every angle. We've had so many suspects turn out to be dead ends that any conviction is going to be difficult at best."

I looked at Walter Jackson to see how pessimistic he was.

He chuckled and raised his hands. "I just find the information out; you're the one who has to make the case."

I said, "We need to find a way to verify that he was calling The Girlfriend Experience. We can't rely on a statement from Thomas Sloan."

Walter said, "I've got about a dozen numbers that are connected to burner phones." He picked up the sheet of numbers Allie Pritz had provided. NYPD tech guys had also managed to grab the records from Allie's phone. Walter had done some reorganizing. Each sheet was arranged by the number that had called The Girlfriend Experience. Two of the phones had called the service only once. A few had called two times. There were three phones that had called the service multiple times. I studied the three sheets of paper. One of the phones had a big gap between a flurry of calls. Last year and this year the phone called in September, October, and November. Then it hit me.

I pulled out my phone and started scrambling to find the calendar. My colleagues just stared at me as I quickly checked each date. Then I looked up and said, "Every call from this phone listed on your sheet was during football season and most of the calls were on a Wednesday or Thursday. Martin's ex-fiancée said he was always looking for an edge in football. Even Thomas Sloan told us the coach said it helped him focus and he called plays better on Fridays if he used The Girlfriend

Experience." I jabbed my finger on the page and said, "This is the phone we need to look at closely. Maybe we can get lucky and connect it to Martin."

Harry Grissom nodded his head. "That's as good a plan as any. Maybe we can find a way to use this young woman you guys found, Allie what's-her-name."

I immediately said, "Pritz. I'm not sure it's worth the risk. She keeps calling, telling me she wants to help. But let's see what we can find out first."

No one lingered after our quick meeting. Everyone had a job to do, and we realized we needed to make an arrest before another girl ended up dead.

# CHAPTER 90

**EACH OF US** jumped on an assignment. Terri tracked down info on the burner phone we were trying to link to Perry Martin. Walter scoured the computer for anything he could find that put Perry Martin in the vicinity of our homicide victims. Even Harry Grissom briefed command staff on what could be a touchy case. Once the media got wind of a string of connected homicides, there'd be a feeding frenzy. They liked nothing more than to report on a serial killer loose in New York.

I drove north to Yonkers, where Coach Martin lived at the end of a quiet street. The coach's house was cute but tiny. I saw his little boy and girl playing in the front yard while their pretty mother looked on from a porch only big enough to hold two chairs. This didn't look like the kind of place where a guy who could spend a thousand to fifteen hundred dollars a night on dates lived. It looked like a schoolteacher's house.

I felt a pang of sadness. The repercussions from a murder affect so many people. The victim, of course. The victim's family is always devastated, sometimes torn apart. The other side of that coin, which few people ever look at, are the effects on the family of the killer. If Perry Martin was our killer, and we got a conviction, those poor kids would grow up without their father through no fault of their own. His young wife would be crushed and doubt every future relationship. I wanted to go tell Martin's wife to grab the kids and leave right now. But I knew I couldn't.

Suddenly I realized how Coach Martin could afford to call The Girlfriend Experience. Then I ran by the Bronxville Police Department to talk to my new friend Detective Ed Horvath.

He didn't exactly seem thrilled to see me. His greeting was "What do you want now?"

"I'm just curious—have you noticed any problems out at the Wolfson Academy? When I was there one day, I heard someone mention some missing money."

Horvath said, "Are you kidding me? Everything goes missing at that place. They lost about six thousand dollars in cash over the last year. The administration fired two secretaries and a janitor over it. Even after I told that goofy headmaster they couldn't have been responsible. What an asshole." Amid the mountain of paper on his desk and on top of the credenza behind him, he pulled one sheet out of a stack like he knew exactly where it would be.

"There were a couple of cars broken into over the year. The burglars knew exactly which ones to hit. They got five hundred dollars in cash from one and a computer from the other. Plus, a couple of the classrooms have been burglarized. The headmaster thinks it might be some of the students. I'm not so sure."

Pieces of the puzzle were starting to fall into place.

# CHAPTER 91

**TERRI MET ME** back in the city. She'd learned that the burner phone that had called The Girlfriend Experience in the fall last year and this year had been purchased from a kiosk at a tiny mall in Yonkers. Not too far from where the coach lived. Terri also told me that Allie Pritz had called her again to tell her she really wanted to help. Terri said, "For once it sounds like we have a cooperating witness who really wants to do the right thing and not just work off charges. She's pissed. She wants justice. This guy murdered her friends."

I looked at Terri and said, "I checked the schedule and there are two more football games left on the Wolfson Academy schedule. One is this Friday. If the coach follows his schedule, he'll call The Girlfriend Experience tomorrow or the next day. Or maybe Wednesday or Thursday of next week."

Terri said, "You don't think Martin would be worried? He's

killed at least three women. He can't be so clueless that he thinks the cops aren't looking into it."

"I doubt he has any idea. I think he floats along in life, following his impulses, and doesn't really consider the consequences. We just have to make a case that sticks."

"If we can interview him and get a DNA swab, maybe the medical examiner can go back over the bodies, find something to link him to one of the murders. But that's a big if."

I said, "I hate saying this, but we're going to have to bring Allie Pritz in on the case. We've already got The Girlfriend Experience phone. All we need to do is have her answer it. Martin would probably recognize her voice since he's called so many times. He should be satisfied everything is okay."

Terri said, "I'll have someone from the Tech Unit work it out so Allie can answer the phone from her house while we keep it in evidence. We'll set up a recorder so any call coming in on the line is automatically saved."

"Then what? Do we let her meet Martin somewhere?"

Terri shrugged. "Don't screw up my idea with good questions."

I snapped my fingers. "That's it. That's how we can absolutely verify it's Perry Martin calling. And what his intentions are. We set up an undercover sting. We pick just the right place here in the city to draw Martin out. We make sure they are never alone. Maybe he'll even say something incriminating. Of course, we'll have a transmitter on Allie and be close by if there's a problem."

"Doesn't that plan scare you?"

"It terrifies me."

# CHAPTER 92

**MY LIEUTENANT, HARRY** Grissom, didn't jump on board with our plan to use Allie Pritz in an undercover sting. At least not completely. He was obviously worried about Allie's safety, as we all were. He trusted me enough to wait until Terri and I spoke with Allie and got a feel for if she would do as she was told. That was good enough for me.

Now Terri and I were sitting in the living room of Allie's apartment in the Village. I'll confess that every time I glanced at the window and saw the fire escape, my stomach did a flip-flop. But sitting in a comfortable chair while Terri Hernandez sat on the couch with Allie made me feel stable enough to continue. Barely.

Terri and I had decided before we arrived at the apartment that she'd do most of the talking. She had a connection with Allie, and basically read her the manual for undercover operations, making Allie acknowledge each point.

I smiled, watching Terri handle this girl so carefully. Terri was tough and could fly off the handle, but she was also patient and caring. It was counter to the persona she tried to project around the department, and I could see that Allie responded to it.

Terri, using her most serious face and voice, started off by saying, "If you're uncomfortable at any time, just get up and walk away. The main thing we're trying to do is tie Martin to the phone line."

Allie kept her eyes on Terri and nodded.

"If he calls, just be cool. Maybe even a little distant. Make him work for everything. We want him recorded."

Allie said, "What if he asks on the phone if I'll have sex?"

"Say you'll think about it. That sounds vague enough and gets him interested."

Again, Allie nodded.

Terri said, "Tell Martin that you'll meet him at a sports bar called The Hockey Stick on 181st Street, a few blocks from University Avenue. Your safety is the overall priority. We know we can cover The Hockey Stick with surveillance and it's far enough north in the city that he shouldn't mind coming down to it. Plus, he'll probably like the idea of a possible college atmosphere."

Once more, Allie nodded.

Terri said, "You'll have a transmitter hidden on you and we'll be able to hear your conversation. It reaches thirty to fifty yards, depending on the environment. Be cautious, but don't be scared. And let him do most of the talking. Maybe he'll say something we can use to connect him to one of the murders."

I finally spoke up. "No matter what happens, don't leave the bar with him. We'll be in there with you somewhere.

If there's a problem, we'll handle it. But stay in the bar no matter what."

Terri and I had visited the place twice to make sure we knew everything about it. There were two doors. The main front entrance and a door toward the rear that was used for take-out orders. There were plenty of places outside the bar to put surveillance teams.

Terri had gone so far as to figure out exactly where Allie should sit at the bar while she waited for Martin to arrive. There were several tables close by that we could sit at. Martin had never seen Terri, and I doubted he'd recognize me from our one conversation.

Allie said, "You really think this guy killed Suzanne and Emma and Estella?"

"He's a suspect. It might turn out to be a wild coincidence. In which case, we'll move on and try to develop a new suspect. I swear to you we're doing everything we can to find and stop this killer. You're really helping us by doing this."

"Are you kidding? I'd do whatever it takes to stop this creep." Allie looked at me. "You don't think a series of coincidences led you to this guy as a suspect, do you?"

I took a moment to give her the best answer I could. "In my experience, I find that coincidence occasionally plays a role in a case. But I'm not a big believer in it otherwise. You can see the trouble we're going to just to make sure we're right."

I didn't like the idea of putting this young woman close to a potential killer. But it was our best option at the moment. I knew all the precautions we were taking, and I had to trust that Allie would be safe.

That didn't make me feel any better.

# CHAPTER 93

**AT HOME THAT** night, Mary Catherine immediately picked up on my anxiety. Reluctantly, I explained to her our plan to use Allie Pritz if Perry Martin called The Girlfriend Experience in the coming days before either of the school's final two games.

She stood out on our balcony with me. She leaned in close and rested her head on my shoulder as I wrapped an arm around her. We stood at the railing and stared out at our quiet Upper West Side neighborhood. Mary Catherine said, "No matter what, you need to be careful."

"I always am."

Mary Catherine let out a snort. "I know you don't tell me everything you do as part of your job. But don't take me for an idiot. I'm aware of the risks you take. I've heard others talk about things you've done. And even though it scares me, it's also part of the reason I fell in love with you. I just want you to look out for yourself as you are looking out for everyone else."

I decided it was time to change the conversation. I said, "Speaking of taking care of yourself, anything new develop with your fertility pre-treatments? I know it was making you tired at first. How do you feel now?"

"I don't know if I'm feeling better or adjusting to feeling tired all the time. I'm starting to feel the stress of the decision. I swear, Michael, I'm not sure if this is the right thing to do. Seeing you work on cases like this scares me. It scares me for the safety of the ten children we have already. Even if three of them are essentially adults. It scares me to think about caring for an infant. The constant attention. The enormous amount of time. What happens to my time with the other kids?"

"All good questions."

"Any chance you want to give me some good answers?"

"The best answer is what you usually tell me: 'Follow your heart.' Or as Seamus would say, 'Trust in faith.' This is not a decision you need to rush."

She squeezed me, then stood on her tiptoes and kissed me on the lips. "How is it you know just what to say to me and the kids when we're feeling our worst?"

"Practice."

I smiled at her laughter. When she rose on her tiptoes again, I was ready for a longer kiss. And I was definitely not disappointed.

# CHAPTER 94

**USING OUR HIGHLY** trained NYPD technicians, Terri and I arranged to have clones of The Girlfriend Experience phone set up at Allie's apartment and our office. The explanation of how the electronics worked made my head spin. But I trusted our tech people. I was confident the phone would alert us to any calls coming in.

That's why on Thursday afternoon, when the phone sitting on my desk beeped, I jumped to listen in on the conversation. Allie handled it perfectly. And although I couldn't be sure, it sounded like Perry Martin's voice on the other end of the line. He was also insistent that he meet one of the girls that night. There wasn't a function; they didn't have to dress up. He just wanted someone to "cuddle with" tonight.

He didn't hesitate to jump at the chance to meet Allie at The Hockey Stick in the Bronx. The call set the entire squad into motion. The fact that we were using a civilian, let alone a college-aged girl, would make our cautious command staff uneasy. Harry Grissom's job was to keep them calm.

Undercover operations like this are generally used in narcotics investigations. Often, a defendant in one case is trying to get a more lenient sentence by cooperating against another drug dealer in a different case.

Police occasionally use ordinary citizens in operations like this. But it would be foolish to think that there is no risk involved. Police work is almost nothing but risk, from pulling a car over for speeding and hoping the driver isn't armed to stepping into a dark alley at night. A police officer's life is all about mitigating risk.

I managed personal risk fine. But the idea of placing Allie Pritz in danger made me nervous. Really nervous.

Terri was with me and said, "How many people do we want on this caper?"

"The easy answer is everybody. The practical answer is we'll use a tac team outside for the arrest, Harry and a couple of detectives from the squad for surveillance. And the two of us inside the bar. That should cover most of the angles. I'm open to other suggestions if you have any."

Terri shook her head. "You've used me undercover a couple of times. I never felt at unnecessary risk."

"For a cop, not a college student."

"A *former* college student who's been running a high-priced dating service. Allie is pleading to be in on this deal. It'll work out."

"But what if it doesn't?"

"If Martin is our guy, this is the most efficient way to stop him. If we wait, it might mean someone else dies. It's a terrible choice, but the kind we have to make every day."

"That doesn't mean I have to like it."

"No, it means we have to *make* the choice. What do you want to do?"

I sighed, trying to buy time. I wanted to run the variables through my head again. And again. And again.

Terri nudged me.

"Okay, okay. Let's do it. But if there are any snags, we cut off the operation right then. No questions asked."

Terri pulled out her phone, dialed, and said, "We're a go."

I knew there was a lot to do between now and seven o'clock, when Perry Martin was supposed to show up at the sports bar. And my heart would be skipping beats until it was all over.

# CHAPTER 95

**I WAS SURPRISED** by the crowd when we entered The Hockey Stick. Thursday nights were busier than I would have guessed. We were in position, sitting at a small table about twenty feet from the main bar. We had a good view of Allie Pritz. And the Tactical Assistance Response Unit outside was ready to go. But I was still nervous.

Terri and I both wore earbuds to monitor the radio and cell phone traffic. Terry's hair completely covered hers. I had one small blue plastic ball that looked like I might have a hearing aid in my right ear. It was a tiny receiver to listen to Allie's transmitter. The larger earbud in my left ear monitored the outside surveillance team's radios. Terri was the only one who could answer the outside team's radio calls. She had a small transmitter mike hidden in the palm of her hand that was connected to a handheld radio in her purse.

I felt like everything was on track.

Allie sat alone at the bar and knew not to look over her shoulder at us. She sipped a Diet Coke and looked up at a TV playing an old Islanders game. There were only four people sitting at the bar. Two older men together and a younger man at the other end of the bar who looked like he was waiting for someone.

I noticed a bartender with a scraggly goatee linger any time he checked on Allie. Why not? Even dressed semi-casually, she was a knockout. Now any time I looked at her, the only thing I thought was how young she was. I hoped my daughters would feel comfortable talking to me if they got into a situation like Allie had. As I had learned with Brian, it's tough being a parent and knowing exactly what's going on with each kid.

I heard the surveillance team we'd sent north to Perry Martin's house and the Wolfson Academy come on the air.

"This is the north surveillance team. We were not able to pick up the target at either location. Repeat, we have not seen the target. You guys won't have much warning when he shows up."

Terri looked at me and bit her lower lip. An anxious habit that few noticed.

I said, "All they were going to do is tell us Martin was on his way. We still have Harry and the tac team outside. They'll give us plenty of notice."

Terri nodded as her eyes slowly scanned the entire bar.

I said, "Are you worried that a six-foot-five, 260-pound man somehow slipped into the bar without us noticing?"

"No, smart-ass, I'm wondering if we'll have problems from anyone if we try to make an arrest. You know how things have been lately. If we start to tussle with this guy, I want to have an idea who might jump in on his side."

I had to acknowledge her superior tactical thinking. Then I looked around the bar quickly. Mostly younger people, probably from Fordham or one of the other schools close by. One table in the back held medical personnel still in their scrubs. The six of them sounded like they were having a great time. That was good. I wanted attention drawn away from us.

I focused on my right earbud to listen to the transmitter we had on Allie, concealed in her blouse. I could clearly hear the TV she was watching over the bar. That meant the signal was good.

There are always so many details that go into an operation like this. Not only safety protocols but to ensure we get what we need to make a case. The entire time, acid ate at my stomach. I might as well have been on a tower looking over the railing at the ground below. That was about how anxious I felt. I had to pull out my left earbud for a moment just to think clearly. I let the little piece of electronics stay on a napkin for a full minute. I needed the break.

Terry's eyes cut up to me suddenly and I knew it was time to reinsert the earpiece. Immediately, I heard Harry Grissom's voice.

Harry Grissom said, "Someone's coming down the street on the same side as the bar. He's pretty far away, but I'd be willing to bet it's our man. It looks like someone put a yellow wig on a minibus."

I looked across at Terri and said, "He's not wrong."

I heard one of the tac team members say, "He just walked past our van. Jesus, Bennett, you need to show more emotion when you're describing someone. It's one thing to *hear* six foot five, it's another to *see* it."

Terri giggled at that.

Terri went up to the bar and grabbed some napkins. While she was there, she casually looked over and nodded at Allie.

Allie returned the nod with confidence.

# CHAPTER 96

**I WAS LOOKING** at the door just as it opened. I kept my head down like I was reading the menu. I didn't need this guy recognizing me, no matter how small the chance. Perry Martin stood in the doorway just for a moment. It was like something had blocked the exit. If there was a fire and he didn't want to move, no one would survive.

He noticed Allie sitting at the bar by herself. A grin spread across his face and he ran his hand through his blond hair. I noticed he arched his back slightly and flexed his chest. Not like he needed to. But it was impressive just the same.

I couldn't keep my eyes from tracking him as he padded across to the bar. I pulled out my surveillance earpiece so I could focus on the transmitter hidden on Allie. Terri turned slightly so she could always keep her eyes on the bar. Martin had never met Terri, so it didn't matter if he looked over and saw her.

As Martin walked up to Allie, I heard him ask, "Are you Allie?"

She nodded and gave him a spectacular smile. She stuck out her hand like a confident real estate agent. Martin shook it, then slipped onto the stool next to her.

We had reached our first goal: verifying that the phone line that had called the service belonged to Perry Martin.

I listened to their small talk and realized I was bothered by a number of issues. I didn't mean to be a prude, but a married man with two little kids at home, dating a girl who looked like she was in college, made me angry. That's right, cops are allowed to feel emotion. Maybe it was because I had my own daughters, but I wouldn't appreciate a guy like Martin bothering them at a bar.

The more I considered him the killer of Suzanne Morton, Estella Abreu, and Emma Schrade, the angrier I became. It just didn't seem right that he should feel so comfortable walking into a bar in New York and talking to a girl like Allie.

He showed no reticence or concern. Allie kept quiet and just let him talk. He tried to ask her questions, but she was smart and came back to him with her own questions. Questions designed to boost his ego. "Do you work out?" "Is everything tight on you?" The questions kept the football coach on his heels and stopped him from asking Allie too much.

In an abundance of caution, I had also given Allie an emergency pager. It had a GPS signal that would go to an app on all our phones. If things went really bad, and she couldn't see us, all she had to do was hit that button and we'd be able to find her fast.

The way things were going, I doubted she'd need that. The

bar had people in it but wasn't packed tight. We had a good line of sight. I had cops I trusted watching the outside of the building. And Terri Hernandez was sitting next to me. You couldn't ask for a steadier partner.

I heard Martin use the word *comfort* several times and realized what he was saying. Maybe that was the new word for sex people were using. I hadn't heard it phrased like that before.

On the transmitter, I heard Martin say, "Maybe we could find a hotel close by. Then you could give me some comfort. I really need to be able to focus tomorrow, and you could help me tonight."

Allie asked a really good question. "Did you have any girls from The Girlfriend Experience that you particularly liked?"

Martin said, "I've never been disappointed with anyone from your agency."

I heard some raised voices and turned to look toward the front door.

The manager was trying to keep someone from coming inside. I saw a group of four or five men arguing with the manager. One of them was trying to push his way into the bar. Then I saw they were all wearing Jets jerseys.

That was never a good sign.

# CHAPTER 97

**I KEPT AN** eye on the growing argument at the front door. I didn't want some loudmouths screwing up our investigation.

The manager, a woman in her early forties, tried to reason with the men. They kept yammering about coming in to see a Thursday night NFL game featuring the Jets. It sounded like they'd been kicked out of the bar last week and told not to come back.

One of the men said in a loud Brooklyn accent, "This is America. You can't keep us out of a bar. Not on a Thursday night with the NFL on."

The manager was professional and didn't sink to their level. She kept an even tone. "I'm afraid none of you are welcome here. Please leave."

That almost did the trick, until the bartender, the one

who'd flirted with Allie, needed to prove his manhood. He shouted from the edge of the bar, fifteen feet away, "You heard her, scumbags. Hit the road."

A skinny dude with a mullet haircut shouted, "What did you just call us?"

Before the manager could turn around and calm down the bartender, all five Jets fans pushed into the bar. The bartender ran out from behind the bar and barreled into them.

Every single eye in the place was glued to the front door. Green Jets jerseys flew all over the entry. The bartender shoved one of the loudmouths so hard he took down two more with him as he hit the industrial-grade tile on the floor like a bowling ball with a goatee.

One of the other Jets fans took a wild swing, which the bartender simply ducked. He countered with a hard punch directly into the Jets fan's face. The man's head snapped violently and he stumbled back two steps. Then he fell over his friends on the ground. The last Jets fan darted out the front door. Apparently, common sense can come to anyone given the right motivation.

I heard on my left earpiece, "This is Tac One. There's some kind of disturbance at the front door of the bar."

Terri used her covert radio transmitter to tell the team it had nothing to do with us and to stay in position. I knew why she'd added *stay in position*. It's tough for cops to sit idly by when violence breaks out. Their instinct is to intervene and try to stop whatever's going on. But this case was too big to risk on a barroom brawl.

Patrons of the bar were standing and moving toward the front door to get a better view of the scuffle.

I could hear something in my right earbud. It was Perry Martin's voice saying, "This is crazy." I turned to get a look at him and Allie at the bar. There were too many people now crowded around my table, cheering on the fight. I couldn't see anything.

I looked at Terri and said, "Can you see Allie and Martin?"

She stood up, but as soon as I saw her crane her neck, I knew something was wrong. I sprang to my feet, where my height helped me easily see over the people crowded around us.

I felt a ball of ice in my stomach. The two barstools where Martin and Allie had been sitting were now empty. Frantically, I scanned the rest of the bar. I didn't see them.

I heard Terri on her radio saying in a loud voice, "We've lost visual. Heads up. Our suspect and our witness may be outside. Stop them immediately."

I pushed my way through the crowd and saw they were not at the front of the bar. I rushed toward the rear. The back door was ajar.

Terri yelled into the radio, "Suspect is out the back door! Suspect is out the back door!"

I didn't waste a second as I burst through the door into an empty alley.

# CHAPTER 98

**I TURNED MY** head to look up and down the alley. I didn't see anyone, let alone a giant man and a beautiful girl.

I don't think the word *panic* can adequately explain what I was feeling at that moment. I stood in the middle of the narrow alley. My stomach felt like a small fire burned inside it. Where could they have gone so quickly?

Terri turned toward one end of the alley and I turned toward the other. I'd only taken a few steps when two of the tac team members jogged around the corner. They skidded to a stop when they saw me.

The taller of the two cops said to me, "He didn't come this way."

I could hear in my earbud Terri saying, "I don't see them this way."

I listened and focused on my right earpiece. I thought I

picked up a snippet of conversation. "I heard them for a second. They gotta be in this area. Quick—start checking doors."

The two tac cops, dressed in bulky clothes to hide their ballistic vests and guns, both started grabbing doorknobs and jerking hard. Some of the doors looked like they went to maintenance rooms. They all appeared to be secure as we worked our way to the main street.

I checked the app on my phone to see if Allie had pushed the panic button on the GPS pager I'd given her. Nothing. How could they have just disappeared in the middle of a crowded bar?

Harry Grissom jogged around the corner of the building and stopped next to me. "Did we find them?"

I shook my head quickly as I tried to think where they could've gone.

Harry got on the radio and said, "We've lost sight of the suspect. Let's get some help in here and start a grid search. We start from this block and work north and south first."

I heard acknowledgments on the radio as well as someone calling dispatch to get more cops in the area to help us search.

My heart was racing and my throat felt like a python was wrapped around my neck. But I wasn't going to let anything stop me from finding Allie. This had been my idea, even if she had agreed to it.

I realized our best chance might be if I was able to use the range of the transmitter on Allie to locate them. All I could do was jog through the area, hoping to catch a voice over the transmitter again.

Terri caught up to me and I explained what I was trying

to do. She held her radio in her hand now and no longer needed the earpiece to monitor surveillance. She pulled the backup earpiece to the transmitter on Allie from her pocket and crammed it in her ear. We split up and started to jog in different directions.

I saw a patrol car whiz by a few blocks north of us. We were starting to get help into the area. It didn't make me feel any better. Until I had Allie safe and handcuffs on Perry Martin, I felt like I was burning days out of my life from the anxiety.

# CHAPTER 99

**I STARTED RUNNING.** Not jogging. Sprinting. I
wanted to cover as much ground as possible. I needed to find
Allie no matter where Martin had taken her. I'd like to say it
wasn't related to the panic I felt. But it was clearly inspired
by the panic. I didn't know what else to do. I was just hoping
to catch a glimpse of them or perhaps hear something on the
transmitter. The transmitter that had been ominously silent
for the last two minutes.

I pulled out the earbud that monitored the radios. I needed
to concentrate. I'd pulled a badge on a chain from my shirt
and let it hang outside so it was visible. I didn't want some
young cop doing some crazy takedown on me just because
they saw another tall guy, even if I was sixty pounds lighter
than Perry Martin.

Once a situation turned bad, it always seemed to cascade

into more and more disasters. I still felt like I might be able to salvage this. All I had to do was find Allie.

I slid to a stop two blocks north, right on the edge of Fordham Heights. That's where I ran into Terri with another detective. She shook her head as we approached each other.

I could hear her radio in her hand. Harry Grissom's voice was clear and commanding. He was organizing all the new arrivals coming into the area to help. Harry's voice blazed as he said, "I want a perimeter set up starting at six blocks in every direction. No male over six feet tall gets through the perimeter without someone who knows this mope laying eyes on him."

I heard someone whose voice I didn't recognize ask where his partner was.

Harry jumped back on the radio and snapped at him. "This isn't a frat party where we're looking for friends. It doesn't matter where partners are. Find this mope and the young woman he has with him. Her safety is all that matters now." That definitely shut down any erroneous chatter on the radio.

I started looking up at buildings, hoping I might see something obvious. Someplace the coach might've taken Allie.

Terri said, "I thought I caught a couple of words as I ran toward you. Earlier, I heard Allie say, 'No.' I don't know what it was in response to. She didn't shout it, but there was an edge in her voice." Terri pointed out where she'd picked up sound on the transmitter.

I looked down the street in both directions. There were a few pedestrians strolling along and a couple of plainclothes police officers hustling past them. Another patrol car raced by on the street. By now, Perry Martin had to know the cops were onto him. That's what I was hoping. I wanted him to see how futile his position was and release Allie.

I started checking every storefront. I couldn't risk leaving any idea alone. Anything I could do to find Allie.

Then I heard it. Just a quick squawk in my earbud. I looked over to Terri, about twenty feet away from me. She was frozen in position, then put a finger to her ear. She was hearing it too.

I hustled closer to Terri and gave her an expectant look.

Terri held up one finger. She had something on her transmitter. Maybe it was the angle she was standing. Maybe it was her younger ears. She could hear them. They were within fifty yards of us right now.

Terri looked up at me. Her eyes moved along the sidewalk. "They're in the subway."

# CHAPTER 100

**I WAS SURPRISED** they'd gotten this far. Terri and I ran to the Fordham Road subway entrance. The detective who was with Terri continued to search the street level just in case we were wrong.

The station was surprisingly busy. I realized it might have had something to do with an event at Fordham University. There were a lot of well-dressed women and men in suits. It didn't make things easier.

I felt my phone buzz. I yanked it out of my front pocket and saw the alert for the GPS application. Allie had pushed the button. I looked down at my phone as I was jostled by people hurrying past me.

The tiny map on my phone showed me that Allie was close by. It had to be somewhere in this station. I eased to the wall to get out of the flow of people, then methodically scanned the station.

Terri started to search near the tracks where a train was just pulling away, headed north.

The signal on my phone froze. I wasn't sure what that meant. My guess was being in the subway interfered with the signal and I was only getting intermittent glimpses of where Allie and Martin were moving.

The chatter on the radio hadn't changed. More and more cops flooded into the area, but no one had seen the couple. It wasn't like we were searching for a nondescript man in a white T-shirt. Someone should notice these two.

I started walking along the wall, past several street musicians. A man with a spectacular beard, wearing a tattered cowboy hat, played guitar. Almost right next to him, a drum line of three young men competed for the few dollars commuters would throw into their jar.

I got frustrated every time I turned a corner and someone jostled me or blocked my view. This place had a lot more corners and nooks than I recalled. Or, more likely, I never cared about them until now.

I checked my phone and the GPS app. The only thing that was on the screen was a small text box in the corner that said WEAK SIGNAL. Satellites could only tell so much. And there was a lot between me and the open sky above.

Another train was arriving from downtown. People started to shuffle into position to get on. I checked my watch. The other train had been out of the station only a minute or two. Someone had seriously screwed up a schedule.

I started walking quickly down the platform, looking

through the crowd that had gathered to jump on the north-bound train. I absently mumbled, "Excuse me," or an apology as I bumped into people while I tried to search the crowd.

I knocked into a stout man about my age wearing a gray suit. I murmured, "Sorry." I kept shuffling along, trying to look ahead of me.

The man snapped, "Be more careful, then you won't have to tell people you're sorry." I glanced over my shoulder at his red face but just ignored him and kept searching.

Then I felt a strong hand on my shoulder. The same man shouted, "Don't turn your damn back on me."

I didn't have time for this. I spun quickly. I slapped his hand away from my shoulder. That really pissed him off. He grabbed my jacket with both hands. A classic intimidation move that wasn't very smart.

Out of instinct and training, I swung my leg up to kick the man's feet out from under him. He hit the concrete subway floor hard.

He whimpered and tried to stand up. Then someone pushed him back on the floor.

That knocked me out of my tunnel vision and I saw Terri Hernandez standing above him. She looked down at the pudgy man on the floor and said, "Stay down, fat boy."

He glared up at her but didn't say anything.

Terri took me by the arm and hustled me away. I fumbled with my phone and saw the GPS signal was back on the screen. It was moving.

I turned to Terri and said, "They're on the train that just left."

# CHAPTER 101

**WE HAD TO** act fast. We jumped onto another train just leaving the station. That caused a few issues. We had no signal coming to the GPS, and Terri couldn't raise anyone on the NYPD radio. We weren't sure if it was because of the range of the tactical radios or the cover of the subway, or if all the other cops were occupied.

I stood right by the door, waiting for the train to make its first stop. I don't know if I hoped to see them in the station, or see the signal. It didn't matter. I had my phone out and in my hand, just staring at the GPS app.

Terri tried her phone and the radio over and over again, but she got no signal. Thankfully, the car was virtually empty. Two city employees in maintenance uniforms sat at the very rear of the train, talking quietly.

My heart was beating a quick rhythm in my chest. I had

never wanted a train to go faster in my life. It felt like we were crawling along.

I turned to Terri and said, "Christ, I could've run to the next station faster than this."

She said, "We've got plenty of cops at street level. As far as I know, we're the only two following the signal."

The train slowed and I saw the lighted station ahead of us. I even bent my knees so I could get a sprinter's start out the door as soon as it opened. Terri looked out the windows at the few people in the station.

The train came to a complete stop and I darted onto the platform. I didn't have to worry about running into people here. Terri turned in one direction and I sprinted directly to the stairs. I estimated I could make it back to the train if I didn't have a signal. But just as I got to the bottom of the stairs, the app on my phone refreshed and I had a clear signal.

I looked back across the platform and yelled to Terri, "Looks like they got off here and are somewhere on the street level."

Terri came racing across the platform. Her radio was still in her hand and she was trying to raise Harry Grissom. Just as she reached the stairs, I heard the squelch of the radio.

Harry's voice was a welcome sound. "Where are you guys? We've got a perimeter set and are doing a grid search."

Terri said, "They took the subway to the next exit north. We're coming out on Kingsbridge Road."

Now I had a good signal on my GPS.

# CHAPTER 102

**TERRI HERNANDEZ AND** I stood just outside the exit to the subway. The GPS showed that Perry Martin and Allie Pritz had walked north at least a block. Terri got on the radio again and called out our exact position and where we were searching.

As we started to jog north, I heard Harry Grissom directing what sounded like an army of cops to start shifting north. It's hard to effectively express how important it is to have a competent boss. I trusted Harry completely. I didn't care how old he was or how many times he had to go to the doctor during a month. That son of a gun knew the city and how to handle dangerous situations. He barked more orders. Just his voice on the radio restored some of my confidence.

Now I was looking at the storefronts and buildings. I was hoping to see something obvious. Maybe another bar. Any place they might've walked into. The signal on my app wasn't exact, but it was pretty close. It showed that they had to be in the area. It looked like the signal had stopped in one place now.

Terri and I looked up and down the street. A cruiser raced past us one block over. The help was coming our way. Then I noticed a shitty-looking hotel. The kind I didn't see much in the city anymore. A tall, skinny building, wedged between a modern office and some older apartments.

The sign on the hotel said THE MALLOY ARMS, and had seen better days. The whole place seemed to have been made in the 1970s. It wasn't only the design but the washed-out colors that told me how old it was. There was a neon VACANCY sign where the *n* was burned out.

I looked at Terri and broke into a sprint. Terri had no problem keeping up with me. As soon as I stepped through the weathered glass door to the hotel, the GPS signal appeared to be right next to me. I realized they were on a floor above us. This was exactly the kind of place I would've expected Perry Martin to find. Cheap, hidden, and no one would ask questions.

The middle-aged clerk looked up at us but didn't bother to speak. His brown ponytail and thick glasses made him look like a nearsighted otter. I pulled out my badge and rushed toward the tiny reception desk.

"Did a great big guy and a younger woman just come in here?"

The man took off his glasses and looked at Terri and me. He didn't hesitate to say, "Yeah. They're up on the ninth floor. Second room on the right after the elevator."

Terri said, "What's the room number?"

"We got no numbers on the rooms. There's only four on each side of the elevator on each floor."

I was about to take the three steps across the lobby to get to the elevator when the clerk said, "Elevator don't work. Gotta take the stairs."

Terri and I raced up the stairs, taking them two at a time. While we were climbing, Terri radioed in our position. We didn't have time to wait for backup. We needed to act right now.

I'll admit I was panting pretty hard by the time we came through the door on the ninth floor. I had enough energy to run down the hallway past the elevator. I found the second door after the elevator. The clerk was right—there were no numbers on any doors.

Terri and I both tried to listen to the transmitter for any clues. It was silent at the moment.

Terri said in a low voice, "Do we knock and announce?"

"I don't think we can risk what he might do. We need surprise on our side." That's when I stepped back and Terri knew exactly what I was going to do. Before I raised my leg to kick the door, Terri tried the handle quickly.

As soon as Terri shook her head, I kicked the door just to the right of the handle. The door and frame collapsed in on itself and I tumbled into the hotel room. Terri stepped through the ruin of the door right behind me with her gun up and sweeping the room.

I sprang to my feet, brushing a piece of broken door off my pant leg. I was frozen for a moment, staring across the room.

# CHAPTER 103

**I STOOD NEAR** the ruined doorway. The first thing I noticed was Allie Pritz sitting by the window, reaching into her purse. She stared at us in silence for a moment. My heart froze as I tried to figure out if she was okay. Then she sprang from the chair, burst into tears, and rushed toward me with her arms outstretched.

The father in me overwhelmed the cop with tactical sense. I wrapped my arms around the sobbing young woman.

She said, "I'm sorry. I panicked and didn't push the GPS button until we were on the subway."

I patted her back and said, "It's okay." I was about to ask her if she was hurt when the bathroom door burst open.

Standing in the doorway, his shirt untucked and only buttoned in the middle, stood Perry Martin. He filled virtually every inch of the doorway. It felt like almost no light got past him from the bathroom.

His deep voice said, "What the hell?"

Terri took a step back and kept her gun up and pointed at Martin.

I released Allie Pritz and pushed her behind me. Then I looked Perry Martin in the eye. This was what I'd been waiting for. Stopping a killer before he could strike again. But sometimes I forget there are other perspectives.

Perry Martin again said, "What the hell?" Then he stared at me. "I know you, don't I?"

"NYPD."

"Why are the cops here? Why did you kick in my door? We didn't do anything wrong."

Terri used a very reasonable voice to say, "Please step out of the bathroom."

"Not until you tell me what the hell is going on." His hands started to shake.

I could see the color in his face changing. Was it fear or anger? Sometimes the response wasn't that different. It felt like it was dawning on the big football coach why we were here. He turned his head slowly to look at Allie, standing behind me.

Allie met his gaze and said, "You murdered my friends." She was no longer scared. She was pissed off. Really pissed off. She stepped around me and tried to kick Martin. Then she hissed, "You're gonna burn in hell for everything you've done."

This was not the young woman we'd been dealing with the last few days.

I corralled Allie and shoved her behind me again. We would have enough problems with Martin if he decided to resist. Allie's insults didn't help.

Martin didn't answer. Terri and I both realized time was

running out. We'd seen it before. The reasonableness was about to disappear. I was afraid to see what was coming from a guy this size.

Terri said, "Down on your knees."

"I don't have a weapon. I haven't done anything wrong."

Now Allie was crying and screamed, "You're a murderer! You can't do anything more wrong than that."

I wanted to quiet Allie down and keep her from inciting a fight I didn't want. But I couldn't risk taking my eyes off Martin. That's why I hadn't drawn my pistol. Terri had hers on target. I might be needed to wrestle him and handcuff the giant football coach.

Martin said, "I know you. You were at the Wolfson Academy."

I said, "Let's not add to our problems. We can go to our office and see about working this out."

"Working what out? Why are you arresting me?"

Terri didn't like the extra chatter. She said very clearly, "Get down on your knees with your hands behind your back. Then you can talk all you want."

I could see it in his face. At that moment, Perry Martin weighed his options. Apparently, he didn't like his chances if we got him in handcuffs and took him to our office.

It was shocking how quickly a man his size could move.

# CHAPTER 104

**PERRY MARTIN GAVE** me a shove. It felt like a force field pushing me away. There was nothing I could do to stop it. I fell back three steps until I was almost out of the hotel room's doorway. Then Martin darted out of the bathroom door to face Terri Hernandez.

Terri used a good command voice to try to get Martin to finally go down on his knees.

As Martin turned to face Terri, I jumped on his back. I tried to reach high enough to get an arm around his neck so I could pull him to the ground. What I discovered was that his neck felt like a thigh. He twisted his body, and I found myself sailing through the air. Somehow he managed to throw me into Terri Hernandez. We both bounced off the edge of the bed and onto the filthy, thin carpet covering the cheap hotel-room floor.

As my head bounced off the floor, I was disoriented for a moment.

Terri had lost her gun in the fall. That didn't slow her down. She was on her feet instantly. She ducked a massive right hand. A haymaker intended to take her out of the fight permanently. As the fist passed over her head, Terri slid to the side and delivered a brutal knee to the side of Martin's leg. In training, it's called a knee spike, and it generally stops anyone when delivered properly.

I saw Terri's technique. It was perfect. And it had almost no effect on Martin. Now he swung a backhand, which Terri ducked again. But Martin was expecting it and used his other hand to grab her by the arm and fling her into the bathroom.

When he turned, I sprang from the floor and hit him like a tackling dummy. In retrospect, hitting a man that much larger than me, who had spent most of his adult life on the football field, didn't make much sense. He turned his body slightly and tossed me into the wall. It felt like the whole building shook. As I slid down the wall to the floor, I prayed that there were reinforcements on the way.

Allie was still standing in the doorway. I hoped she didn't think she should get involved in the fight. She was uncontrollably angry. I didn't blame her. But now I saw I'd misjudged some of her motivation for getting involved in this investigation. She didn't want to just bring Martin to justice; she wanted vengeance. I realized she could never go back to The Girlfriend Experience after knowing what happened to the other three girls.

When Martin turned toward me, Allie took a ceramic lamp sitting on a small table by the door and smashed it over Perry Martin's head. Cheap ceramic shards flew everywhere.

It didn't seem to have that much effect on him, but some shards hit me on the cheek and drew blood.

When Martin turned to face Allie, I jumped up and kicked him in the same leg that Terri had nailed with the knee spike. Finally, he let out a sound like he'd been hurt. A low, guttural growl.

When he turned, I punched him in the face. My right hand connected solidly with the side of his head just in front of his ear. He stumbled and caught himself on the doorframe before he fell.

He glared at Allie, then at me. Then he sprinted down the hallway. Again, he surprised me with his speed.

# CHAPTER 105

**TERRI HERNANDEZ WAS** already in the hallway by the time I was able to get on my feet. We saw Martin hit the stairwell. He hesitated at the landing, then started to climb the stairs. We could already hear someone coming up the stairs. Martin must've heard the same thing and took the only route available.

A single detective ran up to the floor we were on. He was from the local precinct. I'd met him, but I couldn't think of his name. He was a hotshot in a tight shirt. He looked like a rock band reject, with his long dark hair brushed straight back. He kept his pistol in the small of his back. I guessed that was a cool way of carrying your gun now.

He didn't say a word. He just followed us as we climbed the three floors to the roof. Then I paused at the door to the roof. It was one thing to be thrown around the hotel room.

It would be another to be thrown twelve stories to the hard concrete below.

Terri said, "We might be better off leaving him sealed off on the roof. We can wait here for reinforcements."

The new detective with us said, "What am I?"

Terri looked at the young detective. She said, "Reinforcements would be, like, four or five cops. You didn't see him back in the room. You'd just be another body he could toss around."

To his credit, the young detective didn't try to act macho or say anything stupid. He just shrugged like he understood. Since he hadn't seen Perry Martin in person, I didn't think he could really understand what we were trying to tell him.

I thought about Terri's idea. Finally, I said, "He might be able to get onto one of the other roofs or climb down the fire escape. I don't think we can risk it. If we have to, we just stay away from the coach. Keep him occupied without actually engaging him."

This time I didn't hesitate. I turned the handle on the door and shoved it open.

The night air was cooler than I expected. The three of us fanned out quickly on the old-school tar-and-gravel roof. I had to glance over the side of the building to look at the fire escape. Even doing that triggered my acrophobia. Instantly, I felt a little nauseated. On the bright side, the coach wasn't climbing down the fire escape. At least not yet.

I heard a sound and someone grunt. As I spun, I saw the young detective tossed through the air onto the gravel roof. He rolled and ended up on his back. I wanted to shout at him, *That's why we don't carry our pistols in the small of our back.* But somehow I refrained.

The coach stepped out from behind the utility shed that also held the door to the roof. Terri was on one side of him, holding her hands up like she was trying to calm him down.

I jumped forward and grabbed the fallen detective by the collar of his shirt and pulled him away from the coach. He was able to scramble to his feet once I'd dragged him about five yards.

The first thing the detective did was make sure the gun was still in the small of his back, then he ran a hand through his hair to make sure it still looked good. I guess if I was his age, I might do the same thing.

Now I focused on Perry Martin. He was backing away from both Terri and me to the far side of the roof. I knew it faced the street. There was also no way to reach the fire escape from that side.

I said in an even voice, "Let's talk about this. No one needs to get hurt." I noticed a subtle change in the coach's expression. Now he looked nervous and scared. There didn't seem to be any trace of anger left in him.

He yelled, "Don't come any closer."

Terri and I froze in place. We knew that tone—frustration edged with panic.

The coach kept backing away slowly until he bumped into the two-foot ledge that enclosed the entire roof of the hotel. Then he carefully swung a leg up onto the ledge and pushed himself to stand on it. He glanced over the side and then quickly looked back to make sure we weren't trying to sneak up on him.

I'd seen too many suicides in my career. I wasn't interested in seeing another. I held up my hands and said, "Don't do anything stupid, Coach." I gave Terri a quick look and she knew to retreat. We didn't want to overwhelm someone who was so distraught.

Terri eased back toward the door to the stairwell next to the young detective.

We were in an absolute standoff. I could hear sirens below, but right now it was just a suicidal Perry Martin and me. On a rooftop. *Shit.*

# CHAPTER 106

**MY HEART SKIPPED** a beat when I saw Perry Martin wave his arms to keep his balance on the ledge. It wasn't that narrow, but there was some wind up here, and I knew how disconcerting looking over the edge of a high building could be.

I worked hard to keep my tone pleasant and sympathetic. "C'mon, Coach, step down off the ledge and we can talk."

Martin looked at me and said, "What's left to talk about? I know why you broke into my room. I can figure out that that girl was working with you guys."

Just as I was starting to feel like Martin was going to step away from the edge, I heard the door to the stairwell open and bang against the wall. Then I heard a female voice scream, "Jump! Go ahead and do us a favor. Jump! You're a murderer."

I took a quick glance over my shoulder and saw that Allie Pritz had followed us up the stairs. She looked angry. Furious.

Allie looked at me and shouted, "Let him jump." She had a hard edge to her voice.

Now Terri stood next to Allie with an arm around her shoulders. She pulled Allie over next to the young detective so they could both keep an eye on her.

I turned to look back at Perry Martin. Allie's outburst had gotten to him. He looked stricken. His voice cracked as he shouted to Allie, "I'm sorry. I'm sorry everything got so out of hand. I never intended to hurt anyone." He let out a sob but stayed on top of the ledge.

I was now about ten feet from him. There was no way I'd be able to hold on if I grabbed him and he wanted to jump. Either he'd break out of my grip or we'd both go over the side.

Martin shook his head and said in a lower voice, "I know I fucked up. I ruined everything. My family, my career, everything's gone. I even had to steal from the school just to pay for the girls. Once I met that first girl, it was like some kind of primal urge. Or an addiction. I don't know what you'd call it. I had no control over it. And she agreed to have sex with me, but I had to pay her an extra six hundred dollars. I wish I could've stopped right there."

I had to be practical in the situation. If Martin committed suicide, we might not know how many women he killed. I didn't want to give him more incentive to jump, but it was a question I needed answered. I said, "Coach, how many girls did you kill?"

He stared at me like I'd slapped him across the face. A tear did run down his cheek. He started shaking his head like some internal dialogue tormented him. He looked over at me, wiped his nose with his bare forearm, and started to speak slowly.

Martin said, "The first one, Cheryl, was an accident. That was last year. She said no, but I wasn't sure if it was an act. When she pulled away from me, I grabbed her and shook her. Maybe too hard. When I saw she was hurt and moaning about her neck, I panicked. I twisted her head to finish it. Then I dumped her in a garbage truck parked behind the building we were at in Bronxville. Never heard or saw anything about her."

I thought back to my encounter with Cheryl Savage's father. The father determined not to lose another child. At least he'd have some closure.

Martin looked at me. He wanted to talk. I let him.

He said, "Everything seemed fine until a few months ago. That's when I hired Emma. What a sweet singing voice that one had. We went to a motel in Bronxville. She was amazing. She said she didn't mind it a little rough. Then, the next thing I realized, I had my hand around her throat and she was no longer breathing.

"The third girl, Suzanne, tried to blackmail me. She said she'd tell my wife. I'd already used all the money I had or could steal. I flipped out."

Martin mumbled something else, but it wasn't clear. This guy was at the end of his rope.

"The last girl. Her name was Estella. She turned me down flat. She said she'd never have sex for money. Even when I tried to argue the hypocrisy of being paid to go on a date but not accepting money for sex, she wouldn't budge. That one happened quickly. We were behind a restaurant in lower Manhattan. There was no one around. There was some sort of kitchen utensil. It wasn't quite a knife, but it had a pointed end. It was just wedged against the wall. I don't know why I picked it up to look at it. Then when Estella denied me again. I couldn't keep myself from stabbing her. Just once. The look on her face is burned in my memory. I knew I was way out of control, but it was like there was nothing I could do about it. I got rid of her body in the river and just went back to my regular life. I thought the four incidents were separated enough that I might be okay, especially when I didn't see anything in the news about the cops looking for anyone."

He took a step closer to me on the ledge, and I felt like he was about to climb down and back onto the roof.

# CHAPTER 107

**I STOLE A** glance over my shoulder and saw that Harry Grissom and a uniformed patrol officer had joined Terri, Allie Pritz, and the detective who'd followed us. Allie stood between Terri and the other detective. I realized everyone had just heard Perry Martin's confession. On one level that was good. Plenty of witnesses to explain how he'd volunteered everything. On the other hand, I didn't know how the details would affect Allie. It was tough to read her expression in just a quick peek.

I took a step closer to Martin. I slowly extended my hand. His eyes met mine. He was looking for any reason to step down from the ledge and back onto the roof. I said, "Sounds like you need help. We can get you some help."

Martin said, "Really? You'd help me?"

"I promise."

I knew Harry had been in this situation several times. I wanted to ask his advice. But I knew not to turn my back on a suicidal person. I wanted the coach to know he could come down from the ledge. I didn't go into any details about what might happen to him in the near future. But for now, he wasn't going to be a suicide while I was standing there.

I could feel my heartbeat start to settle down. I took a deep breath.

Martin stood up straight and took another half step toward the roof.

I could see his brain working through what might happen to him. He hesitated. I didn't risk saying anything just yet. I wanted him to take that one definitive step toward me. My hand was still extended. Martin leaned in to grab my hand and step down onto the roof.

Then I heard the gunshots. There were two in very rapid succession. One of them hit Martin in the neck. The shock of the bullet stunned him. He reached for the wound with one hand and stumbled slightly. Blood sprayed from his carotid artery. He wobbled on the ledge as I tried to spring forward to steady him.

But it was too late. One foot slid off the edge. He disappeared from my sight silently. The only evidence he had ever stood on the protective ledge were drops of blood.

I spun quickly to see Terri and the young detective holding back Allie Pritz. I immediately realized what had happened. Allie had snatched the gun from where the young detective had tucked it in his waistband. She had gotten off a couple of shots before he was able to stop her.

I had to peek over the edge of the building. Before my

vision started getting blurry and the world started to spin, I could clearly see Perry Martin's body on the sidewalk next to the entrance to the hotel. A couple of uniformed officers were moving toward him.

Then I eased away from the ledge, got ahold of myself, and went to Allie. By now she was sobbing uncontrollably. Her face was a mask of tears, snot, and anguish. I gave a nasty look to the young detective for his poor tactical sense. A gun wasn't supposed to be taken off a cop so easily.

I looked at Terri, who was shaking her head. Neither of us had seen this coming.

# CHAPTER 108

**ALMOST A WEEK** after Perry Martin was shot, I found myself sitting in a car with my friend Sergeant Kathy Figler. I'd been waiting for a chance to find the bullies who had been threatening my sons. Kathy's team had figured out who the boys were after they saw the video from Holy Name. I didn't want special treatment. Kathy assured me that they were more interested in getting a gun away from a kid than just helping a fellow cop. I decided to accept that and was now just along for the ride.

Kathy and I sat in the front seat of her relatively new Ford Explorer.

I'd slipped into the car, leaving mine parked a few blocks away.

As we sat there, one of the first things Kathy said was "You doing okay after the bullshit on the hotel roof?"

"Still trying to wrap my head around it."

"You did a hell of a job. No one can tell when a witness is going to snap. You guys did everything right. Everyone except for the moron who kept his gun stuffed down his pants without a holster."

"For the record, he's not part of Manhattan North Homicide. He's a detective in the Five-Two."

"I think I know who you're talking about. Good-looking kid about thirty with long hair?"

"Sounds like him."

"At least you and Terri weren't hurt." Kathy spent a moment staring at the bruise that covered the side of my face, then added, "Too badly."

"Believe me, after tangling with a former lineman, I feel lucky to have only a few cuts and bruises."

Kathy said, "What about the girl who shot the killer?"

"She's still in custody. Everyone's scrambling to see what they can do to keep her from doing hard time."

"That's a nice change, government employees trying to look at the bigger picture."

"Yeah, I guess this case had a lot of surprises."

Kathy said, "I heard Harry Grissom saved the day organizing cops from a dozen different precincts during the emergency. I guess he's not slowing down after all."

"I doubt there's another lieutenant in the NYPD who could've done a better job. He never hesitates to do everything he can to help us."

Then Kathy sat up a little more in her seat, looking at the park in front of us. She pointed to the basketball court on the far left. "There they are. All three of them together. Perfect."

I watched the three bullies play basketball for a couple of minutes. They looked like they were having fun. They even stopped playing for a minute to help a younger kid with his free throws. Then I said to Kathy, "They seem like regular kids. Why do they even have guns?"

"If I could answer that, I'd save everyone a lot of heartache. I think the draw is just too great. And there's no way we could ever get all the guns off the street."

I just kept staring at the young men on the basketball court.

Kathy got on her radio and told someone to come in on the other side of the basketball courts. We got out of the Explorer and started walking toward the park from the opposite direction.

The boys didn't even notice adults standing around the court until we were almost right next to them.

Sergeant Figler called the three boys over. I liked how the specialized detectives, who generally dealt with juveniles, handled them. There were no threats or intimidation. They let Sergeant Figler do the talking. But the boys weren't interested.

The blond kid told his friends, "Don't say a word. They can't do nothing if none of us talk."

Sergeant Figler said, "Unless we have you on video terrorizing some boys uptown. You know, the ones you showed your gun to. That turns it from kids bullying kids to a felony."

That broke any wall of silence they had. One of the taller boys took a step back and said, "We never had no gun. It was just Mark. He took it from his dad. We said it was a bad idea."

One of the detectives quickly reached across and patted

the boy's beltline and pockets. He pulled out a small, cheap revolver that looked like it would blow up in your hand if you pulled the trigger.

The blond kid said, "You can't take that. You need a warrant to search me." The young man noticed no one was really listening to his complaints. He started to shout, "Help, help, police brutality!"

Everyone stepped away from him except Sergeant Figler. She was just about his size. She said in an even voice, "I'm the only one around you now. Do you really want to claim a tiny woman like me brutalized you? If I were your parent, the first thing I'd tell you is to get your head out of your ass. Then I'd ground you for about a year. Now the state juvenile justice system is going to have to do it for them."

The other boys started to cry.

# CHAPTER 109

**FRIDAY NIGHT OF** the following week, I was back courtside, doing my best to coach the Holy Name girls' basketball team. The crowd cheered as the girls played a fast-paced game against another of our rivals: St. James Episcopal School. The Episcopalian girls looked impressive. Most of them were tall, and all of them seemed faster up and down the court than the girls from Holy Name. Yet the score was tied at 18. I hid my pride that Fiona had scored 10 of our 18 points by herself.

It had been fifteen days since I watched Coach Perry Martin tumble off the roof of the hotel in the Bronx and fall 130 feet to the sidewalk. Every acrophobe's nightmare. The image was still burned in my brain, but my routine was getting back to normal. It reminded me of something Harry Grissom had told me early on in my career in homicide: "No matter what you see on the job, bodies, blood, or tragedy, life goes on. Your family expects a father, not a detective."

It was just one more reason I was glad Harry was my boss. And it didn't look like he was going anywhere. At least for now.

Fiona whizzed past me, headed for the basket. A tall girl with a purple stripe through her blond hair threw an elbow at Fiona. It might've been just a distraction, because Fiona jerked her head to one side and easily avoided the blow. Then she sank the basket.

Before St. James could inbound the ball, I jogged down the court to talk to the ref. I needed to know why no foul had been called for such an obvious elbow. But it's tough to argue with a sixty-seven-year-old nun you've known since sixth grade.

I said in a loud voice, only to be heard over the din on the court, "Sister Lily, didn't you see that elbow?"

The short nun gave me her famous steely-eyed glare. "Coach Bennett, do you want these girls to worry about minor issues or be tough enough to face the harsh realities of life?"

I tried to hide my smile when I said, "I thought you taught English, not philosophy."

"Don't make me teach you not to question the ref." Then she turned, clapped her hands, and St. James inbounded the ball.

I had to laugh out loud as I headed back toward our bench. Why not? I had a daughter on the court plus nine kids and my wife in the stands. And an elderly priest, cheering like he was witnessing the Second Coming instead of his great-granddaughter playing basketball. They all looked happy. I recognized once again that I had a pretty good life.

After our 26–24 victory, I took the entire family to the Fun Zone Grill. It was close to the apartment and they were always happy to see my giant family. Plus, they had an array of games that kept most of the kids busy.

I sat at the end of four tables pushed together. Mary Catherine sat right next to me. We both laughed, watching my grandfather playing Whac-A-Mole with Chrissy. The old man was all smiles. Kids have a tendency to do that to people.

Even the older kids were getting into different games. Fiona was mesmerizing a group of boys by sinking basket after basket in the mini hoops game. Her brothers beamed with pride as more and more kids crowded around the enclosed hoop.

Mary Catherine casually said to me, "Do you really think the bullies are in our rearview mirror?"

"I hope so. We did everything we could. I heard the parents are now very interested in getting involved in their sons' lives. If they follow through, that'll probably be a big help." I didn't voice my concerns about retribution. I had to trust in the system.

Mary Catherine had something else to say. I knew to just keep my mouth shut and wait for it. Finally, after watching Fiona for another few seconds, Mary Catherine said, "I think I'm going to stay on this course of drugs for my fertility treatments. It doesn't mean I've made up my mind. It just gives me a little more time to consider everything."

I kissed her and said, "I want what you want. Take your time."

There was a big cheer in the restaurant. I looked up to see Fiona sink another ball and lights go off around the hoop.

Shawna ran over, bursting to tell us the exciting news.

"Fiona broke the record for consecutive baskets. She's going to get a free milkshake."

I raised my glass of Diet Coke and said, "Here's to our own LeBron."

Shawna looked at me and said, "You mean Lisa Leslie."

"That's exactly who I mean." And that was precisely the sort of thing I wanted my daughters to say.

Mary Catherine and I laughed until she kissed me again. This time it had some passion behind it. She whispered in my ear, "Wait till I get you home."

# ABOUT THE AUTHORS

**James Patterson** is the world's bestselling author. Among his creations are Alex Cross, the Women's Murder Club, Michael Bennett, and Maximum Ride. His #1 bestselling nonfiction includes *Walk in My Combat Boots, Filthy Rich,* and his autobiography, *James Patterson by James Patterson.* He has collaborated on novels with Bill Clinton and Dolly Parton and has won an Edgar Award, nine Emmy Awards, and the National Humanities Medal.

**James O. Born** is an award-winning crime and science-fiction novelist as well as a career law-enforcement agent. A native Floridian, he still lives in the Sunshine State.

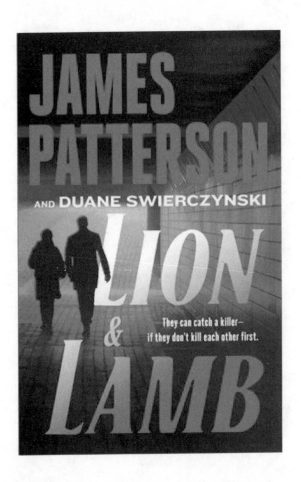

**PATTERSON'S NEXT BLOCKBUSTER
THRILLER SERIES IS HERE!**

Turn the page to meet
Veena Lion and Cooper Lamb,
rival, opposites-attract PIs working the
same intense, headline-making case.

# SUNDAY, JANUARY 23

# THE NIGHT PHILADELPHIA lost its mind, police
officer Deborah Parks was patrolling the Ninth with her
rookie, Rob Sheplavy.

He was a nice enough kid, maybe a little overeager. They'd
been together since just after New Year's Day, when the
red-and-gold holiday decorations were quickly replaced by
Eagles-green banners to celebrate the team clawing its way to
the NFC playoffs.

Now it was just after midnight on a freezing Sunday in late
January, when Philly was at its darkest and coldest. The Birds
were facing off against the Giants, and aside from a few rowdy
drunks with their faces painted green, the residents of the city
had apparently decided to take a collective breather before
tonight's kickoff.

As they went around the Museum of Art toward Eakins
Oval, Sheplavy's face lit up. "Check out that sweet Maserati."

Parks followed his sight line to the sports car, which had
been detailed with a laser-blue holographic wrap. The thing
literally glowed in the street, where it appeared to have
paused at a stoplight at the far end of the traffic circle. Only
problem: The traffic circle had no light. But still, the Maserati
had come to a dead stop, nose slightly out of its lane.

"What is up with this guy?" Parks said. "Look, we're going to pull up a little closer and I'll check it out. You stay here."

"Wait—can't I come with you?"

"I need you to hang back. And don't touch the radio!"

Parks hated being rough with the new kid. But he had a tendency to go rogue, and she knew something was off about this even before she climbed out of the car.

As Parks moved closer, she could see someone slumped behind the wheel of the glowing vehicle. Was the driver passed out drunk?

No. The body language was all wrong—his head was tilted at an unnatural angle, his shoulders were completely still, and there was no sign of breathing.

Parks glanced back to make sure the rookie was where he should be. "Stay in the car, Sheplavy!"

If the rookie heard, he didn't respond.

Steeling herself, Parks moved to the driver's side, hand near her service weapon just in case this guy turned out to be (a) alive and (b) drunk and pissed. But she knew that would be the best-case scenario.

Parks called out to him, trying to wake him up. The driver didn't stir. She reached in and touched the side of his neck with two fingers. The man's skin was ice cold, and there was no pulse.

Parks had forgotten to put on gloves, and when she lifted her fingers away from the driver's neck, she was surprised to find them tacky. She looked down at her hands and realized that the city's new LED streetlights had made the body look as if it were covered in shadows.

But it was blood. *So much blood...*

# MONDAY, JANUARY 24

*Transcript of private conversation between Cooper Lamb and Lisa Marchese, senior partner at Kaplan, DePaulo, and Marchese, captured using an ambient recording app on Lamb's smartwatch*

LISA MARCHESE: You're seriously going to walk away from the biggest murder case in Philadelphia history?

COOPER LAMB: Why don't you try Veena Lion? She's the best. Well, second best, if I may be so immodest.

MARCHESE: Maybe we already called Veena.

LAMB: Nah, she'd never work for you guys. She hates big law firms even more than she hates authority figures.

MARCHESE: You've had no problem cashing our checks in the past.

LAMB: And in the past, the checks have been generous. But when it comes to…what did you say? "The biggest murder case in Philadelphia history"?

MARCHESE: Ah. I see. You're negotiating.

LAMB: Of course I am. I wouldn't want you to lowball me simply because I'd kill for this job. I loved Archie and I pretty much bleed Eagles green. I bet on them every week, even during their not-so-stellar seasons. And I've had a massive crush on Francine Pearl ever since that music video where she's wearing that…ah, never mind. But yeah. I'm all in. Wait, what are you writing there?

MARCHESE: How's this for a retainer?

LAMB: That is…impressive. Lupe, my faithful friend, I think that will keep you in dried salmon treats for months to come.

MARCHESE: So we have an agreement?

LAMB: Just one thing. Two things, actually.

MARCHESE: Go on.

LAMB: I'll need full access to the team. And the owners.

MARCHESE: You don't honestly believe one of Archie's own teammates murdered him, do you? Or the Sables?

LAMB: Maybe I'm a huge fan *and* milking this situation for all it's worth.

MARCHESE: I'm sorry, what?

LAMB: Maybe I promised my kids some autographs.

MARCHESE: But—

LAMB: Or maybe I'm really good at my job, and you should trust my instincts.

MARCHESE: (*Sighs*) Fine. What's the other thing?

LAMB: If you hire me, I'm not going to stop until I find the truth.

MARCHESE: That's what we want.

LAMB: Even if the truth is very bad for your client?

MARCHESE: (*Slight hesitation*) That's what we want, Lamb.

LAMB: You've got yourself a private eye, Marchese.

*10:01 p.m.*

**"TRUTH IS,** this case is a flaming garbage fire," Veena said, then downed half the martini. It was cold and bracing and exactly what she needed.

"Please," Cooper said. "Not with us working together as a team."

"Cooper, the only thing worse than being on a team *with* you is being on a team opposite you. Which is why I wanted to meet."

"And here I thought you just wanted to tie one on. Speaking of..." Cooper looked around for their server, who had departed only a few moments ago.

"We're friends and all, but I want to establish some ground rules," Veena said.

"Perfect. This calls for a drink."

"Rules first, drinks after."

"Okay, fine," Cooper said with a slight pout in his voice.

"We share everything. I mean every last shred of intelligence."

"Done."

Veena blinked. "Really? That was too easy."

"Not at all. It's the smart move. I mean, my man Victor can grab anything he likes from your files—"

"Just like my number two, Janie, can from yours."

"See? So we're saving valuable snooping time. Anything else?"

"Yes. We need to agree that we won't trust anything that comes from Mickey Bernstein."

"Done," Cooper said. "I hate that tall handsome prick. He's nothing but a haircut, a Penn degree, and a last name. What else?"

"No bullshit, now—who do you think killed Archie Hughes?"

"My gut take right now, based on the available facts?" Cooper asked. "Some of which came from Bernstein's initial report?"

Veena made a sweeping *The floor is yours* gesture with her freshly manicured hands.

Cooper nodded. "It was a random carjacker. He saw the fancy Maserati, not the guy behind the wheel. Once he realized who he'd killed, he took the Super Bowl ring to pawn it for some getaway money, but then figured out it would be like tattooing *Guilty* on his forehead."

"Interesting theory. So this random carjacker is also a master criminal who can evade dozens of surveillance cameras in the area and knows how to elude the cops in a citywide manhunt?"

"Eh, beginner's luck," Cooper said. "This is probably the guy's first time, which is why Mickey B. and his goons are having so much trouble finding him. And until they do, the entire city will continue to lose its collective mind. So that's my take. Who do you like for this?"

"Oh, the wife killed him," Veena said. "Absolutely."

"Really."

"No doubt about it."

Cooper made a *Give it to me* motion with four fingers.

"Let's put aside for the moment *why* Francine Pearl Hughes definitely murdered her husband," Veena said. "Instead, let's discuss why they'll never arrest her."

"I don't know. Could it be because…she absolutely didn't do it?"

"No. It's because this city loved her long before any of us had even heard of Archie Hughes."

"True. Francine is Philadelphia's sweetheart. What was that cringey soul trio she used to front?"

"You're pretending like you don't remember the Puritones, but I know you do."

Cooper smiled like a boy caught in a fib. He was completely unaware that their server was approaching as he broke into a horribly off-key rendition of the Puritones' hit "Cross My Broken Heart." Veena considered Cooper a highly talented investigator who had many skills across a variety of disciplines. Singing wasn't one of them.

*"I'll swear it to the ennnnnnd,"* Cooper crooned, *"cross my broken heaaaaaaaarrt!"*

"So glad Lupe isn't here to see this," Veena said.

"Can I, uh, get you anything else?" the server asked.

"Only my dignity," Cooper said, his cheeks slightly red. "As well as another round."

"Not for me," Veena said. She downed the second half of her martini.

"Come on, one more," Cooper pleaded. "Cross my broken heart?"

"Nope." Veena left cash, including an incredibly generous tip for the server. "By the way," Veena told her, "don't go home with him. He's a gifted orator and can probably talk you into it, but do yourself a favor and pass."

"I'm mortally wounded," Cooper said, clutching his chest.

"What business is it of yours?" the server asked. "Are you his ex or something?"

"Maybe someday," Veena said.

For a complete list of books by
# JAMES PATTERSON

VISIT
## JamesPatterson.com

 Follow James Patterson on Facebook
**@JamesPatterson**

 Follow James Patterson on Twitter
**@JP_Books**

 Follow James Patterson on Instagram
**@jamespattersonbooks**